Javada Rings True

by

Lloyd DuBé

First published by AuthorHouse 05/06/04

ISBN: 1-4184-6751-0 (e-book)
ISBN: 1-4184-4313-1 (Paperback)

This book is printed on acid free paper.

DEDICATION:

To my dear brother George whose premonition of his upcoming inter-dimensional passing propelled the writing of this book to it's completion.

May you rest in the arms of the one you love, be sweet.

WARNING:

Only the brave-hearted, open-minded ones who thirst for knowledge will be allowed to pass the guardians within, and enjoy the bounty.

CHAPTER 1

Approaching the Segna, an interdimensional portal, I felt the resistance. Yet the flow surrounding and nudging me towards the experience. The approach was always similar, as the reluctance to let go of the familiar rose. Yet the exhilaration of the experience, always new, unique in its manifestation called irresistibly.

It was several jugas (a time-consciousness measurement) since my last calling into service and yet like yesterday. Time had changed in my evolution from boundaried segments to interlocking, flowing constancy.

My last training work on Javada had begun a transformational attitudinal evolution, unknown in its direction.

Javada, my home planet, was commissioned by the universal body of planets known within the limited realms as Galaxium, to research and document the motion and nature of a phenomenon relatively new in it's recognition.

Until now the origin of creation was a domain reserved for the intellectual exercises of the philosophers, spiritualists and naturalists. There was a general consensus, an agreement as to the existence of a force, an intelligence, a divine program in which all creation was governed, sustained and kept on a positive evolutionary course to its destiny. Galaxium had incorporated this approach into its constitutional governing body. respecting above all else, each member's right to evolve to its optimum potential.

Planets, which had not evolved to this level of consciousness were monitored and approached only when a majority of its inhabitants were aware intrinsically of this state of being.

Until now the decision of approach was a scientific decision based on studied data and past experience of success and failure. Premature approach had resulted in disaster, as contact had an immediate quantum effect on power levels, all levels of life on the planet. If the self-centered, fear-based tendencies had not been purified to the degree of acceptance of more than the known, the power would be channeled into destructive, limiting directions. Conflict would rise along with the technological quantum leap to self-destruction. This was of constant concern. All factors could not be taken into account to 100% effective levels.

Recently something new came into being at the critical approach time. As all studies pointed to contact initiation time, while reservation forces exercised their responsibilities, an unexplainable phenomenon would occur. An emanation, felt by the most sensitive, seen by aura readers and registered by the most sensitive monitoring equipment came from an uncharted segment of the universe. The emanation appeared to envelope the planet under consideration in a sort of energy field.

The effect on the planet was almost identical to contact, a quickening, an increase in energy levels of the inhabitants, a speeding up of tendencies whether growth full or destructive. The result in the Galaxium quarter was that their involvement was made necessary at all speed. The reservation forces agreed as there was no real choice, the results would transpire with or without our influence. Our influence now would be a reaction rather than an initiation. Less responsibility in the eyes of the conservative. The source of the emanation was now responsible.

Since this phenomenon had come into effect, the transitions appeared to take place far more effectively, with less disturbance. Possibly due to the less intense approach to the process by Galaxium, a sense of destiny, a movement into a direction heralded by this unknown source. The planetising process began to change from one of scientific analysis-based decision making to one of monitoring, observing and waiting for the emanation to take the first step at which time all the transition-aiding forces within Galaxium would unhesitatingly "kick in".

One of the most socially felt results was experienced within the scientific community. Unlike the psychic and religious based who felt this newness as a fulfillment of prophecy, the scientific community wanted to know more about the emanation. Was it really as positive, helpful and benevolent as it appeared or was there a catch? Was everyone being lulled into a sense of complacency, a sense of trust, undermining the fruits of effort? These concerns resulted in a realignment of scientific resources towards researching this new phenomenon being popularly referred to as Mahaj, meaning "The Greatest One" in the oldest known language.

Highly-tuned sensors were all aimed at the section of uncharted area, probing, collecting data, watching, listening, resulting in reports upon reports. Theories began to surface, ranging from an alien society to a freak of nature reflecting our own collective psyche.

The Mahaj became the focus of communication throughout the known worlds. Then a strange occurrence: As the probes began registering the surges, wainings, sounds, light forms and motions of this strange area, a change.

All emanations ceased. There was a sudden drop in the recently accelerated energy levels. The concerns in Galaxium were increased by the instant effect on the newest planetary members. Their positive evolutionary processes began to slow and some even turned into the most-feared, D-evolution.

It was then that my planet, Javada, was approached for consultation. We were known for our long-standing interaction with the Mahaj. Our people had long since adopted a co-operative mode, acceptance. The striving which existed among the young was directed towards developing channels of communication with this force, we felt created, sustained and ultimately destroyed. We accepted its wisdom and developed processes aimed at developing trust and awareness, forms of motion channeling Mahaj rather than our limited wills.

I had been accepted as a member of the U.I.A., the Universal Intelligence Agency, quite sometime ago, but had not been given a great deal of work due to the scientific focus dominating the Galaxium mentality. With these recent developments, however, a call went out for any unconventional approach to solving this problem. If the emanations ceased, everything would fall back into the old scientific pressure systems which were beginning to be seen as archaic, out-lived, limited in scope. The excitement of unlimited potential felt in the waves of emanation had taken root. The question was posed to the leaders of Javada. What can be done to restore the quantum field influence, first to the de-evolving planetary segments and eventually to the restoration of the previous planetising process.

My briefing was brisk, short and to the point. Our motions were always spontaneous, focused on channeling the Mahaj rather than conspiring a particular outcome. I was told to simply rely on my intuitive skills, past training and the general understanding reached by the governors of Javada as to the reasons for the upsetting condition. The general consensus was that the Mahaj simply did not want to be probed as there was no need for it. Understanding its make-up would not improve its beneficial nature. Furthermore, understanding it or trying to, would be a futile effort. Much like one of your sophisticated sensor units turning on you, I told the Galaxium representatives in my address, and trying to figure you out. The created ones never fully understand their creator, only by moving easily and in harmony with their program, will they successfully fulfill their destiny.

Our advice was seriously taken into account and as there were no other feasible options presented, a program of sensor de-activation was initiated. The route was well taken, within a solar month all sensors were re-aligned to their former planetary projects. A surprising turn of events then happened. The emanations not only resumed from the uncharted segment but new centers began to emerge from a 360 degree arena. We were suddenly the center of a flood of emanations.

The results were, of course, spectacular. Every segment of society was touched and enriched. The planetising program not only restored itself to its previous growth but planets formerly considered as potential in the future began to show signs of readiness for contact.

It was a beehive of activity, more training programs were set up, students from the far reaches of Galaxium gathered and were taught the most recent technologies involved in aiding new members to understand the quantum leap process they were experiencing.

Galaxium was growing dramatically in its influence and power as each new planetary psyche seemed to fill gaps previously felt. A sense of [Yes, now we are really on the right track].

Of course, having been instrumental in contributing to the course of events leading to this condition, Javada was looked at with great respect and favor. As it's emissary and active member of the U.I.A., I found myself favored as well. My assignments became far more pleasure-oriented. I was sent to observe and document planetary systems which had long out-grown their growing pains. The societies I visited were peaceful, co-operative and involved in Galaxium's objectives. I was beginning to feel like a pampered monarch. Our way of seeing and relating to the Mahaj were being studied and accepted. The skeptics however still held power. Though tolerant, questions of validity still arose. Healthy debate, we called it.

You might be wondering, how could all this happen due to such a simple turn of events. My planet simply seeing the nature of the Mahaj, suggesting such a straight-forward solution. Well, this was the exact initial response from the Galaxium governing body. Why would a highly developed scientific body become an irritant to the Mahaj? Now what is to be done with all these highly developed scientific minds who hungered for observing, studying and analyzing theories and then interacting from this platform of knowing with the intriguing Mahaj.

I invite you to step back in time to the gathering of invited representatives from Galaxium and the elders of Javada.

Close your eyes, and feel yourself approaching my planet. To facilitate your emotional readiness, Breathe in, with the thought "MA" expel with the thought "HAJ". Several times.

Now open your eyes, and we will continue the journey. As we approach, our first impression will be, the RINGS of COLOR surrounding Javada. These rings were never studied scientifically but were probed by our psychics, felt, and understood. Each ring was a boundary much like Gargoyles guarding the entrance to a spiritual center. Only those ready for the experience within, could pass through easily.

We are now passing through the outer ring, the ring of Sincerity. The color of Turquoise surrounds us. We feel its coolness as it passes through each cell of our being, finally reaching deep into our psyche to determine the level of our sincerity in our approach. Do we come with an open mind willing to observe dispassionately, absorb what is shared and leave the reflective process involving judgment of any sort until a later time, if at all?

Our levels are registered and we gently pass into the Aura of the second ring. This is the Ring of Courage.

The color Beige emits a hazy light shield around each of us and probes our aura's for signs of how we face challenges. Is there an angry tolerance of the condition or do we see our challenges as opportunity for growth?

Our levels are again registered and we somewhat abruptly fall into the pool of the third ring.

It feels like bathing in warm milk. This is the Ring of Physical Readiness. The milk seeps gently into our bodies enveloping each muscle, down-loading its memory, seeing the history of the body in wholeness, all in a micro-second.

Did we live a Sedentary or Active life? Were we self-abusive or had we found our balance. Not deprived, yet, not over indulged.

Our levels are again registered and we float free, down towards Javada. As you may have noticed, the challenges we just faced were quite gentle and unobtrusive. It was not a pass or fail type of program. A simple observation of the status of our evolution. Passing and failing are competitive exercises which have been purified for quite some time on Javada. We found that competition drain the collective psyche and co-operative efforts to aid in the evolution of others, enriched it.

It was, therefore, to each individual's interest to help in whatever manner was presented by the Mahaj. Not helping from the platform of what we thought was needed in the situation, but a spontaneous knowing which way to move, what to do and having the courage to move easily and quickly with the wave as it crested. The results always turned out beneficial to all involved.

A commitment to mutual benefit rather than winning. Javadians do not consider pride worthy, rather a limitation to their spontaneous nature. Too high a self-image weighs a great deal, inhibiting one's ability to dance on the spontaneous waves of the Mahaj's ocean.

The dance is the thing, not the destination of the journey, just the joy of the dance. Here and now.

As we lightly touch down, our first impression may be the sweet, haunting odor of the Pickdaylias blooming. It is their season. As they bloom they draw nectar drinkers from all parts of our system. The insects are not bound to the atmosphere of the planet, but fly to the many orbiting moons. Each having their own worlds to evolve in, yet gathering here for a short while to drink. This is considered a time of sharing, an ideal time for our visit as well as the Galaxium conference about to begin.

The hum in the air from all the insert flyers seems to have an orchestration, a pattern like the background music in a symphony. Then the birds, exotic creatures here, sing their joyful tune as they periodically stop their feast. Somewhat unfortunate for some of the insect population, but this is the chain of life as it is everywhere. The Javadians considered themselves extremely fortunate as they no longer had any predators. That time is over. We now stand at the head of the chain, with a sense of responsibility for all below.

"BENEVOLENT MONARCHS", you might say.

Through the beehive of atmospheric activity, we now see three separate groups of Javadians approaching our newly arrived group. Each having its distinctive coloring led by an elder with probing character features. Reading, almost the sense of seeing through us, perceiving something deeper, hidden.

As we notice, the color of each group corresponds with the color of one of the rings we just passed through.

TURQUOISE, the leader is calm, gentle, moving with determination, yet as if flying, responding to currents.

BEIGE, the leader is steady, powerful, perceiving us with the courage of one who faced many challenges and knew the outcome always reflected the approach and attitude.

MILKY, the leader is agile, almost nervous, anxious to get on with it. There is work to be done, the energy and vitality shine through brilliantly.

As the three groups surround us, we might wonder what next? A sense of something important unfolding, then an emission from each group, a barely visible beam surrounding each one of us, drawing us individually towards our group.

The readings of the rings has obviously determined this phenomenon. We will each be taken into the group experience most beneficial for us at our particular point of evolution.

I was not being spared the experience, a never-ending thing. Each time I entered my psyche was probed, the needed experience found putting the machinery in motion. This time it was the emotional, courage, BEIGE RING calling. I surrendered my will, my thoughts, my body, knowing the experience, the outcome was all harmonious at this time.

I was taken to the preparation quarters where I settled in, was fed, relaxed in the sweat rooms, bathed in the crystal pools, massaged, and finally led to the DREAM ROOM. I quickly fell into a deep sleep and dreamt.

The dream was scattered, many fragments all revolving around my eldest son. Our contacts now were few as he was intensely involved in the planetising program. His skills as a genetic gardener were well known so a great deal of his time was spent traveling to the far reaches to devise, and supervise the environmental growth patterns of emerging planetary systems. Places where life on all levels was being engineered at its seed stage. Any spare time was spent with his mate and two children. He was totally immersed in the nesting part of his life. As a result there was little time for old Dad. This situation was a challenge for me as my emotions drew me to him and his family, yet the limitations of our physical reality put obvious boundaries on contact. This condition was reflected in the dream sequence.

The excitement of taking a journey together, somewhere relaxing, possibly fishing, exploring the things we enjoyed individually and then naturally as a team. Yet there were obstacles. In one sequence, I was waiting in a high-terrain vehicle, wanting to get going, yet, no son. I moved into a room finding him bathing in a child's play pool, smiling, having a great time, yet I was full of the feeling, "What are you doing we are supposed to take off on our adventure?" Obvious impatience with the situation. Not accepting things as they were unfolding but wanting them another way. A challenge to be consciously resolved.

In another sequence, there he was, lounging around with his friends in a trance induced by one of our powerful hallucinogenic plants. I felt rejected, not part of the group. Almost feared, accepted tolerantly, yet not really wanted. Not a pleasant feeling.

Once again, a gap, in age obviously, in pleasure patterns and priorities. Again the challenge of acceptance of the condition. In the final sequence, I decided to go up the distant mountain on my own, a feeling of relief, a recognition of following my own path, my own destiny, leaving my son to his.

Dreams were seen in Javada as direct channels, communicative cables between our conscious and unconscious parts, the perceiving mind of the physical and the psyche, the part of the whole, the part of us in union with the Mahaj.

The messages were held in reverence as gifts guiding us to correct actions which would aid us in our evolution to facilitate a harmonious passage through life to its ultimate, unknown destiny.

My dream, this time, clearly showed me the necessity to let go, follow my own light, knowing all was as it should be with my son. He was going through what he must. My responsibility, now was to my own ongoing journey.

My journey up the mountain, who knows, we might meet there and enjoy each other's experiences when the time was right. When we were each full, emptying ourselves to each other. Nourishing each other with our diverse experiences.

Once again, allowing with faith in the outcome, although difficult at this time, knowing all was as it should be.

CHAPTER 1

The day had a shimmering brilliance, a freshness, as a tropical storm had just passed overnight. The storms here were fierce, as if they were a sneeze from the Mahaj. Everyone and everything found shelter and hung on. Now, a sense of relief, a coming back to life's normality.

As we each come out into the Javadian sun, we feel drawn to one another. It is the time of sharing our experiences. Each one with their own individual perception of their Ring Aura encounters.

We gently settle around the TRUTH STONE in a loose circle finding our own comfort zone. Without intending to, we settle in three groups, each group in front of a stone arch with a seat below, a simple curved stone suitable for sitting on. As we each become comfortable in our space, we see three figures approaching from a distant temple-like structure. It's our three ringleaders, each still projecting their respective postures but now with an auric hue surrounding each, TURQUOISE, BEIGE and MILKY and a misty white, almost invisible flowing light surrounding them as a group, interweaving and heralding the next steps as taken. They have just finished their morning preparations, a small meal, a stimulating herb drink grown on the south side, the sun side of a nearby mountain and a group meditation preparing them for this gathering. A very important time for each newcomer as this is an initiation into the Javadian Ring of Truth. A time of truthful encounter with each other and the presence of the Mahaj. The seeding of a process much revered on the planet.

As each leader takes his respective arch seat, we notice a slow glow begin from the tip of each arch gradually seeping down each side finally closing the ring. Then an emanation encompassing each group in its respective aura and color.

At the center of the circle of Arches lay a circular flat stone, a platform, a sort of stage. We notice the inter-twining connecting misty white light which brought our 3 friends has now settled in this area. Gently shimmering, as if waiting, watching, probing. A respectful hesitation in anticipation for what is about to happen.

Each of us, I'm sure, has an idea of what might happen next. Probably each leader would give us an address and we would be on our way to further explore this fascinating world. Well, Surprise.

The Javadian Sun, suddenly dims as if overloaded for an instant, then a brilliant flash, a bolt of shearing, lightening-like essence stands resonating between the sun and the platform. The misty white presence is now bright, almost blinding, yet the feeling is soothing, supportive. Another flash, this time from the platform, over through and around the milky auric area of the gathering. The choice has been made, personally, by the Mahaj. The first to rise and share will be our physically oriented leader.

True to his character, he responds agilely like a tightly-wound spring finally released, bounding up on the stage without hesitation. Then a moment of stillness, a time of reverent introspection, a short but powerful meditation, connecting with the individual manifestation of the Mahaj within each of us. We each feel the inner force, a warm surge.

The process has now really begun. The address begins, His voice is low, deep with the resonance of a drum, felt deeply yet not confronting in its feeling tone. It seems to elicit an automatic respect:

"Each here, gathered, for the experience has been brought by the Mahaj, each motivated uniquely. We all have our stories, our histories, but what we have in common is the interest. Our time to open to the unknown, all that is asked of you is this openness. All else will unfold according to your individual psychic program. Everything which has happened to you to bring you to this moment was not a haphazard accident but a flowing directed journey orchestrated by the Mahaj. I have been sent to impress the importance of a healthy physical condition in order to facilitate the spontaneous motion of the Mahaj.

As you begin to consciously channel the flow into your realm of reality, much like fresh, clear mountain water flowing through you, the condition of the water as it flows out of you will depend on your physical, mental and psychic cleanliness and health. The clearer you are, the clearer the outcome. The healthier and fit you are, the more energetic will be your individual manifestation into your reality.

Our physical preparation programs here on Javada are aimed towards this goal. As those of you who have been drawn by the milky ring aura are well aware of by now, the program starts with a physical cleansing. A time spent fasting, simple subsistence on a herbal mixture prepared specifically to detoxify your body. A time when all of your normal patterns are dropped, introspection for our minds, an observation of the physical symptoms as a lifetime of built-up poisons are released. Many of you felt some discomfort initially, but soon replaced by the warm flow of the Mahaj supporting your step towards a more harmonious way of life. A small price to pay for an approach to an experience carrying you to realms beyond the known.

When this stage of the program is complete, guidelines as to nourishment are recommended. Easily assimilated sources of energy are outlined bringing us to the next phase in our program. Instead of describing this stage, I'll show you".

At this point, he leaves the stage in a deer-like bound and takes his seat in the Milky Arch. Instantly, a spiraling milky beam emanates from the peak of the distant temple towards the stage platform. As it reaches the stone, an image forms. We can see our leader moving slowly through a forested path along a stream, we hear the water, the birds, the insects, a most pleasing scene. We can even smell the humid forest air. An intriguing holographic projection, almost more realistic than reality. He moves along the path seemingly, unconcerned with where his next step would land. The walk of trust, complete faith in his balance. More of a dance than a stride. Then an opening, a birth-like frame, bursting out into the open and there lay the ocean, a bright sunny day, a shoreline with rocks, logs and sand. A challenging terrain yet without hesitation, he leaps into the shoreline with an obvious appetite for the experience.

Bounding from rock to rock easily, no delays, no consideration for the next step, yet each step lands on a firm footing. A physical portrayal of the infamous "Leap of Faith". The Mahaj is obviously in charge here, more than guiding but actually doing the motion. It reminds me of my lucid dream experiences where I felt such a surge of faith in the flight, that I surrendered my will as to where I wanted to fly to the Mahaj. I simply lay back into a feeling and was carried ecstatically to places I would not have been able to envision. But it was the feeling, the joy, the ecstasy so strong I found myself moaning, then sounds coming from so deep almost a yell to the heavens of appreciation. A place hard to leave and yet existing within me to be experienced when ever the Mahaj granted it.

This flight feeling is what I saw in his face as he faced each challenge, each bound, each completed exercise. He plays with sticks in a martial arts fashion exercising all parts of his body. The stick seems to be a part of his own form, an extension, no possibility of dropping it. He throws stones with amazing accuracy not really aiming, just throwing at something, the stone seems guided often hitting many objects before stopping.

This reminds me of a myth passed down many generations on a planet I once visited. It was believed that a special being, close to the Mahaj, possibly one with the Mahaj, appeared to a warrior who was preparing for a battle. His forces were badly outnumbered and he was concerned. The being known as Krishna held out his hands and emitted a ray of light saying.

"Here, I give you divine accuracy, simply aim in the direction of your enemy and fire, I will guide your arrows. Your faith is all that is needed".

The warrior went into battle with his forces, firing quickly without hesitation, each arrow found it's mark and the battle was won. A similar process was at work here. Faith in the Mahaj had become an integral part of the warrior training program. As peace ruled in Javada for a long, long time, the warrior training was used mainly for physical fitness as well as the corresponding mental attitude towards any challenge. Aim, Fire and allow the outcome to take its course.

As he approached the end of the work-out trail, the images dim and draw back in a slow spiral to the temple's peak. The leader again takes the stage to conclude.

"Our bodies are extensions of the Mahaj into this physical reality. As nature is spontaneous, they must be in top condition to easily channel the power. Physical impediments interfere with this motion and prevent the individual from experiencing the ultimate joy of surrendering to the guiding flow. Learn to move with disciplined abandonment. This is done by focusing your mind on the Mahaj within you and allowing the power from within to move, direct and protect you. Stay flexible, rigidity inhibits. This physical practice will in time affect your complete approach to life, no matter what the challenge. Finally manifesting the ultimate Life Style where you become one who does nothing and yet nothing is left undone. No longer carrying the weight of responsibility, free to lay back into the protective arms of the Mahaj and be carried to undescribable heights, individually experienced in your particular Dance of Life".

With these words still ringing in our consciousness, we watch Him flow back to his Arch Seat with the retracting Milky Aura. I had taken my warrior training with the Milky Leader some time ago in my preparation for entering the U.I.A.

The Javadian Code of warriorship had been demonstratively instilled in me at that time. The ways of moving with and unleashing the Force of the Mahaj were tempered with the Code of non-interference. Our Mode of Behavior held us to a defensive posture only. Allowing anyone challenging to evolve and only if attacked, use our knowledge to stop the attacker, then limit the attacker from causing harm, and finally initiate a healing process into the relationship. Enemies draw on one's psychic powers while allies enhance. The collective psyche is then nourished and all benefit. Once again seeing challenges as opportunities for enhancement as we each as individuals are directly affected by the collective.

A focus on constructive resolution rather than victory and defeat. Simply seeing the wholeness of the situation rather than simply the individual's position.

I remembered when I was fresh out of the U.I.A. Academy and was given an assignment to observe a planet recently admitted to Galaxium. It was still embroiled in conflict based on religious, ethnic and cultural differences. Private property was blindly defended. The society was still alienated from itself and the Mahaj. Yet there was a segment which opened to the Mahaj and even though Galaxium felt approach was premature the process of initiation into membership was implemented.

Many of the inhabitants were conscious of the potential benefits and co-operated, however there was still a loosely organized warrior segment who felt their authority challenged. My mission was to confront, appraise and bring this fearful segment to the bargaining table. As the group respected power and saw negotiation, compromise and co-operation as weakness, my approach would definitely lead to confrontation. But being young and eager to test my warrior wings I approached the situation eagerly.

As I neared the settlement hall my first impression was the stench. All around the structures were bodies in various stages of decay. Oh yes! I thought, this was a place where differences were settled with finality. Little, if any, consideration for the vanquished. I swaggered confidently past this area, through a square-dark doorway, into the courtyard where the congregation had gathered. Undoubtedly to witness another unwanted guest's quick and painful demise. Well, I thought to myself, I've just been trained by the Best in the Galaxy, what have I to fear. Yet an inner sense of unease, not absolute confidence. As I continued to move towards a figure sitting on a seat commanding a view of the entire gathering, I was abruptly stopped by a hulk of a being.

There was no denying this one his pleasure.

"No one approaches the power point in this hall without a contest".

The look in his eyes as he spoke left no doubt that there would be only one standing at the end of this contest. The other would decay.

I replied with a slight tremor in my voice.

"I come in peace, to talk, to see if there is any way to resolve our differences".

He left no doubt in his reply.

"Fight or Leave, we will spare your useless life, today".

I saw no choice, if I turned and left, the credibility of Galaxium would be compromised. I stepped forward.

The Hulk reached slowly for his blade, a huge piece of steel with ritualistic engraving still tainted by the blood of his last challenge. As I was unarmed, physically, I saw a smaller, darkly clad figure approach carrying three blades. I was to choose my weapon. My stick training on Javada prepared me for the use of a blade. I chose a smaller, shorter weapon than my adversary. Speed and agility would be my only chance, as I was far outweighed, and out muscled. As he began to swing his blade almost playfully, pleasurably, I felt toyed with.

I took the Javadian Warrior Posture designed to enhance the flow of the Mahaj in movement as well as presenting the most formidable projection upon the enemy. This was it, outweighed, out numbered, I felt like Krishna's warrior and remembering his experience of Faith, I moved forward.

Just as the Hulk raised his weapon to strike the first blow, I saw a strange glow coming from the figure on the power-point seat, his hand was raised, a murmur went through the congregation replacing the previous shouts of challenge and encouragement to their hero. The figure moved calmly, slowly, down a flight of stairs, approached us watchfully and ceremoniously touched the Hulk's left ear taking the blade from his hand with no resistance. His voice was low, strong and confident, the survivor of many battles undoubtedly. This was obviously the leader.

"I will deal with him". He spoke into the Hulk's ear. The congregation was silent now. Their best, their Leader was taking the stage. Obviously an auspicious occasion, a treat and I was to be the dessert. This sudden change threw me into an unbalanced space of mind. I'd had time to intuitively access my former opponent. I'd felt his strengths as well as his limitations. His size and weight could have been used against him. A sketchy strategy had been formulated, a weak point was seen and would have been pursued. Now I faced a smaller, quicker and mentally superior opponent, and no time to access as he was already moving towards me. Why had he decided to step forward, had he sensed my strategy and its excellent chance of success? Was it the Javadian Warrior pose? Was he aware of it's channeling nature? Strength being drawn from the inner essence allowing the warrior to relax into its surge and concentrate on the visualization of the outcome, rather than the limitations of the conflict. Yet here I was in a reactionary position. No choice but to let go into the Mahaj and follow its motions without interference.

Our blades met in an ear-piercing clang. A quick hit, then withdrawal to strike again. I felt his blows were not full, he was holding back, probably to measure and draw me into the offensive. I found myself doing the same. No retreat, no advance. A simple mirroring of his tactics. Blocking, striking, conserving strength. Waiting for a change, an opening, an opportunity for advance.

The dilemma here was that if I lost the battle nothing would be accomplished. The group would feel superior and continue its resistance to the newly formed alliance. On the other hand, if I won decisively, the defeat could simply antagonize and deepen the rift. A time when the Mahaj would have to manifest a solution. To facilitate this possibility, my approach had to be one of openness, yet staying alive. Then, there it was, an opening, my opponent had swung his blade with the anticipation of my block, but I'd slightly lost my balance and inadvertently stumbled to the right. As his blade met no resistance, the momentum of his swing carried too far and his left side was momentarily open and vulnerable. A chance, to sever either his left arm or strike his throat, a killing strike. I instinctively swung in the general area, not choosing, yet taking the opportunity. Our eyes met, he knew precisely what was happening and was waiting in that split second for the extent of my strike. I felt my blade connect with his shoulder but glancing upward towards his throat, the kill area, would this be the end? Just as the blade began to cut in, a shudder from deep within, a pulling back, merely a shallow cut about three inches long. The warrior, I faced, knew he'd been spared yet cut. His eyes showed a wonder, why? I also wondered, the shudder from within had interfered, avoided death, yet made its point clear. Would the battle continue? I readied myself for an onslaught now fueled by a hurt pride. Yet as he approached I sensed no anger. The congregation however was not pleased. They seemed to feel, their leader, humiliated by the gesture of mercy. Simply marked, yet alive. What did the Mahaj intend now? My question was quickly answered. I felt the arrow strike my back, knocking me forwards, headlong into the leader's waiting blade. The pain shot through my body like a bolt of lightening, then a sense of faintness, a numbing feeling. My head spun, I was losing consciousness. My time had come, so early in life, yet death undoubtedly here. If the arrow wasn't a lethal blow, then my opponent's waiting blade would soon end it. Just another addition to the waiting pile of decay. Then blackness.

A warmness returning, a faint glow like moving through a forest, after a fresh snowfall under a full moon. A dimness in my sight, but a feeling of warmth inside. No physical sensation, as if bodiless, yet this energy body from inside, So Real, So Comfortable. Then familiar forms, smiling, welcoming, beckoning me into a direction, a feeling drawing me towards a distant light, more felt than seen. This must be a lucid dream, I'm aware I can move by will alone, I can fly, My most pleasurable experience. The flight becomes effortless carried not self propelled. Laying back into the arms of the Mahaj, trusting. Bursting with rapture, now flying backwards through aura's of ecstasy. Stars, Moons, Suns flashing past me. Then turning to see the direction of the flight. Not really caring where I was going just so happy to be where I was. These dreams, always so fleeting, always waking too soon. But this one was going on and on, maybe this dream won't end, wonderful, I like it. Yet always ahead of me, the Light now closer, brighter. So easy to let go, surrender, into this feeling. How could I possibly resist? What more could I want. Absolute abandonment. Laughter, release, all happening simultaneously, then the thought, maybe this is death but I just couldn't remember, how I got here. No matter, I'm here finally.

Now, entering the light, feeling its essence moving around and through me, like tiny explosions that felt so good. The feeling of coming home, tired, to the warmth, the welcome, the final release. The light seemed to be absorbing me, slowly losing individual consciousness, a merging with more. Yet no sense of a loss instead a sense of me. Becoming expansive. Like a drop of rain merging with the ocean, becoming one with it. Feeling the motion of it, the filling, the ebbing. All happening in this New Sense of Being. The final relaxation, releasing the hold on life. The "AH", Home at last. The tension of life in form gone just a sense of belonging. A sense of destiny fulfilled. Nothing to pursue. All past impressions dimming, no longer necessary, as survival here was completely effortless. Effort would simply pull one out of this place. Why? The concept of Bliss, Now Manifest.

So this is who I really am. A being in total union with the Mahaj. The sense of all-knowing, not pondering, searching for truth, just a complete sense of knowing. This state of being was an obvious gift, a granting. Not earned, not a result of effort. Just an awakening to reality. This is how it really is, not how it appeared to be.

Suddenly, a change, a tug. The sense of individuality returning. An emotion of separating, becoming an entity unto itself. A sadness, having to leave such a paradise. Yet a knowing that it must be. Taking another rush at it, something left undone. Another tug. The light was dimming replaced by a rainbow colored stream carrying me. Then slam, I was back in form. I felt my skin feeling contact with what it was separate from. The sense of separation back again. The pain in my back, my immediate cringing reaction to it. Always a challenge to embrace pain. Yet knowing that to be free of it, it must be accepted, nourished and healed. When the pain is in you, avoidance is impossible. Shrinking away from it, traumatize the surrounding area as well, magnifying the effect. I began breathing into the hurt feeling, relaxing. It became bearable.

Then I opened my eyes. Where was I? Slowly memory of the battle began coming back. Looking around, there were no decaying bodies. So I didn't end up in that heap. Then I heard a gentle voice calling "Father, He's Awake". It came from a dark corner of the room. I could just make out a form, small with long, golden hair. A female, probably my nurse, I thought.

A door opened and in strode my opponent. He now wore a flowing robe, looking gentler without his warrior armor. A look of concern was obvious on his scarred face. I saw the scar my blade had left. It was healed over, but stood out distinctively as the light from the nearby table lantern fell on it. I thought "He can't be too happy about that", but to my surprise, his voice sounded soft, compassionately concerned.

"So, you're back among the living."

I thought. The other felt better, more like living. Here the challenge and pain go on.

I replied, "I guess you didn't finish me off, couldn't bring yourself to rid this world of such a beauty, huh?

My attempt at humor through the pain brought a look of pleasure to his face. He came closer, reached over and touched my forehead.

"The fever has broken, it looks like you'll make it after all. We had our doubts for awhile there. My daughter "Rea" would have been disappointed if you were taken. She's become quite attached to your ugly face, what she sees in it is beyond me."

Rea, shyly, bowed her head and started for the doorway. Apparently uncomfortable with her father's teasing remarks. "She's done a good job, treating your wound and watching over your trickle of life". Catching her before she reached the door, "Thank you, Rea, your kindness is appreciated". Raising her head slightly, I saw a flicker of a smile, a warmth from her eyes, and she was gone. Silently like a shadow.

"Don't be fooled by her gentleness, she is a fine warrioress but like her mother, is not too social. A loner, always with her animals. She rides like the wind, a fine huntress". I was surprised at the warmth in my host's voice and his obviously friendly demeanor.

"What happened out there and how did I end up here?" I queried.

"You're a strange one", his face showed puzzlement.

"You came into my encampment alone, challenged me, fought well, had your chance to finish me, yet didn't, and then your God cuts you down before us all. What could I do but take you in? I'm curious as to your reasoning and motive."

I replied, "My God cut me down, what are you saying? You think my God took one of your warriors and shot me in the back with his bow? Sounds to me like your shirking responsibility."

I felt strangely secure, but puzzled at this explanation.

His face had become stony - no expression.

"I do not lie, no one in my forces cut you down. It was not an arrow. I have never seen a wound like yours before. It was more of a burn than penetration. None of our weapons could do that. It was something else, and it came from beyond our settlement hall".

I sensed the truth in his voice. Odd, I thought, I'd heard stories of the Mahaj interfering in similar situations, but why?

Yet, why not? The results were all favorable. I'd had an incredible experience; been drawn into the very essence of LIFE, rested there, absorbed what was there and now lived on with a conscious memory of what lay ahead when this was over.

And here I was talking with the leader of the rebellious faction. Laying in his protection, healing. Furthermore, accepted and favored by his daughter.

The Mahaj had once again manifested a masterpiece of creativity. I remembered in the heat of battle seeing the dilemma of winning or losing.

This was the mutually acceptable way through.

I replied with sincerity. "Thank you for taking me in and caring for my wound. I hope I can repay you in some way".

"You can start by explaining what happened here, but now you need rest. There is plenty of time for the explanations. Let your flicker of life become a flame, then we shall talk".

My days of recuperation were somewhat painful but peaceful. My host slowly warmed to me and introduced me to many of his warriors as well as their codes. Although very intolerant of anything which appeared to be weakness, there was openness, deep down, to comradeship and honor, a space where true friendship could grow.

My challenge was to heal and at the same time create in roads of communication through which a mixture of our ways could find enough common ground to make us allies.

My days with Rea were warm. There seemed an automatic understanding between us despite our obvious differences. Were we soul mates, was the future simply a continuance of a past relationship, a continuance beyond our concepts of time and reality? This concept was spoken of a great deal among the Javadian youth. As a coming together of souls in such a fashion would be the ultimate nourishment and support for a male and female growing in the eye of the Mahaj.

Yet, this was not the right time to pursue this possibility, possibly at a later time, somewhere. A connection like this, if in fact it was, would create it's own magic. The sequence of events in each of our lives would conspire super consciously to bring us together to fulfill this part of our destinies. A warm feeling of acceptance came with this approach. No need to hurry, allow the flower to bloom in harmony with its nature and environment.

Seeing my wound as a gift from the Mahaj rather than an unwanted infliction of fate, speeded my healing process. Watching the consequences as they unfolded reinforced this premise. Galaxium was treating the fledgling relationship with the warrior faction with a great deal of care. Not pushing for any immediate changes but always ready to respond to any opening or need. My host saw this as well as the obvious benefits to his people from interaction. Once again allowance and co-operation were showing themselves as the most growth full approach to conflict.

Yet for me, the question, had I in some way pushed too hard in my approach? Being shot down so dramatically was not usual. I did swagger possibly over-confident in myself bringing on such an extreme reaction. Had I been gentler, slower, a bit more cautious, I might not have been confronted so directly. All academic postulations.

Toying with the possibilities, would I change the happenings now if I could? I realized I would not. The experience of touching in so deeply, bathing in the universal sea had somehow enriched me. There seemed a stronger current inside now. A deepening peace. A change from faith into an understanding. Still a faith, but now being built on the solidity of experience.

A Javadian psychic, at a later date, did a reading around the event and added even more depth to my understanding. Events like this in the past had always heralded important future events in the lives of those involved. This process was a preparation, a quantum leap in its influence on the psyche. Powers, depths of understanding, mystic abilities. All these sorts of seeds were planted during this time of near-death. Like genetic programs instilled to be accessed at a later, appropriate time. I began to feel a specialness around the happening and an excitement in the anticipation of what might happen.

I never did get around to trying to explain the occurrence to my host. He seemed to understand the futility of it all.

For a strong, self-willed being, his acceptance of the unknown aspect involved here surprised me. But what should surprise me after all this? The unfathomable was becoming common place and that daughter of his, Rea, riding like the wind, through the mists of my mind - where would we meet again?

CHAPTER 2

The Truth Stone was calling me back from the adventure with my warrior faction now living in my memory, yet so real, so accessible, an emotional memory, an experience I'd built on over the years. But here we are again, sitting around the Stone, the Arch Seats now silently waiting for the next surge.

Our introduction to the Javadian Physical Readiness Program fading away taking a side seat in readiness for our next stage.

The Beige Auric Ring Cloud floated gently as if on the winds of time, hovered over us all, then funneled itself down into the Beige Arch Seat signaling the rise of our Beige Leader. She stood tall and strong, yet reserved. Unlike the Milky Leader's eagerness, she approached the stone stage circle slowly with her right hand holding her heart area as if guarding it or perhaps waiting for her guidance to come from within.

As she reached the center, the cloud swirled furiously as if warning any possible threat of the potency here. Then settled into a layered multi-level hue of Beige in a spiral around our leader. The impression of protection was the dominant feature. We might wonder, why? Standing before us, she appeared strong, capable of facing her challenges unaided, yet a sense of vulnerability.

Our heart warrioress, willfully choosing to be open, vulnerable, able to sense with the sensitivity of one letting down her guard, trusting yet protected psychically. The mother of all the love-goddesses which had passed through my life. All those who had teased, treated, tortured and taught me along the way. The one who knew the deepest emotion yet supported all the levels leading there.

Her voice resonated not with the authority and vibrant vitality of our Milky Leader, but a soft permeating warmth which had an almost paralyzing inner effect, eliciting a response almost like a child hearing it's mother's warnings, directions and encouragements.

"I've come to speak to all of you, gathered here, about the Javadian approach to the phenomenon we all know as LOVE. That emotion which takes so many forms, rules most of us from our very first days. As children love keeps us close to our nourishment, our parents. Love opens our minds to their guidance. Comforts us through our growing times and binds us to our parent's ways, positive or negative depending on the level of evolution of the parents. Love makes the home the most precious place for us all.

Understanding this, you may see why and how you have gone about re-creating this Love-Home throughout your entire life. It becomes a place inside you, which is then projected out at different times of your life to re-create itself in your external reality. Why do you naturally seem to love certain settings, certain people, certain challenges. Many of us, spend our entire lives moving from one comfort zone to another even if they become reiterating and not growth full. Love, then can become a blinding, limiting force bound by its own pattern. Have you ever known someone who came from a violent family, abused from inside it, always re-creating violence in their life. They may not like the reality, yet inside they find comfort in it - home if you like, a sense of belonging.

A pattern, destructive, not growing, yet very difficult to change.

Then there is the child who grew up in a very emotionally - loving environment given support every step of the way. Almost smothered by the expressions of the feelings. Seemingly perfect, moving out of the protective enclosure of nurturing into the surrounding environment. Projecting out a reality creating warmth, security and that same aura of comfort. External realities are however unstable, subject to one constant, that is change.

As life goes on, loved ones grow, leave, die or simply evolve on another path. Being left alone, that loving home gone, what now? A life of memories, sadness, missing someone. Even the perfect start in life, can therefore end in unfulfillment.

What then is the answer? Loved or neglected. Inside, deep inside, we are all the same. The true Home of Love.

A true lover must be a warrior. The truth of the situation must be found, understood and unconditionally accepted.

The Mahaj has shown us, those of us who are willing to let go of our concepts of how things are, or how we want them to be, that a stable, dependable, loving home does exist. Deep inside us all, a place not influenced by the transitory nature of our external reality. When this place is found and given priority in importance all else begins to fall into place. Oh Yes!, even our external love relationships thrive in this aura. We each, individually, can then give of ourselves into the relationship not looking to the relationship for our comfort, but, already having the inner comfort, we give that to the collective. The collective, no matter what kind of relationship it is, will thrive because it is constantly being nourished, not drained by the needy. Filled by the Full.

Of course, with this fullness, completeness, there is not such a hunger for relationship. We each become an entity unto itself. Stronger in our independence, yet caring in our natural expression of ourselves, our true selves. That part of us which is one with the Mahaj, the source of this thing we call love.

When the expression of this thing we call love, is expressed back to its source, an ending is felt. The circle is finally complete. Everything living within that circle is also complete.

This approach to your life may sound simple, straight forward, easy to accomplish, yet as you step on this path, you may find it is far more challenging than any other journey you have taken as a warrior in life.

You will come face to face with all your fears. Shadows waiting to haunt you for you've had the courage to step outside the security of your comfort zones. Those limiting factors which eventually bring you pain. The Mahaj wants you to fly free of them and constantly coaxes, nudges, sometimes pushes demonstratively. Getting free is obviously the first important step on the journey to the center of the heart, the abode of love, pure and simple. Uncontaminated by attached emotion".

She was now a dancing, flowing goddess radiating that clear love zone she spoke about.

Courage was being emitted, like waves washing a pebble beach. Felt deep inside, inspiring one to look there and see the intrigue.

She continued, encouraged by our obvious thirst for more.

"These fears have created neurotic patterns which have their own momentum of self-preservation. When approached, recognized and seen as conditions to be outgrown, their self-preservation mechanisms will undoubtedly arise.

Here is where the inner battle begins.

Try approaching a part of your life you know is disharmonious, causing you more discomfort than comfort. An addiction to a substance or a relationship which causes more grief than happiness. Simply walking away from the condition just never seems to work. In the case of the substance, you might find yourself free, yet taking a look at yourself later you'll probably find you've simply transferred your addictive nature into another relationship with something else. The cravings are simply refocused but they live on. In the case of the relationship, leaving it without resolving the part of you which reached out and created the original condition will probably just bring you into another relationship down the road with a similar set-up, similar outcome.

This is a battle of consciousness, consciousness being the greatest healing tool available to us. As we shine our consciousness on these murky portions of our lives, the Mahaj comes to our aid. We take the first baby steps toward clarity and freedom. We are met and helped by forces beyond our imagination".

She was now smiling as if remembering some part of her own process she was going to undoubtedly share with us.

"Once, walking along a distant shoreline, I ran across a small bird who was doing the oddest thing. She was dipping her beak into the ocean and drinking. Now I knew birds did not particularly like salt water, but there she was slurping away at the ocean. I cleared my throat, caught her attention and asked.

"Why are you drinking the ocean?"

Seeing a small tear in her eyes, I felt her sorrow and listened to her story.

"Three days ago, I laid two golden eggs right here on this shore, where my family has laid eggs forever. Yesterday, the sea monster who lives over there", she was showing me a distant island, "came and took them. He just laughed at me when I threatened to drink the ocean dry if he didn't give back my children. Well the sadness in my heart is so great, that I decided I have to try. So pardon me, but I must get back to my mission".

With this, she started drinking the ocean. What a sense of hopelessness I felt as I heard the monster's jeering laughter floating over the water. What hope could she possibly have?

Then there was a sudden darkening, a great shadow, I looked up and there was this gigantic bird. His wings reached from horizon to horizon. He settled down gently behind his sister bird. She didn't even notice his presence as she was so intent on her work. To my surprise I saw the great bird reach over her and simultaneously in perfect synchronicity begin drinking. The ocean receded slightly. The sea monster had seen the going's on and stood watching with a look of growing concern. Was his home being endangered? Would it be drunk by this little bird and her helper?

He decided not to risk it, reached into a deep hole and brought out two golden eggs, swam up to the little bird and humbly placed her eggs before her and swam off dejected.

At once, the great bird spread his great wings and flew off unnoticed by the little bird. The little bird, now, gleefully, pranced her dance of celebration, turned to me and said.

"You see, that big bully, knows what I can do when I'm determined".

All was well, I saw the power of my determination and the power it could unearth.

Yet the question arises, what in this reality we call life is worthy of such determination and power? If we create realities with it which in turn limit our potential, then we've done ourselves disservice. Of course, in the case of the little bird, her determination for self-preservation of her species was undoubtedly harmonious.

Those of us, in the nesting process, need physical support systems for the propogational stage of our lives to go smoothly. To give our fledglings the benefit of a healthy, happy start. When this stage of our lives is over isn't it limiting to carry on building the nest when it is no longer really necessary. Our illusions of security and comfort make it appear very necessary. But if the process, in fact limits our growth, what use is it all? There may be no harm in being comfortable but when the fear of losing it becomes the primary emotion and therefore our determination is focused on this form of security, the power of this process can become limiting and dysfunctional. A time to take a good look at our lives and re-align our priorities. Commitments and determinations are incredible avenues of power - use them wisely.

I suggest that our experiences in commitment and determination throughout the early stages of our lives may be practicing flights. Not unlike the short flights, young birds take around their nests, strengthening their wings developing stamina. The real excursion is yet to come.

When the transitory nature of the physical reality is seen and understood, the necessity of finding something stable, not transitory, becomes the logical pursuit. But where to look, everything perceived extraneously is transitory, in constant change, had a beginning and for all intents and purposes will have an end. Even the mechanism that we perceive and experience the external reality with will someday end.

What option is left? The only place left to look is within ourselves. Now comes the true test of commitment and determination. Simply glancing inside has little effect. This must be seen as the beginning of an eternal journey. One which must be acknowledged, settled into and enjoyed. You're going to be on it for a long time. Once the commitment to the process is made and the determination to achieve this seemingly impossible feat is made, like the little bird we must make our effort with the faith that the Mahaj will come to our aide.

Once our experiences on this journey show us that we are being helped, in fact, what we actually do is very little in comparison to our helper's part, our faith turns into knowledge. A true understanding as to how things really work. A sense of surrender, letting go into a process beyond our limited comprehension. What a release, a burden dropped, a feeling of lightness lifting us, carrying us, where to? Who cares, its all in the getting there, the journey. Possibly there is no destination other than the joy of the voyage".

The feelings I was having as she spoke of the journey were similar to my flight to the Mahaj after being shot down on my warrior friend's planet. The joy of flying through star systems, feeling them inside me, then finally resting in the bosom of the universal sea gently ebbing and filling. Could this be the journey's end? Resting, being absorbed, losing individuality yet becoming so much more.

"You see," she said, now beaming around her closing remarks.

"My message is really quite simple even though the process may not be. After a life of setting goals, achieving results and gaining skills in dealing with our external world, the time must come when you simply let go and trust. Not blindly, but consciously. Conscious of the importance of this new stage in your evolution. Knowing that all you can really do is make the commitment and then voluntarily participate with the process as it unfolds. Sounds straight forward and easy doesn't it?

Good luck to each of you".

Her message seemed so simple, yet pondering on its ramifications, the depth of what was introduced was unfathomable. Too much, to really comprehend, but its direction was clear. The rest was up to each one of us in our individual approach to the ultimate common denominator.

The mists of Beige slowly receded with our leader to her Arch Seat, then on back to the temple from where it had come from.

This brought us to the time to hear from our final leader, the Turquoise Ring Aura. What more could be added? The need for a healthy, strong, agile physical form was made clear. Moving spontaneously on the currents of the universal sea could challenge even the fittest. The need for a strong, brave heart and spirit to move towards fulfillment of our ultimate destiny was made clear. The final challenge of coming to terms with our true purpose of being, not just tending to our physical responsibilities and comfort, but taking our steps into our final dance.

The truth stone had suddenly become translucent as if it were changing before our eyes, the arch seats with the leaders were losing their individual color codes and becoming almost vibrational in appearance. A sudden darkening, then a resonating whirring sound from the far off temple. A change was taking place from the emission center, throughout the physical arena we were all in. The previously solid stage setting was losing it's solidity, now barely visible, yet still present. Then a hazy emanation descending from the dimmed sun simultaneously touching the top of the temple and the Turquoise Arch seat area coming to rest in the center of the former stage area.

We were witnessing a graphic demonstration of a physical reality dimensional transformation. A picture is often as effectual in presenting a conceptual point as a lengthy dialogue. Here it was, a demonstration of change from a common agreed on reality into something new, different, but undeniable. Graphic enough to open the mind of the most doubting. As my senses observed the changes, I felt an inner quickening, almost a tension similar to fear. Approaching the unknown, always confronting. How we enjoy settling into stability, the common agreed upon framework we call reality.

The introduction of newness never failing to elicit this self-preservational phenomena. Yet here I was, still me, still observing, even though my former physical body state was changing, becoming vibrational. As I glanced around, I saw my fellow journeyers were experiencing a similar transformation.

Then the voice, a haunting wail, as if coming from a resonance scale beyond our hearing capacity, tuning itself slowly to our common vibrational hearing mode. Changing from unintelligible impressions similar to the sounds we hear inside ourselves in deep meditation, to a flow of impressions slowly becoming audibly understandable. A calming feeling and there before us stood our Turquoise Aura Leader. Not invisible, yet not clearly defined. Much like a flowing mist, taking form, then moving into an almost unperceivable state.

"Pardon, this sudden change but what I will be presenting to you is not in the common framework of what most of us consider reality. You have each been placed temporarily into a stage of your own ethereal energy body. Introducing you in this way, saves me a great deal of time explaining and convincing. Experience is undeniable unless you doubt even that. In that case you're hopeless. Too immersed in the physical. Caught in the web of illusion which keeps you on the wheel of birth after birth. The process which brings you here over and over again until the boundaries holding you weaken enough to facilitate an easy transformation into your constant, unchangeable self. The two previous leaders have laid out the groundwork of preparation to prepare you for this inevitable experience. Your long-awaited step into immortality.

This body has no end, no limits other than those you bring from your physical life. Strong desire patterns which do not easily dissipate. Necessitating an approach to the purification of your desire processes. Desires thrive on consciousness, the more you feed them, the stronger they become. Starving them, on the other hand, weakens them. However, a great deal of discomfort can be involved in a wilful approach to the starvation mode, even though this may be the most effective.

There is an alternate approach, that of re-alignment and being conscious of your desire processes. Watching them as they rise in you demanding satisfaction. Then as you approach satisfying them, observe the patterns created around them. Patterns which live on, grow stronger as you feed them with your committed actions.

Pleasures experienced creating a need, a craving to re-experience. Soon the patterns limit your spontaneity creating a predictable re-play of events leading to a re-experiencing of what you feel to be the most important events in your life, excluding all those events which lay in the field of potentiality, left unexperienced because you're too busy replaying your old, familiar desire patterns. Once seen as the trap these desire patterns really are, what can be done about them? They resonate so powerfully in you, demanding your attention. Wanting to live on. Self-preservation, a part of you firing automatically - feed me, feed me.

This may be a good time to look around you, take a good look at the fruits that you grow on this tree. Watch the young creating their particular patterns, see how the middle aged settle into their familiar pleasure modes, then look to the elders who still feel the needs but begin to reflect on the futility of their life-long pursuits. Soon, only too soon, it will all end and what is left but a shadow of a life satisfying the needs of a body-mind now coming to its inevitable end. Worm food, nothing more. Do you consider this a fruit worthy of eating, worthy of savoring, worthy of investing your precious consciousness, a life-time of consciousness on?

There are those who would say, "Well, this is all we know. What else is there to do but satisfy our needs, our desires, be as comfortable as possible and then hopefully pass on to heaven. It's all out of our control, out of our hands".

Those of you gathered here, now know there is more, much more and it is in your hands. It is your will, that can re-align your desire mode, set your goals on another avenue of pursuit, bring your attention onto a process not bound by pattern, but designed to free you, draw you into an unlimited flight. An endless journey, blissful every step of the way.

Desire is an incredibly powerful process in our lives, realities are created by them. If they are aligned to only the physical domain, the results will be predictable, limited in their potential at the very best. Probably painful for most, because of their unfulfillment. Undoubtedly a poor gambler's risk.

Yet when this process is re-aligned to the growth into your infinite self and the unlimited nature of this experience, the miraculous will unfold. All that is required is your commitment and willingness to co-operate. The rest will unfold like a rose in the spring sun. Powers await to turn your small step into a gigantic leap.

Every little step will show itself as willingness, a readiness for the final leap taking you beyond the limits of the known. The final step, however, is in the hands of the Mahaj. Like a beam from a far off star, presenting itself to us individually. All we need is the courage, understanding and will to step aboard. Letting go of our self-inflicted limits, that's our part. The rest is the wonderment of the universal plan. Desire is the key, trust opens the door, our commitment takes us in, our true identity waits inside, unlimited and growth full in nature.

We must come to see, our subtle form, our mind, our persona, that part of us which can identify with anything and become anything. Most of us choose to be a physical entity, which we undoubtedly are at this particular time. But that is where most of us stop. Could we possibly be more? We, here, can now see that we are more. Our subtle form can now re-identify itself. The transition will not be immediate but once seen, the truth can no longer be denied. Stay open to your infinite self, let your mind move into this newness, explore it, become familiar with it. Finally live there.

Like the worm, seeing its butterfly nature losing interest in digging in the dirt begins to weave its cocoon, certain of its transformational capability. Then leaving its old familiar form and becomes its potential.

Fulfilling its destiny, becoming a cosmic butterfly with wings powerful enough to explore the far reaches of the unlimited universe. Soaring gracefully on the powerful winds of the ever-present, beckoning Mahaj".

CHAPTER 3

As our leader's voice faded into the realm of the past, a hazy dimness settled over the congregation, a stillness as if asking us all to reflect on the profundity of what was said, what was relayed. How quickly our minds re-frame our familiar realities. I'd had this experience before, many times before, but each time it was as if it were the first. This time it felt a little more familiar and now a memory came to me. A time I'd spent with an old friend who now lived most of his time in the ethereal aspect of his being. The boundaries between his realities had faded to the extent of easily moving between realms. In his company, it seemed easy to follow the transitional process. As if his efforts had made cosmic in-roads. He always enjoyed company on his voyages, being well aware that someone open could gain strength in their own ability to transform by the effect of doing it with him in their initial stages of initiation.

My adventure with him some time ago was like a dream. Segments of experience, rather than a continuum of events, one leading into the other. His service in the Galaxium quarter had evolved through the U.I.A. and was now independent of any group. He had over time manifested on many planets in physical form, done extra-ordinary things, things referred to as miracles, occurrences a step beyond the normal limits occurring at that time. This was done to gain a level of respect and authority so that at times of transition, his form could be projected and help in the trying, difficult periods. The trust given would aid the process in the trusting.

This time he was being called to a place where he'd taught the ways of the Mahaj for a period of time, but the times were disruptive, in the early stages of development, much distrust, much selfishness, territoriality was emphatically protected and in the early stages of his life, he was executed in a slow and painful manner. The whole event was a dramatic historical occurrence referred to in stories passed down through generation after generation. So I began relating to him as my martyred friend. Martyrdom had become an almost revered form of death. The high level of values held by those who stood firmly by their beliefs and their willingness to serve at all costs became an example many strived to live by.

However most of the social order still maintained it's reverence of power over their fellows and held firmly to systems of control which perpetuated violence and death. There was little importance placed on the inner journey. The only institutions which flickered these ideals were religious orders built around the myths formed around the lives and teachings of those like my martyred friend. This was our mission this time round to monitor and support in any possible way, the flicker even though it was still in the belief stages rather than committed to experimental process systems. It was hoped that the flicker if fanned appropriately would become a flame inspiring more of the society to change it's priorities from self-centered gain to the gain individually experienced in the service of the Mahaj.

Initially by serving his representatives and eventually seeing the wholeness of existence and their unity with the entirety.

My near death experience on my warrior friend's planet seemed to have laid the ground work for a relatively easy access to entering the ethereal body experience. Through meditation, breath control and visualization, I was able to bring my form vibration to a point where my martyred friend, I called him Marty for short, could reach through the boundary and pull me into his ethereal vibrational dimension. In preparation, I would fast and meditate to purify the body and mind for several days. Toxic waste in either form would make the passage difficult in its initial stages. Much like a space shuttle with any loose parts breaking out of the atmosphere.

The force of the transition would shock the craft so intensely, that these loose parts would fly free until only the solid form holding tight would smoothly break through.

Let's say the loose parts are any physical remains of toxic input as well as mental disfocused thought forms drawing us back into neurotic desire modes.

I dropped into the preliminary stages of meditation quickly as I practiced this part almost daily. Following my breath to the heart region, focusing my attention here, as this was considered to be the central dwelling area of the Mahaj in all Javadian thought processes. By focusing and holding here, the intent to participate in the process if it was in harmony at this time was presented to the Mahaj. It was, as I felt a warm, tingling emanation from the center, then a corresponding glow in the Tishra Roi region commonly referred to, as the third eye. The linkage between the light and the resonating word of the Mahaj had been made. Then, the sound, an inner hum, growing in intensity until all external sound was blocked out fading into that constant oceanic rhythm. I felt the current of life, building, building, a slight hesitancy, something I forgot to do, a small thing which suddenly seemed so important. I saw it at once as a mental diversion, trying to disfocus me, then a surge and I was through. No longer feeling my physical limitations, now drifting as if on a cloud in readiness. Here there was a peace, a dream-like observing, watching somewhat removed, separate yet full of an almost joyful expectancy. Fear did not enter this place of existence. The perfect platform from which to observe dispassionately even the most confronting events. I felt Marty approaching even before I saw the swirling, brilliant light form, a beam reaching into my transitional state, then millions of sparks exploding all around me, feeling like tiny pin pricks, not painful, almost pleasant and then the pull - breathtaking.

There we were, standing side by side at our destination. No travel time, he always said we were everywhere already, all we had to do was see it in the ethereal. The challenge was to let go of our limited vision in order to see the reality. In this case, Marty had visualized us at our destination and by surrendering myself through the meditation I was able to move into his reality and experience almost like his shadow.

Me, I thought, a shadow, Ha! So full of self-importance, must be quite a dark shadow.

Marty, reading my thoughts, assured me.

"You're doing quite alright for a fledgling, do you see that building where all those vehicles are gathered around? I want you to go there and observe, I have some preparations to make. In your present form you are barely visible, but to those there who are sensitive, you'll appear as one of the security people. This will give you access to wherever the Mahaj takes you. Flow freely, but you know all about that, don't you?".

He always enjoyed pointing out my little time and experience in the U.I.A. as well as the over-dramatic occurrence on my warrior friend's planet. Marty felt that the Mahaj had shot me down for not flowing loosely enough in the situation. I used too much of my own will with a little too much assurance and pride.

I replied with an inner sense of joy at once again being here in company with one I respected and always felt very comfortable with.

"Well, I never seem to be able to flow quite as freely as you. But then you're almost invisible nowadays. Why don't you keep in touch?"

"Busy! Busy! Busy!". He replied with a smile knowing full well that he was never too busy to manifest to anyone needing his company. In fact it was always me who was too involved in my life's limitations to open up to the pleasure.

"Is there anything I should know about all this?". I queried.

"Nope", he was almost flippant. "Just play it by ear".

Saying this, he moved into a swirl and headed off to a distant hill with an opening. I wondered what could he be preparing for, preparations were not usual for his inherent spontaneous nature.

As I began moving towards the grey, official looking building, I felt a sense of numbness, my preference would have been to visit, share experiences. Marty's experience throughout the galaxy always stretched my comprehension of reality. I guess that's what we call growth, and growth was definitely one thing I was totally committed to.

Even though that growth was often disturbing. In it's very nature, to grow means to change, to become more, and how can that manifest without leaving the old, the familiar behind. That was always the rub, the price. Learning to detach quickly through practice by seeing the nature of it all. Growing in the experience of "of letting go" in order to move easily into the new. To learn that and the freedom it brings is one of the most important self-skills to be developed in dealing with a constantly changing environment. Only when grounded in the essence of our true self, the transitional process stops. Or does it? Possibly our sense of the unity brings stability but the stability itself has its own inherent growth nature. "Beats me," I thought, as I moved through the archway towards a buzz of activity. I passed official looking beings dressed in similar uniforms. Obviously a gathering of warriors. The type of weapons that ripped through the flesh, left gaping holes through which the internal fluids drained, were displayed everywhere. Javadians had long since evolved past anything like this. There was such an ignorance in the thought process supporting the concept that if you simply eliminate the fellow beings who stand in your aggressive way, you would be free of interference in having things the way you wanted them. It was far more complex than that. Bodies would be replaced. The conflict would continue, in fact, the resistance by its very nature would grow.

Yet here I was, witnessing beings who supported a process, we as a collective had grown through. I wondered, were we being monitored by beings who had out-grown our particular natures. Were we considered archaic in our ways of being. Seeing this possibility, a sense of tolerance came over me. How could I aide the growing process here, for that is what I would wish from a collective evolved beyond me and mine.

This inner shift seemed to create an energy surge in my heart region, I felt drawn to a stairway leading to a room bordering on a stage-like platform. An obvious place for the leader or leaders to gather in preparation for addressing the gathered. As I approached the door, I began pacing myself to the external rhythm of motion around me. Being invisible to most, opening the door could draw unwanted attention. These people were alert, watching for anything abnormal, wary of any unseen threat. A few feet from the door, it opens, a well decorated officer holds the door open momentarily as he finishes a conversation with someone inside. I always enjoyed these subtle manipulations by the Mahaj. It always made me feel in harmony, moving in tune with the divine hand. In that motion, there was little if any self-will, just the sense of being carried, an experience which made the letting go of the preferred easier.

As I was swept into the room, unseen up to now, I felt the tension, the aura of self-importance, a mission, ideals held which seemingly transcended the needs of the individual. What was going on here was for the good of the collective rather than just an imposition of will upon others for self-gain. How we play with these illusions of grandeur when in fact most everyone gathered here was probably supporting, protecting or enlarging their worldly nest. Their small part of their particular environment worthy of standing up for with their very lives, they felt. Not only felt, but felt self-righteously about. Reminded me somewhat of a young fellow, I'd recently seen on a shuttle, who was completely caught in a love web with his young female friend. An obvious mating ritual. What I saw was his self-righteous protective stance. So uncomfortable, so vulnerable, so unstable. Scanning his environment for possible threats to his shaky ego-stance. Yet through his obvious discomfort trying to maintain an aura of control. She seemed to be enjoying it all, I quivered inside, probably seeing myself in my youth.

Yet in this atmosphere, the wrong glance, a word taken as a challenge, the unstable ego ready to do battle for something meaningless, but not in the eyes of the emotionally involved. To them this was all that mattered.

I found myself drawn to a far corner of the room, three men stood looking my way, had they perceived my approach? I never knew when my ethereal form would take on a visible appearance in this play. Would I remain a detached observer or would the Mahaj bring me right into the melodrama by reducing my vibrational frequency level. It seemed that in this case, I was being drawn into the scene, as different persons were glancing my way, noticing me, possibly just as a vibrational nuance.

But no, one of the three men was beckoning, well, here we go, I thought, relax and flow just like Marty said. My universal translation implant was functional and my response language translator was also intact. I approached with the surety of a veteran security type. The look of intense concern, fully committed to protect at all costs.

One of the men was reaching out his hand in a handshake mode, I wondered if I had made enough of a vibrational transition to do this. I took his hand and felt his energy-body. Slow yet strong, firm with conviction. Here was one who completely believed what he was doing here, was honorable in harmony with his life and his society's. "We've been expecting you, after a short speech from Beno on the necessity of attacking now, we'll be leaving. Our intelligence has informed us that our approach now will be successful. You'll be in charge of personal security for Beno and his company. Has central intelligence briefed you on procedures?"

All I could say was, "Yes", assuming procedures were similar to personal protection standards formulated in Galaxium for situations like this in societies at this level of evolution.

Beno was obviously the un-uniformed political-type standing slightly off to my right looking my way. Was it puzzlement on his face or just the concern of being in the hands of a stranger in what appeared to be a dangerous situation unfolding.

My obvious superior in this particular frame continued.

"Beno will be meeting the people, highly exposed only until we reach this side of the boundary tunnel. The area from that point on has been fully secured and is well guarded. On the other side you'll escort the party to a safe place where we've set up a temporary command headquarters. I'll be leading the attack,

Meisha, here", he was pointing out his comrade standing at his left who curtly saluted, I returned the salute, no intimacy here, I thought, "will be sweeping the area ahead of the cavalcade".

I saw that Meisha was very rigid, solid but inflexible. He would play the game straight by the rule book. Efficient but not intuitive and spontaneous in battle.

"Kwan Yen will be sweeping the rear of the cavalcade". A smaller yellow-skinned man with piercing, searching eyes appraising me. His greeting was more cordial, my translator registered. "May your day with us, be uneventful".

Yes, I thought, in the security business that was a good day. I replied,

"May the ripples of our cavalcade be small".

He had the maturity to see preference in swimming in ripples rather than surfing on a raging sea. A seasoned warrior who'd seen his share of the results of rushing head-long into battle, now preferring to hang back, letting the younger take the foreground.

"Here is a map laying out your route, you'll have a pilot you can give it to at the departure time".

Standard procedure I thought.

"Good luck men" wished my unnamed superior as I saw Beno move through a door onto the stage area.

The stage was set up quite well, I thought, I'd been accepted to play out my small role and would have a good vantage point to observe whatever it was I was here to observe. I'd witnessed these types of occurrences, many times before. What could be different about this one?

Here were all these committed beings, committed to their particular view of the situation. Obviously there was an opposing faction in the play who were also as committed to their viewpoint. The situation appeared to be headed for a direct confrontation. An attack, I wondered, would it be as easy and successful as my superior seemed convinced of. In my experience it hardly ever was.

Well, to protect a few individuals even in the worst scenario shouldn't be too difficult. I'd play out my part, simply and straight forward. My U.I.A. training was quite extensive in this particular field. My Javadian training would intuitively keep me aware of any danger to my wards. I was thankful, I'd not been put in charge of the attack. Working around the issues involved in that scenario would have been difficult. Simple protection could be dealt with, without violence. Slipping through and around obstacles had been my specialty in this field of encounter. Since my warrior-planet experience, the Mahaj always presented me with an avenue circumventing direct confrontation. A side door which would always magically open, an escape route, a way out. Some might say, the cowards way out, yet the job always got done, mostly uneventfully.

The Javadian's greatest battle was with their own ego. That part identifying with their image in the group. The warrior who would rather die than lose face in his or her community. I felt I was surrounded by many of these here.

I'd dealt with this personal issue many times. When the feeling of pride and identity with the outcome, rose inside in a situation, instead of acting immediately on it, I found the results were always more appropriate, if I stopped, looked objectively at the external factors as well as my internal urges. That moment was always enough to allow the Mahaj to re-frame the situation and give me the way out with personal integrity intact. Moving with the universal currents, the will of the Mahaj, had become far more satisfying than the fleeting acclaims of an impressed social group. Sometimes leading to an alone place but never a lonely place. Always in good company. A guiding force which never failed to show the wisdom in surrendering one's personal will in uncertain situations and follow the obvious route clearly shown without personal ego involvement. The secret seemed to be able to see the Mahaj in all aspects of the play, in the stage and in all the players, then relating directly to that in a co-operative mode. A powerful, growth full vision of reality always supported by a harmonious outcome.

The pleasure of being a conscious part of the play rather than one of the unconscious. From the outside, all seem the same, caught up helplessly in the arising sea of physical phenomenon leading to the undeniable conclusion. However, being conscious that the Mahaj was always playing with the events as they unfolded gave one the sense of surety, the inner faith to move with the subtle currents and to glean out the pearl being offered. After all each event like this unfolded for that reason. Growth and understanding were the real opportunities here. Not territory and power. Yet few would see that in to-day's events. Such a pity, I thought, to miss the presence of the painter's hand. To only see the picture from the perspective of the painted. Too immoveable for me, I thought, catching myself, feeling a little pride in my understanding, but then I had all the advantages. How many times had I been caught up in the battle and not seen the true nature of the war.

The inspirational speech was predictable.

Starting by pointing out a few recent atrocities committed on his people, an assurance that all efforts for resolution of issues had been made. Now that all alternatives had been exhausted, attack and resolution through force was not only the most logical option but was deemed harmonious by the priests of their spiritual leader who had been a great warrior in his time.

Well, it all fit very nicely, the fault lay on the shoulders of the enemy and God was on their side. A comforting thought for all concerned.

I wondered if there was a similar gathering going on somewhere on the other side with a similar stance. Must be a confusing dilemma for anyone up there listening.

None the less, the gathered warriors ate it all up, cheered Beno's address and enthusiastically prepared for battle.

Throughout the address and even now I sensed something familiar in the ethereal field. I just couldn't put a finger on it. But there it was almost like sensing the approach of an old friend. There was an intensity in the field unlike that of Marty.

As the troops gathered in and around their heavily-armored vehicles, I took my position in a smaller somewhat over-powered but extremely maneuverable all-terrain vehicle at the head of Beno's highly decorated parade-like vehicle. The area must be secure indeed, I thought, we stuck out like a sore thumb. Beno, his company and driver were settling into their showmanship stance, getting as comfortable as possible. I was beginning to wonder where my driver was, I didn't relish the idea of trying to figure out the route on the map and drive all at once. Might end up in the wrong place at the wrong time. Just then I saw a slight figure break from Beno's immediate group, approach my vehicle and climb into the driver's seat. I voiced my relief.

"Just on time, I guess I shouldn't give you the map, until we get to the other side of the tunnel. Security, you know".

I wondered at my feelings of humorous warmth to this soldier who seemed so familiar and relaxed.

As my driver turned to reply, I was surprised to see an attractive youthful female. Apparently pleased at my surprise she replied.

"Yes, security above all else, after all that is my family you're guarding. My name is Cinda, Beno is my father. He thought you might enjoy a member of the family showing the way and ours". She added reassuringly.

"I'm also a capable driver, I race for sport and know these mountains quite well. Feel secure now?"

I almost lost the pun, but catching my breath replied.

"That was very nice of him, isn't he concerned that I might be distracted by someone as beautiful as you?"

The flirtation was tolerantly accepted.

"He knows a man of your discipline is not easily distracted. I'll also do my best not to distract you in any way". Her eyes showed a slight glint of pleasure at the immediate warmth between us. The warmth was partially due to the fact, I was sure, that I'd not been in the company of a woman for sometime. My biological response was only too obvious. Taking her helmet off and tossing her reddish curls down around her shoulders didn't help matters in any way. This is shaping up to be quite a trip, I thought.

I felt someone at my right elbow, it was my superior.

"I see you've met Cinda, she's as capable as any man we have. Expert in the martial arts, as well." I was beginning to feel a little toyed with, seeing a little lechery in his expression. He obviously felt I was on a pleasant cruise, well guarded, no where near the battle. A nice, soft visit with the first family in their secured mountain retreat.

"You can give me back the map, if you like, Cinda knows the way."

"I'd like to keep it, if it's all right." I didn't want to be totally dependant on Cinda, just in case I lost her.

"Certainly, keep it as a souvenir." He seemed quite jovial, as he strode off assuredly to his waiting armored truck.

As I turned my attention back to Cinda a shadow fell over her, someone had approached and stood near her, too near I thought. She noticed the presence, looked up at the young officer standing there.

"Oh, hello Feda, its been awhile, how are you?"

"Fine", he replied, "You look well, I guess it's finally here, what we've been waiting for."

"Yes", Cinda showed concern, "You're part of the fore-front strike force, aren't you?"

"Yes", Feda replied enthusiastically.

"We've trained long and hard for this opportunity."

He was obviously seeing this as a chance to step up in his hierarchy of command. Battle had a way of doing that if you survived.

"Could I see you, after this is all over?"

Cinda's response was warm but reserved.

"Sure, send Mela, my parents like her. She can take me to where you are, we can visit for awhile."

"Good". Feda was now straining at the bit.

"I must get back to my men. Take care, Cinda."

"Yes, I will", she replied, "May Moham shine his protective light on you."

"Thank you." He bounced away, waving his farewell.

The procession was about to get under way. People had lined up along the roadway to the tunnel and were waving different banners, different colors, it was all very Gaelic, too much like a celebration, I thought, but then it was always like this. The enthusiasm, the assumption of victory, the bolstering of the spirit for the upcoming trial.

"Seems like a nice fellow", part of me feeling I might be getting too personal.

She replied.

"Oh yes, he's very nice, I'm sorry, I didn't introduce you."

"That's quite alright, I'd rather remain somewhat of a shadow anyway." At any rate, I thought, I haven't even made up a name, yet. Maybe I should, we'll see if I need one. One will come to me then, I'm sure. I could call myself Mo, but that might be getting to close to identifying with Cinda's protective spirit.

A sharp, shrill blast suddenly resonated in our ears. As I turned I saw Beno had leaned over his driver's shoulder and given us a blast from their horn, as he grinned playfully, obviously enjoying himself. Well, why not, I thought here he was the center of all this attention, surrounded by comrades and family. Living in harmony with his sense of duty and destiny.

I playfully nudged Cinda.

"Daddy calls, I guess we'd better move it."

"Yes Sir!" I didn't know if she was directing that remark to Daddy or me.

As we slowly moved down the roadway towards the distant tunnel, I scanned the gathered for any possible threat, everyone seemed harmlessly waving their support, taking the opportunity to enjoy themselves. The majority appeared to be workers of the land. Weather-beaten faces, large strong hands, not people who thought too deeply about life, politics and evolution. Survival was their main concern. Beno's administration had apparently provided this to their satisfaction. I sensed little possibility of threat here, but somewhere, I could just feel it, it was there.

I'd noticed an occasional glint, like the sun reflecting off glass on a hillside up to the right of the tunnel.

"What goes on over there," I pointed out the hill area. Cinda momentarily took her eyes off the road and gazed in the direction I'd pointed to.

"Not too much, some sheep herding and some recreational area's for all terrain vehicles."

That's probably it, I thought, a reflecting windshield, but then again, it just might be a surveillance glass, watching us, co-ordinating an attack. No way to be sure.

I checked my map instead of bothering and distracting Cinda from her driving, saw that our route took us to the other side of the hills when we exited the tunnel. Good, no chance of an encounter, at least with that particular potential threat, yet I would have secured a vantage point, like that. Meisha's scope didn't seem to reach that far. Possibly the level of surveillance technology wasn't developed enough to function at that distance.

I was familiar with equipment so sensitive that I could count the number of pimples on the face of one of the young soldiers ahead from that distance. Boys, I thought, playing with such a precious opportunity, life. The chance to evolve to immortality, by simply focusing their life-force appropriately, instead here they were marching straight into the possible end of the opportunity.

No ideal, value or belief was worth that, they all dimmed at death. Yet the soul, the inner self, always waiting to be approached, experienced, played with, offering the step into immortality. Yet here I sat with a young lady who while believing in some form of spirituality was still living a life committed to the values and ideals of her family and society.

How could I reach in and change all that? It just wasn't that simple. Somehow evolution had to bring her to first question all these values, then move away from them towards the truth in whatever way it would reach out to her. I wondered, was that happening someway, now? Not turning to her, so she wouldn't have to return my look, wanting her full attention on the driving although it was very straight forward and slow at this time.

"Where did you study the ways of Moham?"

Her reply was automatic, unthought.

"My parents, brought in a special tutor when I was very young, she knew all the old ways. She taught me about the life, the teachings and the miracles as the foundation. When I was older,. she showed me some rituals and exercises which were designed to keep me true to the ways of Moham."

I was surprised, there was wisdom at work here, some hope. A shadow passed slowly across our windshield, looking up I spotted a large greyish bird hovering over our cavalcade, it slowly dipped its left wing catching an air current, circled us as if eyeing watchfully. I felt a protective aura.

"Is she still with you?"

The words almost fell out of my mouth.

"No", there was a slight sadness in her voice, "She passed on to the higher realms a short while ago."

The protective aura grew stronger, looking up to the circling bird, I thought, Cinda has a protective spirit watching over her evolution, I wondered if she was aware of it. As I gazed at the bird and extended my senses, feeling its strength envelope us, I saw that Cinda had taken her focus off the road and was gazing at me with a look of puzzlement.

"How did you know?"

"Know what?" I feigned ignorance.

"You know, that Rhona is still here, with me in spirit." Wanting to avoid a direct discussion of the how's of it all, I replied.

"You're very fortunate to have such a powerful guide especially in times like this."

"She speaks to me in my indecisive times", Cinda now spoke through a trance-like facial expression.

"In fact, she just assured me of your integrity. She wants me to trust you completely, you will do nothing consciously to ever harm me or my family in any way."

I felt thankful for the support, trust was a very powerful key, I might need to use it in a critical situation.

"Do you also feel the presence of Moham in your life?"

"Not like Rhona, Rhona is his servant, so my directions come through her. His teachings are my guidelines in life, but his presence is for those who have passed on."

I felt an inner sadness for the conscious denial of the possibility of direct experience. Yet here was a connection, an openness to the unknown, although contaminated with a belief structure limiting the possibilities. I wondered do I do the same in some other way. Fragments of belief's standing between me and the Mahaj, getting in the way. Much like rocks in a stream, creating swirls and pools, illusory yet so real.

By this time, we'd almost passed the cheering well-wishers and were approaching the darkness of the tunnel entrance. Our forerunners led by my superior had already passed inside, out of sight. Rhona suddenly dropped straight down towards us like a bullet, wings tucked in then with a shriek, pulled out of her dive almost touching the top of our vehicle. As she flew off, I saw a lone large wing feather drifting down, hanging lazily in the still air. It passed our windshield to my side, I reached out almost instinctively and plucked it out of the air. Synchronicity, I thought, like events falling together separately to create a reality, a single reality.

I felt the flow and knew where the feather belonged. But the intimacy; was I opening up a can of worms? Nevertheless, pushing aside my inhibitions I spontaneously reached over, took three strands of Cinda's hair created a quick braid and inserted the feather.

"There you are, now you too can fly."

Cinda's look was a mixture of surprise, hesitancy and wonderment. Extraneous magic had obviously not played itself out this dramatically in her life before now.

"Are your hands always in the right place at the right time?" She said teasingly. I almost felt embarrassed, moving unthinkingly on the wings of spontaneity often put me in situations like this, where all I could do was play it by ear.

"I like to think so, my dear."

As I said this I felt the celebratory, psychic field changing. A heavier, darker sense was coming in. The ominous, waiting hole in the mountain seemed to be emitting a radiation unwelcoming. I could almost hear the words.

"If you enter here, do so at your own risk and you better stay awake. Pull free of your little romantic fantasy and stay in touch with your intuition. Observe dispassionately and all will be shown."

Cinda had also felt the change, swirling her braids up quickly, tucking them up in a tight knit, she slipped on her helmet transforming herself from a seductress into a young warrioress instantaneously. There was an awareness here now, a readiness to respond.

Entering the tunnel, I felt the warmth of the air from the blazing sun suddenly cool. As our mood, a cooling, a focusing.

The tunnel itself was dimly lit, yet enough light to see soldiers standing aside watching us pass, then a small group with a vehicle. All seemed to be well secured, as I settled into the standard Galaxium security practice of gazing into the eyes of each soldier reading his or her expressions. Most here were expressionless, concentrated on observing as well, scanning for anything abnormal. Efficient, dispassionate, security types, I thought.

As we rounded a slight bend in the graveled, relatively smooth roadway, I sensed a change, a quickening inside. Everything was still the same, no change, lone soldiers with a small group some distance ahead. Yet this feeling, was I picking up on something or was it just the tension of being so enclosed, almost claustrophobic. The image of moving through what could be a large crypt. Then I noticed some of the lone soldiers had their eyes turned away, upwards as if avoiding contact. This was unusual, one here, this one was of the norm, but here again, one looking up, very unusual. There was no way to read these few, nothing else about them was abnormal.

Spotting a lone male soldier coming up on our left, a short distance before the group with a vehicle, he was avoiding looking at us, eyes at a slight upward gaze. I quickly reached over between Cinda's arms and pushed hard on the horn, the soldier looked down, I caught his look.

What I saw and read sent a cold shiver up my spine. These eyes were not dispassionate, they were fiery, shifting restlessly, possibly startled by the blast, yet there was something else, fear, like a trapped animal ready to strike.

There behind him, a small rock formation with an unusual dark pile of earth as if it didn't belong. A feeling more than a physical observation as if it covered the remains of a tunnel now concealed.

By this time, we'd come in too far to turn back. Kwan Yen's security forces were almost half-in, a comforting presence yet these oddities, quite discomforting.

"Cinda!" I barked, "Is there any other way out of here, other than straight ahead?"

"No" she replied, obviously startled by the sharpness in my voice. "Is something wrong?"

"I'm not sure, but I would like an escape route, just in case."

"Well", she seemed to be pondering, remembering. "There is a tunnel, my friends and I used to play in. It came down from the hill area you asked me about earlier. It was quite narrow and rocky but we had great fun exploring it with our flashlights. Once Feda and I got separated from the group and got turned around sort-of-lost, I guess. When we came to the end, we thought we were trapped but we could hear an engine, then the sound of a passing vehicle through the wall. Feda dug away a small hole and we saw into this tunnel. We didn't come through, backtracked, and eventually found the entrance. That was a long time ago.

We were approaching the small group of soldiers with a vehicle, their backs were to us, leaning over the motor.

"Where is this tunnel?" My voice was tense, tense enough to draw a questioning look.

"I'm not absolutely sure, but I remember seeing a distance marker, I think it said five Km."

She was sensing my tension.

"Is there something I should know?" I'd noticed we'd just passed the four Km. marker and were almost on the group busy fixing their vehicle or so it seemed. I'd worked with my fear and had come to terms with much of it through the Javadian understanding of its nature. We considered it a tool once old neurotic patterns built around it had been purified, and I was now feeling its presence in a pure, instinctive fashion, beyond imaginative conjuring I curtly replied, now taking an authoritative stance, no time for explanations, all I needed from her now was quick, obedient response.

"No, just be ready. We may need to find your tunnel. Bring it back in your mind. Replay it to be sure. Do we have flashlights?"

"Yes", she assured me, "they are standard equipment."

We were passing the mechanically involved group, I needed to reach these men. I stuck my head and shoulders out the window.

"Having difficulties?"

One, older member turned slightly towards me. His look was steady, maybe too steady.

"Nothing serious, we'll have it fixed and ready to go in minutes. Thank you for your concern, sir."

Applying a little more pressure, I offered.

"I could leave a mechanic with you to speed things up."

A younger soldier turned quickly, nervously.

"No", the strain in his voice was only too obvious. "Sergeant Hyde is capable enough to deal with it."

I needed time, not a premature confrontation, yet the older soldier was now looking at me reading my response, his hand resting on his weapon.

I smiled, "Well, suit yourselves, if you can't get it fixed, flag down one of the rear guard."

I disengaged contact, came back inside and hoped I hadn't pushed too hard. I was now convinced we were in deep trouble here. No time to corroborate identities, as they seemed to have the area under their control, yet no attack. The trap had not been sprung. How much time did we have?

As we drove on, the older soldier was talking into a transmitter, yet the message was not coming through our radio band, a look of concern on his face. My adrenalin was starting to kick in, Fight! or Flight!

How much time did we have? Much too vulnerable, this could turn into a turkey shoot.

Touching Cinda's shoulder, turning her slightly towards me, I looked directly in her eyes for impact.

"We're in deep trouble here, there is going to be an attack any time now. We must get to your tunnel and out of here. When you get to the marker pull over so that the opening to the tunnel is hidden by Beno's truck. Then get one of the guards with a shovel and dig it open enough to crawl into. Take your father and his company through and out. I'll take care of things here and follow. Wait around the entrance. Stay well hidden up there."

According to my calculations the entrance came out close to where I'd seen the reflections, yet there was no choice, a lesser threat. Cinda was questioning, taking liberties due to our recent past intimacy.

"I'm not sure Beno and some of the younger one's can make it up through there, are you sure this is necessary?"

I felt a surge of impatience. "I'm absolutely sure, it's the only way. Just remember Rhona's words and do as I say." Her glance was apologetic and the concern for her responsibility was setting in.

I'd better be right, I thought, or I'll have some explaining to do. Pulling the first family out of their comfort, into a long difficult climb to where only Cinda might know. I was trusting the memory of a child. What if she'd dreamt the whole thing. Anyhow the Mahaj had not shown any other option, this had to be the side door. The way out avoiding direct confrontation. The confrontation would occur, there seemed no way around it for the rest of the troops. However, my ward who was undoubtedly the targets now in the center of the tunnel, most vulnerable, must slip away, out the side door. I felt concern for all the others, probably all in the passage by now. The trap would be sprung soon, hopefully not too soon.

As we came around another bend, I saw the 5 Km marker in the gleam of our headlights. We'll have to do this quickly, I thought, we're almost certainly being watched. As we ground to a stop across from the marker, I jumped out, kicked the rear tire in anger and started waving to the guards in the truck behind Beno to lend a hand. I saw Cinda moving towards her father's truck, a few seconds later she came past me with a guard carrying a shovel. Two guards from behind arrived to help with the feigned flat tire.

"How can we help?" These men were sincere, trying to be helpful in their service, to be trusted.

"There is no flat tire, but go ahead and pretend to be fixing it." I wasn't about to explain further. Their training had taught them to do as they were told in situations like this without question, I assumed.

As Cinda passed me with the guard, her look was concerned and frustrated.

"I think you'd better have a talk with my father, he's not convinced of the wisdom of your actions."

Scanning the tunnel wall, I asked.

"Do you see the area of the hole?"

Her eyes moved along the rocks, searching.

"I think that's it right here."

There seemed a small hole up about four feet with a small trail leading to the roadside. Probably used by small animals living in the tunnel.

"Go for it, I'll deal with your father."

I wasn't looking forward to dealing with an irate, aristocratic, probably head-strong politician at this point. My mind was on when the sound of the first shot would herald all hell breaking loose.

As I approached Beno, he moved away from his small group which included two women and two children and placed himself in an obvious power stance. He was definitely going to challenge my decision. I didn't have much time, wondering how the Mahaj would facilitate this touchy situation. Direct confrontation would probably simply antagonize him, yet the severity of the situation had to be made clear.

"What the hell is going on here?" His voice was authorative, yet I sensed a slight unsureness. A doubt.

"We will be attacked any moment now, you know my level of training. There simply is no time to explain all the details. You will have to trust me."

I needed something to happen for the final convincement. I remembered how he had looked at me, back at the stage area. There was a look of puzzlement.

As I thought back to the setting, I felt a change in myself. As if I was moving back into my ethereal form, touching back into that transcendent place where there was no involvement, no importance to any of this. It's transient nature apparent with the knowledge that it will work itself out. As I moved back into the feeling, I realized how involved and absorbed I'd become in such a short period of time. Beno was now looking at me with the same puzzlement.

"Who are you or should I say what are you?"

I realized in the moment that this man had a sensitivity, he saw auras and felt their changing patterns.

"There is no time to explain now, all I can say is that I'll do you no harm, however, this area is full of those who will. You've seen my light, now will you trust me?"

He really had no choice, if he was sensitive enough to perceive my changes, he must sense some of the danger here. He was also a man of wise decisions to have reached his level of influence.

"All right," he said to my relief. "What do you want us to do?"

My directions were short and to the point. I wanted him to do a quick clothing change with one of the guards and then follow Cinda, unquestioningly. He apparently trusted his daughter's abilities, quickly agreeing and moving away. Cinda arrived with a look of success.

"It's ready, is my father?"

"Yes," I assured her, "he'll follow you, just don't give him any time to think about his decision."

Moving out of the sight barrier of Beno's truck towards our stalled vehicle, I scanned the area, saw no immediate threat, yet I felt it there somewhere.

The soldiers had taken off the wheel and were busily replacing it with the spare. Glancing back I saw Beno and his company leaving his truck, now dressed as a guard, the women were also dressed as their attendants hiding the children with their frocks.

"Strip a few of the nut bolts and push it out of the way, we'll continue in a few of the following vehicles."

The larger of the groups, grabbed the wrench, gave it a couple hard thrusts and swore at the tire, telling his fellows to push the useless thing out of the way.

"Hurry up," I yelled, "We can't keep the enemy waiting forever."

By this time, the last of Beno's company had passed out of sight, I moved to the hole rolled three large rocks around it and moved back to Beno's truck. Spotting the commanding officer in the truck, I asked.

"Who is closer to us, here, the commander of the rear guard or the front?"

"The rear guard commander, is about ten vehicles back, would you like me to radio him?"

"No, I'll wait here for him, carry on." I saw the questions in their eyes, wondering what was going on, why all these changes.

The cavalcade continued on, slightly faster now, to catch up to the front guard who were waiting a short distance ahead. The delays and transition seemed to take forever. Yet little actual time had passed. I only hoped we weren't spotted, a necessary gamble. If we were, Beno would be in even more danger. Now unguarded. I'd have to follow as soon as possible.

As I sat waiting, guarding the hole, I could almost see the tunneler's aiming, ready to begin their onslaught. What else could I do, but warn Kwan Yen personally, then leave it in his hands. Five more trucks to go, I thought I heard a shot, probably an engine back-fire. If there was one shot I'm sure there would be more. These men all carried fully automatic weapons. Then there it was, Kwan Yen's command vehicle, ominous in its size, heavily armoured, black now showing the greyness of the road dust. Kwan Yen stepped out looking irritated.

"What's going on here, why the delay, and where the hell is Beno, why aren't you with him?" That's a lot of questions to answer I thought.

"You're going to be attacked any time now, they'll be coming through the walls of the tunnel. Prepare yourself.

I've taken the necessary precautions to safeguard Beno and company. You're the ones that concern me. No cover here."

He was looking at me, disbelievingly yet wondering. He'd probably been sensing something wrong too.

"No harm putting the troops on full alert, but your in shit if nothing comes of this."

He'd quite nicely placed full responsibility on my shoulders, yet showing himself as co-operative. Quite a tactician, I thought, hoping he was as capable in the field of command.

"If nothing comes of this", I replied, "I'll be most happy to eat shit." He grinned momentarily, then began barking orders to his seconds. I knew our hand was now played, as the orders hit the air waves, they would be monitored necessitating a decision to either attack or retreat.

"Could I have two of your most trusted." I requested.

He waved his hand at two soldiers in the truck following his.

"Where are you going now?" He questioned.

"Up, along with many before the day is done, I'm sure. I need this area well secured. Beno's life depends on it."

I started moving towards my hole in the wall.

"Don't get lost, I'll need you around for the barbecue." I knew exactly what he meant, the sheep would be safe today. The two soldiers moved quickly yet with the caution of cats in uncertain terrain.

We quickly removed the three rocks, I motioned one through, climbed behind him and signaled the second to follow. On the other side, we blocked the entrance as best we could.

I didn't want anyone guarding the hole too closely as this might just draw attention, if the battle went against us.

As we proceeded up the dark hole, on our hands and knees, I finally heard it, the chatter of the kill machines. We'd gotten out just on time. I wondered, what sequence of events had brought these two to me. Relatively safe for now, yet who knows what lay ahead. Nonetheless, what lay back there was certainly deadlier at this time.

CHAPTER 4

As we slowly climbed, the passageway began to widen slightly, the air became a little fresher. We must be approaching a cavern. Then a glimmer of light ahead and we stepped out into an enlargement about twelve feet high with a small portal to the top letting in the light like a beam creating a spot light effect on the floor. There was a small trickle of water pooling just to the right of a boulder bordering the extreme right side of the area. A good spot to keep an eye on our entry point, I thought.

I signaled the spot to the man following me, instructed him to set his radio frequency on 12Khz as we all did and use it only if someone was coming through assuring him that I would send a replacement as soon as possible. He seemed surprised by the consideration, almost uncomfortable, as he had supplies for days with him as well as the fresh water. Severely trained, I thought, probably could sit in one spot on surveillance duty for days without moving. I'd heard of these types - wouldn't even move to shit. I was just trying to make him a little more comfortable than that. I would appreciate the similar courtesy if I were in his shoes. Yet, there was nothing comfortable in war. Survival was the prize.

While the front man went ahead to determine our route to the top, I took the opportunity to rest. Settling in beside the large rock, taking a drink of the fresh mountain water, I felt removed from the intensity below. Yet knowing individuals were facing their personal trials, their tests of strength and courage. I turned to my comrade who had settled in for his stay. His eyes gazed in the direction we'd just come from, probably wondering if we would be followed, were his comrades safe?

"Do you have family, back there?"

His answer was brief.

"Yes sir; mother, father, two brothers and a wife."

A lot, to live for, I thought.

"By the way, if anyone comes through don't confront them, just signal me and we'll deal with them up top. I could hear my front man scrambling back over the loose rocks, as he neared, I saw a look of concern on his face.

"There are three paths out of here, I can't tell which one will get us out."

Reassuringly I took his flashlight.

"No problem, I'll check into it, take a rest with our friend here."

My feeling was that a party as large as Beno's would leave some trace in passing. Part of my concern if we were followed.

Glancing back as I moved off, I saw the two men huddled together sharing a light for their cigarettes, the match illuminating their hardened features, each lost in their thoughts yet feeling the comfort of comradeship. Rounding a slight bend in the cavern I saw the three possible exits, one left, one about center and one to the right. Their angles all seemed about the same. There were some spider webs on the left passage but high enough in the opening to get around. The middle one was lined with small rocks, checking for scrapes or any disturbance, I saw none. The right path showed signs of bats or similar creatures, yet again no sign of disturbance. Cinda must have been extra careful at this point realizing if she'd be followed, they would have the same dilemma as I was having. She was also testing my training, I could almost see her challenging eyes.

"Find us if you can, security man."

Alright, I thought, time to check into the Mahaj. Moving back a few paces I found a comfortable patch of sand, sat down facing the three exits and settled quietly into myself. The meditative trance was surprisingly immediate. The warmth of the Mahaj crept up slowly, gently from the heart area, touching first the inner well-spring, the feeling was like a burst of cool, spring water gushing upwards, the inner sound was like the wings of a thousand birds. Upwards to the third eye, a flash of swirling light and there was Marty, smiling at me.

"Haven't gotten completely lost in your play down there, yet?"

I felt a little foolish, knowing I'd been drawn deeply, almost too deeply into the physical play with all its emotions. My feelings towards Cinda, my concerns for my comrades, now here I was, back at the beginning. Gazing into the transcendent, beyond it all, eyes of the one who brought me here.

"Almost", I replied, "a very intense situation. Difficult to stay removed. How do you do it?"

"Practice, son, practice," he was teasing me, now.

"Now comes the real test, I want you to go back down through the tunnel, observe. There will be someone waiting for you at the entrance. My curiosity spoke.

"Who?" I couldn't imagine who would want to see me, here. In fact who even knew I was here. Marty was being evasive.

"Not someone I particularly resonate with, but he seems impressed with you. You'll know him when you see him."

His inner projection slowly dimmed, replaced by a comforting pale yellow aura. I bathed, drifted and came out refreshed, centered. The inner glow was now shining in the middle passageway. Thanks Marty, I thought, I needed that and now I know which way Cinda had gone. Yet I couldn't follow. Back down there to witness the horror. Why? To meet whom?

Turning from the way out, I returned to the two men waiting patiently by the rock.

"The middle tunnel," I told my front man.

"The party's gone up that way, be very careful not to leave any trace of your passage, just in case things go wrong here. When you get to the top report to Cinda, directly, tell her I'm not finished down here, but will be up soon. If there's any danger, don't wait for me, head for their mountain retreat." Wishing both men success, I headed back down the narrow tunnel, almost a reverse birth. As I crawled down in the dust, alone, I felt a change coming on inside myself.

Here I was making a choice, some might say it was a mad one. Basing my decision on what some would call a hallucination. At times like this, my greatest challenge was dealing with my own doubts. I'd experienced this type of phenomenon so many times yet in critical situations like this one, the doubt, the incessant doubt. Was it truly Marty in my inner vision or a psychic projection like a dream? Either way was it to be trusted? On one hand my physical duty lay with the first family, protecting them was my first direction, it lay in harmony with the ethereal projection creating the physical reality here on this planet.

Yet, here I was trusting my inner self, the inner vision, leaving them unprotected, waiting up top. My feeling was that they were safe for now, Cinda seemed quite capable in covering her tracks. It followed that she would keep everyone safely hidden and secure up top as well. But in the final analysis, my Javadian training had instilled the over powering confidence in the inner manifestation of the Mahaj through meditative insights, dreams and visions. While the external reality could be manipulated by any archetypal forces at work in the universe, the inner-self was fully committed to the Mahaj, whose nature was completely trustworthy. I was betting my life on it. I probably always would. An eternal commitment. Now the test of determination and action. In the resolution, I felt a comforting re-assurance, the mental debate was over. An inner warmth, a surge running through my body. A transformation was taking place in me as I approached the tunnel entrance. The Mahaj was bringing me back into my ethereal form, my transcendent self. I could feel my concerns fading, my involvement in the physical play here becoming dream-like, illusory in nature. Why concern myself with the scene ahead of me, it was a temporal condition, like a worm in a cocoon, about to emerge as a butterfly. There would be many going through their personal transformation. Death left no choice.

The rocks at the tunnel entrance came apart easily, so easily, this was always a sign that I was headed in the right direction, the harmonious way. The path of least resistance. Crawling through I could hardly feel the gravelly surface. Feeling, yet not really touching.

Stepping out on the roadway, I saw what I'd expected. The ravages of the battle. Now still, except for the occasional groan of someone in pain. Normally I would have gone into the healer mode comforting doing whatever possible to lessen the physical discomfort aspect in the transformation. Instead I was being drawn quickly back to the main tunnel entrance. Something important lay there waiting. I could feel it. Cool and steady, beckoning. Rounding a bend in the roadway, I came on a burned out truck, riddled with bullets, I saw three men, two were slumped lifelessly in their seats. The third had crawled out on the hood of the vehicle, still alive, with blood gushing from his mouth. Yet, to my amazement, he was talking into his radio, still giving orders. So caught up in the battle, using his last breath to perpetuate the temporal, still not seeing the step he was about to take. As I passed, now completely in my ethereal form, I felt his eyes gaze blankly my way. His face showed surprise, was he seeing me? He slumped slowly, lifelessly onto the hood, slipped gently off and fell with a dull thump on the roadway. As the body lay there, I saw something else, a rising energy form.

The ethereal form of the man was disengaging. The persona was in obvious confusion. A lifetime of identity, changing. Moving from the now lifeless to all that was left. A form not previously experienced. So caught up in the physical life, not knowing about this one. I sensed the fear, the apprehension, what is this, where do I go, why is this happening?

So brave in battle, yet now in the face of the unknown, near hysteria. Then I saw it. A beam coming from the direction I was being drawn to. As it gently settled around what should I call him, the dead man? Hardly, yet there he lay. I sensed a quieting, calming effect. What was he feeling? Whatever it was, he was accepting it. A process beyond thought. The smell, like a garden full of blooming gardenias in the cool evening after a hot day. So sweet and the sound of small bells, tinkling in the wind.

I could see the ethereal beam changing color and shape. It had become a rose-red lounge chair, waiting. The man now calmly settled himself into his carriage, laying back, I could almost feel him relaxing, letting go of all the tensions inherent in physical life, trusting, possibly for the first time.

The beam began to retract carrying its guest, as if on a cloud, back to the tunnel entrance. I curiously followed. This was quite different from my near-death experience, but then why should the unlimited, limit it's creativity. What was happening here was undoubtedly appropriate. Just seeing and feeling the almost instantaneous transformation in the man's psychic emotional state made the benevolent nature of the beam apparent.

I could hear the chatter of gunfire just ahead. A young soldier ran past me towards the battle, as he passed I saw his determined, committed look. There was no doubt in his mind, he was on the side of good. As we moved past a stalled truck, we ran headlong into two soldiers wearing different uniforms, obviously the enemy, they turned, pointed their weapons at us and began firing. The young soldier returned their fire. I could feel the pieces of metal passing through me, a strange sensation. The dead one seemed now oblivious to the whole play, just laying back with his hands behind his head, resting. Seeing the illusion for the first time. The young soldier however, was more involved. He was caught in a crossfire, bullets were tearing through his chest. At the same time, he'd centered his fire on one of the enemy who was slowly slumping into his death crouch. I was sure our young comrade was dead while he stood there, so many wounds. Yet the look on his face, not pain, just surprise. Once again gazing towards me and the carried one.

I half expected the beam to move to him, take him but instead a piece of it separated out encircled the dead enemy soldier and drew out his energy body, placing him in another seat alongside the other and continued on its journey. I followed, glancing back to see what was happening to our young comrade. What I saw was unexpected, no beam, no bells, no carriage. As his body fell, his ethereal form stood. Again the surprise, the confusion, the panic, but suddenly a glow, a sparkle from his heart area, the same response, quieting, a relaxation, but here even more. A seeming grin of satisfaction, a look of at last. Home at last.

Then a leaning backwards as if something was there to lay back into. I felt a familiarity here, almost like my experience of laying back and flying backwards through the star systems to the universal sea where I lay. Then I saw the sparkling intensify, become brilliant, a flash and he was gone. All I sensed now was a familiar presence, friendly.

I turned back to my two, now ethereal spirits, enjoying their ride to wherever we were going. Off in the distance, I could see the pin of light, the entrance to the tunnel, in this case the exit.

The horror I'd expected had somehow been transformed into a divine play. A look into the process of perpetuation. The non-ending drama of life and death or should I say life in its many forms. Transformations, all with an underlying benevolence, evoking a sense of trust, a faith in the outcome no matter how horrendous the events leading up to it. For me, I had been spared the emotional turmoil. I'd been placed in an emotionally transcendent state from which it was easy to simply see it all unfold with minimal thought, no judgment. Time enough for that later, if at all.

The battle which had raged here was now over, the outcome unknown. Had the enemy been pushed back into the tunnels to the surface? Were they anywhere near Cinda and her party? It all seemed far away now. In this state of being, physical, emotional concerns seemed dim, part of another dimension. I was having an adventure in another one, one which was presenting unlimited possibilities. Yet all the bodies, embracing the death process, each being taken, where? My sense was that there was a duality at play here. Some chosen to move to one end of the tunnel, some to the other. What lay waiting and what was the criterion involved in the choice. I felt after death there was one final destiny, the universal ocean I'd been taken to, the final rest, the absorption, the loss of an individuality and the gain of eternal infinite-beingness, our own true nature, finally revealing itself, and all this but a play, a dance, a learning to let go into. What I was seeing here was that even the letting go was a gift given in a divinely creative manner.

I moved through an area of intense confrontation, bodies lay everywhere, some actually embraced in their death struggles with each other. I was stepping through a pool of water which reached up over my ankles. Looking down I realized it wasn't water, it was the life blood of all these men. In my ethereal form I sensed the collective energies of the blood, not exactly as a physical sensation, but a psychic impression. On Javada I'd spent some time practicing the art form of carving, psychic carving, a form of art bridging the inner creative genius and the physical. Allowing the flow of infinity to move through your hands and create works of art beyond the cognitive, limited realm of the known. For me, the results were usually tools aiding me in dealing with challenges arising around me at that time. The tools seemed to release incredible powers from within me and focus them on the root of my challenge, bringing quick resolutions to the conflict. The final touch to an art piece was almost always blood. I would inadvertently cut myself and bleed on the piece. The blood seemed to be the empowering ingredient, the catalyst bringing the power tool into full bloom. I felt the same sense, stepping through the blood of all these men, now gone.

Was I witnessing a great piece of art, here? A psychic creation now empowered by the sacrifice of so many. A possible insight into the ultimate perfection of creation through destruction. I was walking through the symbol of the ultimate sacrifice of those who had passed here, yet in reality was it a sacrifice, when so much had been gained. I'd witnessed the process of continuance, divine continuance. My comrades just ahead were blatant examples of this. Neither would willingly step back into their former realities. Lost in the bliss of their release, their surrender to a feeling so ecstatic, all they could do was lay back and smile contentedly, finally carried. No longer responsible for the journey.

We were quickly approaching the end of the tunnel, the warmth of the fresh outside air touched us, welcomed us along with a line of ethereal beings standing on each side of the passageway. My comrades were glowing with the look of seeing old friends, the feeling of kinship. As we came out into the fullness of the day, I noticed an incredible change. Coming into the tunnel sometime ago, this had all been dry, parched desert, no trees or vegetation, just dust. Now I witnessed a lush, almost tropical oasis stretching off into the horizon. Groups of beings were lounging in the sun, eating the fruit from the trees, berries from the bushes, sipping on who knows what. A joyful chatter filled the air, in a harmonious lilt with the singing birds. A lot like Javada, I thought, some transformation. My comrades were now standing watching their carrier beam disappearing through a natural archway of trees and small brush with blooming lengths of ivy holding the leaves tightly bound. The resulting passageway beckoned colorfully. My comrades moved ceremoniously towards it, I followed. A slightly orange hue emanated from the opening along with the sound of flutes and strings. Sounds like a party going on, wonder if I should be crashing it. Oh well, what have I got to lose at this point. Might get a free drink of nectar? I suddenly felt quite thirsty, no sooner thought than a young girl dressed in a flowery red and green dress ran up offering a golden goblet full of some liquid.

I took a drink, how sweet yet sour. Sweet to the taste yet sour to quench the thirst. Ah, ambrosia. Nice, I thought, and I haven't even passed the flowery archway. What delights might lay waiting inside? My comrades had passed through, it was now my turn. Holding my goblet up to the arch, I saw a mirror, in it I saw the tunnel behind me, I toasted.

"Here's to the past and all its taught me, here's to the future, unknown yet so enticingly welcoming. Here's to the here and now. A constant presence. Becoming constantly more pleasurable."

I was getting poetic from just a few sips of this ambrosia. Some powerful potion. I stepped through the archway, felt a tingling sensation a lot like the ring probes entering Javada. Unobtrusive, yet quite perceptible. What I then saw still resonates in my memory.

Gardens, fresh water pools, wild life, beings vibrating on the edge of invisibility, yet still having substance. Senses with which to enjoy their environment. All this mingling peacefully. The air was full of joyful interaction. Quite a contrast to what I'd just passed through, what we'd all just passed through.

I spotted my two comrades being led quite ceremoniously up a small hill. I thought I might as well follow along instead of just aimlessly rambling about. Although that would be a pleasant enough alternative in this environment.

As we came over the crest of the hill, I saw what must be our destination. On a knoll overlooking the gathered vista, was a throne, a living throne, vibrating much like all the beings around this place. The colors, sounds and feelings coming from the area were mesmerizing, drawing one closer. There was no denying this call. I saw someone sitting on the throne, but was still too far away to see specific features, just the general impression of this stage. Everything seemed to be vibrating on just this side of the visually perceptible, occasionally fading, then growing stronger, more detailed.

The throne had a sense of warriorship, the presence of authority, to be approached with respect. Yet there was no sense of fear. The kind of respect solicited without the use of fear, just the recognition of power, respectful power.

As I got nearer, I could see my comrades had come to the foot of the throne, had raised their arms and then lay face down before the one sitting on it. I heard the faint whisper, as if on the gentle breeze, MOHAM.

So this is where I was, in the court of Moham. I knew little of this persona, this god-like projection worshiped here. He did rule with the sword, I knew this much. Cinda had not been too specific, but what I'd understood was that his teachings were the standard introductions to the universal ways. His persona was of the soldier ilk. Dealing head-on with one's inner challenges.

Backing away from nothing in the pursuit of inner union. The sword of fire in one hand, slashing through the obstacles of illusion, the offering of divine intention in the other hand.

My interest surged to meet this one, as I stepped forward. Just then the vibration became detailed and I saw the features of the warrior sitting before me. Amazement, beyond amazement. It was no one other than my old warrior friend, the one who sent me on my unforgettable journey to the universal sea, even though he denied responsibility for that. None of it would have happened had he not lived there.

He was grinning that old grin of satisfaction, seeing the surprise on my face, my old wound glistening in the ethereal hue.

"Surprise, Birthday Boy, did you get killed in there, too?"

I knew he knew better. I decided to play the game.

"Oh yes, kind sir, will you accept me in your gracious court and let me live under your protective eye?"

He roared with laughter.

"Oh yes, you are always welcome here, but I know you are still bound to your duty. However someday, if you like, I have much to show you."

Stepping down off his throne, he gave me one of his crushing hugs, the kind you feel for days.

"So are you enjoying your little visit, here?"

As he spoke, he waved his hand over both of us, looking up I saw a rainbow of sparkles forming from horizon to horizon.

"Powerful stuff", I guessed.

"You really are a god, here."

His face went suddenly serious.

"My followers by their transference make me what I am. My responsibility is to them. You can understand that."

Oh yes, I thought, I understand the principle of transference very well. I'd spent a large part of my Javadian training exploring the phenomenon. When someone in a time of need or confusion reached out for help to the Mahaj through one of his representatives, the Mahaj would respond with a flow of power making anything imaginable possible and more. As long as one could keep their focus on the representative, the flow would go on. The only possible contamination was the tendencies of the representative. When pure mountain water passes through a passageway, it is only as clear as the interior of the passageway on the other side.

"This is quite a gathering you have here."

I found myself changing the conversational drift.

"Yes, a gathering". His face had lightened.

"Just a short rest, they deserve it after their trials in there. Facing the end of all you know to be real armed only with faith is very intense for most. They each in their own way called to me in their moment of confusion and so you see the gathering. Drifting aimlessly, confused, through the universe for eternity is not near as pleasant as what's in store for all these."

I wondered what was in store for them but didn't ask. My host, however, reading my thoughts continued.

"That's a long, deep subject, let's just say we're dealing with the field of unlimited potential. Come and visit with us, soon. Rea has been asking about you. She wants me to create an adventure for the two of you. I think she might be getting a little bored playing in her back yard. Not enough challenge for her. I'll show you some of my new edge experiments if you like, it will give you an insight into the creative possibilities of visualization."

An exciting prospect, I thought as I answered.

"Yes, soon, yet we do have an eternity of time to play, don't we?"

His form faded, then returned.

"Take nothing for granted, son."

The son part made me feel welcome yet a little manipulated, I answered.

"Yes, I've taken the safety of my ward back in the physical for granted, I should return, but one thing, Marty must be on the other side doing something similar with his followers. Why don't the two of you resonate well together?"

My warrior friend had taken an almost aggressive stance, his eyes were stern yet thoughtful.

"Your friend, I know he brought you here, has some strange ways. He lazily lays back and allows everything to unfold with little personal involvement. I, on the other hand, enjoy creating, playing with the field of unlimited potential, experimenting. I also feel responsible for my creations and constantly improve them. You'll see when you visit us. Now, let me help you in your return to your responsibilities.

Careful not to get too caught up in the scenario. Cinda is a wise and powerful soul. Her will can be very influential in the psychic as well as the physical. I look forward to welcoming her when her time comes for transformation. Now close your eyes, move into your meditation."

Taking a final glance around, setting down my goblet, I did as he instructed. I felt the familiar heart glow, then a rising, an orange hue and there was my old friend inside me now. His thoughts spoke directly to my inner senses.

"Farewell, stay in touch with yourself. Here we are close, almost inseparable."

My meditation continued in swirls of colors, emanations of feelings, divine emotions - the kind that linger into the days they usher in. Much like powerful dreams affecting the feeling tone of the following day.

I felt myself being lifted, carried as if on a soft cloud, then settled gently on a firm surface. Opening my eyes I found myself back in the escape tunnel sitting in front of the three cave entrances.

As if all that I'd just experienced was a dream, a psychic projection, but now I saw a rainbow of sparkles shimmering around the entrance of the left tunnel. Moham's parting piece of humor, knowing I would be confused as Cinda had gone up the middle way according to Marty's direction. What was I to do? if I disregarded this new direction, it would show a lack of faith in Moham's guidance, yet Marty brought me here and was guiding me another way. Quite a dilemma. I decided to go back inside myself, deep inside myself, my way of asking the Mahaj directly for the appropriate action. For some time little happened, intermingling light forms, a blend of colors in the spectrum between pale yellow to dark orange. It felt like an inner mingling of my two friends each presenting their ways, their unique approaches to reality. Both very real, yet uniquely individual. Deeper, I must touch the common place. The place of wisdom where all individuality merged into oneness.

I felt drawn inward, inward until I was a small spark, a star in a sea of darkness, all inclusive, independently full of everything. I'd been taken to the place beyond dilemma. No choice, just perfection. Then the loss of all physical sensation, floating in spirit.

Two forms suddenly formed. My two friends floated before me, holding each others hand. Above them, I saw a ball of swirling light, gently moving towards me in colors changing from pale yellow to dark orange. The light form was radiating over and encompassing my two friends. I felt a sense of unity. As if there was only one being here, not two. The ball of light was suddenly deep inside me. I felt its wholeness, my friends now as a part of me, their forms now integrated within me. As if this is where they came from and now have returned to wait for the next scene. The next time they would emerge and play with me as if they were separate from me and each other.

The intensity of all this power, this new way of seeing my reality, was almost overpowering, yet felt right, not to be contained or fully understood, just accepted and moved with. The power and magic of this vision would unfold itself creatively in my living. I accepted it and felt at peace.

Opening my eyes, I found myself no longer in the tunnel but in a meadow. A beautiful white creature stood before me. The evening sun radiated a reddish glow as it reflected off the horizon clouds casting a hue almost like a rainbow over my horse-like creature, I recalled a mythical creature known as a unicorn. One spiraling horn coming out of its third eye pointed up towards the heavens. Front legs with glistening sharp hooves which could turn into wings to fly to the heavens.

The symbol of unity, one horn, not two. Unbound, unlimited, a creature of the land yet free to leave it at will.

It tossed its regal head, the mane flew freely in the dimming light casting sparkles of light-flashes across the meadow. Moving slowly, looking back at me, wanting me to follow, heading to a small knoll on the other side of the meadow. Then reaching it, standing aside, beckoning me to come and sit.

As I reached my appointed seat, a small stump perfectly formed by nature, the unicorn lowered its head presenting it's horn an arm's length away. I reached out and touched it respecting its power. A flowing sensation, through my arm, into my body, centering and stopping in my heart area, where the glowing ball of color still resonated. A sense of unification, the inner and the outer.

The unicorn now glowing with the same hues of color as my inner ball, gently raised its head and looked at me. I felt the union, the love, the power, then as if sensing her duty here had been fulfilled, she stood high above me on her hind legs, kicked her front legs ceremoniously clicking her feet and leapt high into the air. As her hind legs left the ground, I witnessed a transformation, her front legs changed into two long flowing wings and she flew. Once in a circle around me, then off over the meadow, up higher and higher, finally disappearing into the clouds, orange-yellow from the sunset, bordering the distant mountains.

My eyes stayed on the area of her disappearance, almost feeling sad, yet so full, parting such sweet sorrow. The sweetness of feeling blessed with such an experience, the sorrow of feeling a part of myself flying away possibly not to return, yet sensing no real separation. Separation only in the physical, an eternal bond in the ethereal.

Then I saw it, a stream of light forms rising from my left, I sensed this was the general area of the entrance to the main tunnel. Moham must be on the move. As I glanced to my right, I `saw a similar phenomenon yet different. The light forms here were like brilliant white flashes flying off quickly leaving a trail of pale yellow in their wake.

Marty must also be completing his mission here, sending his ward off to wherever they must go.

I was being given a compete view of the process. Liberated souls flying off to continue their experience, elsewhere, under the protective, guiding eyes of my two friends. I settled back and watched, felt the joy falling from the sky as if it all was now in me, a part of me.

The former dilemma in the cave, transformed into this. A co-operative exodus, staged synchronistically. Leaving the choice to the inner manifestation of the Mahaj, always the right choice. As the light dimmed into darkness, the two trails gently faded, the final forms disappeared as the unicorn. The same sense of letting go of all those, I really hadn't known yet felt at one with. As the darkness deepened, I closed my eyes and felt the inner ball of color. Although I saw my two friends, I heard one voice.

"You've now witnessed the unity behind this duality. Although each trail of souls will be taken to various stages of being to aid in the process of evolution, the final stage will be unity, harmonious oneness. This might all be illusion, yet what a divine play. Play your part with the joy of knowing the outcome. Your friends will always be here with you, as will I."

I opened my eyes, finding myself alone in the darkness, yet full of company. The darkness felt comfortable, safe yet I knew, not for all. Somewhere near, my ward, my responsibility lay hidden, waiting. I must play out my part, knowing it may be illusion to me but quite real for them. All the emotions of individuality with all its concerns must be laying heavy on them at this time.

As I stood up, I realized, I had no idea where Cinda and her company were. I could stumble around here on the mountain side forever and not find them. Once again the need for guidance. I was sure it would come. I simply had to be aware enough to catch it. The color ball inside seemed to be the connection now between this physical reality and the magic of the other.

I turned slowly in the direction where the trail of souls as well as the unicorn had faded into obscurity, just the darkness with clusters of stars emerging. The sense of distance, so far off. Where had all gone? After all the busyness, the seeming importance, the inner excitements, all that was left was silence. Then I saw a huge, full moon rising over the distant mountain peak casting moving shadows over the hillsides and the meadow. Like phantoms gliding across the land heading for some unknown destination, a gathering to talk of adventures from around the galaxy. To laugh, to dance in the silvery hue of the moon.

Then, I felt an inner surge of the Mahaj like a powering up to extend itself into the external, to create a reality of guidance. Helping me to find that needle in the haystack.

My eyes were drawn to the moon as I gazed at it I saw a faint speck, then a dot. Something was approaching me, as if from the moon. As it neared, I could see the wings beating fiercely, hurriedly, the whole body straining on the air currents.

I sensed its need to get to me quickly, a sense of desperation. It was smaller than the unicorn, then I recognized her, Rhona, Cinda's bird-spirit. As she reached the edge of the meadow, she shrieked once, swept past me, I turned and followed. My guide had arrived, all I had to do now was let her take me through the darkness now illuminated by the moon. Rhona's desperation concerned me, was something wrong, was there a threat. I hurried not taking the usual Galaxium security precautions.

Rhona had led me to a small trail probably formed by the creatures of the forest leading down to a river, I could hear the sounds as it rippled over a rock bed. It must be shallow, shallow enough to cross, I thought. Rhona had taken a perch on top of a tall tree overlooking the area. As I reached the water's edge I saw the water was swift but indeed shallow. The moon showed an easy crossing, but the light would make me very visible and vulnerable. I felt myself quite physical again moving towards my physical responsibility, the imminent encounters and challenges on this dimension once again.

CHAPTER 5

Stepping into the water and the moonlight I moved as quickly as possible, not concerned with the sounds I made. The river sounds would most certainly drown out mine. Getting to the other side, uninterrupted, I moved quickly up the bank to a small clump of reeds and stopped for a moment to rest and re-connect with Rhona.

The rustling coming from my left drew my attention but seemed light, like a small animal moving down to the river to drink. Then there he was, a soldier standing no more than ten feet from me, peering down at me, I heard Rhona's shriek and knew I was in trouble. This was not an ally, to the contrary, he wore the uniform of the two men in the tunnel who had fired through me.

As he looked down at me, surveying what he'd found, I saw a sinister grin coming to his face. He'd found a prize, an unarmed prize. What was he to do with it. I saw him slowly raising his weapon, an archaic killing machine to me, yet quite efficient in inflicting pain even death. Was he intending to kill me and take me in as a dead find or just leave me here for the creatures of the night. Either alternative appeared quite dismal. Normally I would have sensed his presence miles away, yet I didn't. The Mahaj had not warned me in any way. Rhona must have seen his presence yet she led me right into the trap. Was I supposed to be here, it almost felt like it. Yet to simply accept death seemed fruitless.

What the soldier did not know was that Javadians never carried weapons. This did not mean they were unarmed and defenseless. It simply meant, they were no longer burdened with heavy weapons and ammunition. I was, to the contrary, armed with a most fearsome weapon known as a reality disruptor. It was a Javadian contribution to the U.I.A. some time ago, a quantum leap in the evolution of settling potentially hazardous incidents like this one. The weapon lay in the psyche of the warrior completely undetectable to be used only when absolutely necessary.

This, I thought, may be one of those situations. Yet if the Mahaj let me slip into this mess so easily, there may be an underlying reason. A part of a process, necessary, in order to achieve a most important end. These thoughts flashed through my mind, as I saw the soldiers finger tighten around the trigger of his gun.

I flashed back to my initiation to the Javadian reality disruptor when I was quite young. It seemed like such an awesome responsibility. It was the time after the Milky leader had taught us the ways of physical readiness. Our bodies had been purified through cleansing, fed with herbal potions and strengthened by the regular daily physical training in spontaneous intuitive motion. The dance of the Mahaj as we knew it to be.

A strange occurrence began to emerge for me. A very raucous Bird-like creature, much like a reptile yet part of the bird family began stalking me, interrupting my meditations and lucid dream times. These were all very important processes in my development, so the interferences were a growing concern. One day a deep forest meditation was interrupted just as I was entering the deep trance stage, my most enjoyable experience at this time. I was dejected, feeling helplessly victimized by these creatures and yet knowing they were a part of the Mahaj. Why were they allowed to disrupt me when I was following my training program sincerely? Walking out of the forest onto a sunny meadow, head down pondering the situation, I ran headlong into my Milky leader walking with the Beige leader. They were both smiling at me. I felt they knew my dilemma and were there to help. In fact, they knew it was the time for my initiation into the powers of visualization.

Following their instructions, I went to the ocean shoreline, found a soft patch of sand, sat in meditation for a few moments and petitioned the Mahaj to guide me through this dilemma. My instructors assured me, I would be given a tool. Then suddenly it was there, interesting how when the need is great the solution comes quickly if you know how and where to look.

A large seventh wave had swept in a strange looking piece of driftwood. It was straight, long enough to be a walking stick, but had unique knot-like eyes or buttons. My instructions were to put my attention on the tool and allow it in time to reveal its power to me. I kept the stick with me for some time, carving in it, sanding it, polishing it. Putting my energy into it whenever I felt the draw. Meanwhile the creatures continued their harassment until one day I couldn't take it any more.

I had come to the end of my night's sleep cycle, entered the lucid dream stage and was flying unbound through beautiful terrain. High above everything feeling boundless. Warm turquoise oceans, hot sand beaches, steaming green jungles, all lay below to explore. Drifting on the endless currents of the Mahaj, feeling the joy. Through it all, I was aware that I was in my dream body, unlimited, unfettered by the restrictions of the physical. A sense of wanting to stay here forever, then the raspy sound of my tormentors.

Waking, I saw them all gathered in the trees above my bed. The fury of being disturbed, drawn away from my heaven, back to this, my tormentors.

My stick lay beside me, grabbing it I leapt up furiously waving it at the creatures. They seemed quite entertained by the display of abandoned anger, jumping about and squawking joyfully.

I remembered my instructions in dealing with anger, how it actually fed my challengers. The art of constructive resolution was to draw back from the anger center and allow the inner self, the Mahaj within, to emerge and resolve the situation. Settling myself, drawing my concentration back inside, I asked for resolution.

As I sat there, the agitating effect of the creatures seemed to dim. I found my thumb had unconsciously moved onto one of the buttons. I felt the time had come to use this unknown tool on my tormentors. I pressed hard on the button. I felt my senses dimming, a peaceful warmth was creeping in replacing the previous uproar of anger, a feeling similar to my lucid dream tone. Looking down at the stick, I saw a dim turquoise glow coming from one of the eyes. It reached slowly up towards the creatures, who were now sitting quietly watching. As the glow touched the clawed feet of one of the creatures, he hopped up as if burned and flew off squawking his displeasure. The others seemed to sense the discomfort of their fellow and followed. I was left in silence, sweet silence. The creatures never did torment me again as my instructors assured me that I had faced the challenge and learned the lesson they had come to teach me. After all they were sent by the Mahaj to prompt me in the direction of learning the art of bridging the physical and the psychic power field.

Over the next few years, my stick revealed many powers similar in nature in dealing with irritations, then actual threats, always in defense, in response with the goal of peaceful resolution. What became apparent was that no actual harm was ever done, the results were always growth full.

Once I'd developed confidence in using the power projections in their many facets to deal with my challenges, I was shown how to immortalize the tool which had become somewhat cumbersome. Everywhere I went I had to carry my stick, my psychic projection tool. Much like a soldier burdened by his heavy weapons and ammunition.

Through the art of visualization, I was able to transform my training stick into what was known as a reality disruptor. Stored deep in my psyche, I could access its powers at will projecting them at my challenge for immediate resolutions.

All Javadian warriors had their own individual psycho-physical bridge tools, but the resulting inner reality disruptor was the same, the flow of psychic power changing the threatening reality into one less so, leading to a growth full situation in harmony with the will of the Mahaj.

All the warriors were however cautioned in its use. Many situations may appear hazardous but in fact are simply guidance frames to quickly place us in postures and places where we can perform our service to the Mahaj most expediently.

Was this one of them? I had little time to decide, as the soldier's finger tightened.

Suddenly, my reality disruptor came into my mind's eye. There it was in full detail. I felt it forming slowly in my right hand, its weight, its substance so real yet invisible to everyone but me. My finger had unconsciously found a button and was tightening as if in synchronicity with the soldier's finger on his gun. While this process was taking place, I'd instinctively rolled into a firing position presenting as small a target as possible to my opponent. Then a very strange thing happened, the soldier raised his weapon and started laughing at me. I suppose the sight of an unarmed man pointing an imaginary weapon at him was too hilarious a sight to remain serious enough to want to kill him. My disruptor had done its work without doing anything. The threat had been neutralized, at least temporarily. I was still captured, in the hands of this now rolling in the aisles with laughter soldier.

"What are you going to do, shoot me with your finger?" he roared almost hysterically. Obviously the tension of the confrontation was releasing itself in him cathartically.

My reply, however, still had an edge of uncertainty.

"It's not a bad idea. However, I won't shoot you, if you don't shoot me."

My attempt at jest was having its effect. My opponent had lowered his weapon, almost dropping it in his fits of laughter. I wondered how long it had been since he'd had a good laugh like this. Good therapy.

"No I won't shoot you. You're too funny. Maybe I'll keep you as a pet."

Better a pet, than dead, I thought. Meanwhile my opponent had relaxed to a point of vulnerability. It would have been quite easy to disarm him with an eel-lunge, a standard U.I.A. move starting from a lying position, constricting the body into a tight coil, rolling forward and as the feet hit the ground, lunging forward. It was a very quick move and carried the hitting power of all one's body weight on impact. However I hesitated.

Why was I put in this position, just for a good laugh, possibly but not probably. Yet this opportunity would soon pass, I had to decide, now. As I began coiling my inner energies for the lunge, I sensed an emanation coming from the trees. As it reached me, touched me, I saw an older, grey-haired woman in my mind's eye. As I again hesitated, she spoke.

"Let yourself go into this, it is very important that he take you to his camp. You will know what to do when you get there." Her face dimmed, then faded away.

I was sure it was the ethereal projection of Rhona, as she shrieked in the trees and flew up and over us. The soldier was again distracted, perfect opportunity, I let it pass. Standing up slowly, I raised my arms in surrender.

"I'm your prisoner, what is your will?"

His face showed an uncertainty. No longer laughing, the choices were obviously being weighted. I didn't like what he said.

"Your just too much trouble to drag around. I've been sent to perform a specific mission and you'll be in the way."

We both heard the rustling coming from a clump of trees, someone was approaching. The soldier had gone on full alert, aiming his weapon at the emerging figure, then another and another. Three women quickly crossed the opening between us and encircled the soldier who had lowered his weapon. Their communications were low and hurried. The soldier seemed to do most of the listening, then turned to me.

"It's your lucky day. My comrades here will take you to our camp, I may see you later, if you're still alive." I felt his threat was to keep me docilely submissive to my new captors.

"Thank you, I'll present no problem."

I'd had my opportunities for escape but knew now I was right where I was supposed to be, but did not know why, yet.

As the soldier moved quietly, cautiously down the river bank, crossed the river and disappeared on the far shore, my three new captors approached. The smallest of the three stood directly in front of me, while the two larger, older, stood on each side, their weapons not pointed at me, yet in a ready posture. There would be no escaping these three, yet I felt no threat from them.

The younger spoke.

"You're the one in the tunnel who did the gaze-scan, are you not?" I assumed she meant the readings I'd done on the soldiers I passed and detected. I decided to be evasive.

"I was in the tunnel, but don't know what you mean by the gaze-scan." Her voice was powerfully assertive and irritated.

"Don't toy with us, we know more about you, than you realize. It was because of your skills, our mission failed and yet so many lives were lost."

I sensed the truth in her voice, and decided to co-operate.

"What do you want from me, I was only doing my job, you can understand that?"

"Yes", she was calmer now, "we understand duty, but your allegiance lies in the wrong quarter, you must be shown this, follow me." The speaker took a short lead, I followed, the two older women fell in behind me.

The trek led us up along the river to constantly higher ground. The leader was agile, almost Javadian in her movements, balanced. My sense was that she spent a lot of time watching and moving with the animals of the area, knowing the terrain and how to move through it with minimal effort. The ones behind me moved noiselessly, almost not there, yet whenever I glanced back, there they were watching me. A very tight unit, intuitively moving together, no conversation, just knowing where they were going and how to get there.

The leader's words still rang in my ears about my misplaced allegiance. It was a natural reaction. Her view of reality placed me as a committed soldier embracing the entire dogma surrounding Beno and his administration as well as the spiritual teachings of Moham. This she felt was a misguided process. She was correct, of course, for different reasons than she thought. She, I was sure, had her own particular dogma, political and spiritual, which led her into conflict. Dogma of any sort usually does. The process itself lies beyond the realm of right and wrong. To me it was all wrong, anything leading to conflict and violence cannot be right. Yet if everyone was wrong what was right?

In my opinion, it was the movement away from conventional belief systems into the realm of experience. Experiential experimentation with openness. As much openness as could be mustered up. The openness coming from an inner trust, a willingness to change. Then watching experience slowly erode standard, rigid beliefs replacing them with a belief in one's own innate potency and its unity with the Mahaj.

Yet, I felt, no one here would be open to leaving the comforts of their particular way of seeing things, hardly anyone, anywhere was. I realized, I too clung to the experiential reality of the Mahaj, although broader, much more encompassing, still a comfort zone, a bridge over troubled waters and as we crossed the river on a shaky, rope bridge I saw its usefulness. The river below was a torrent of rage, impossible to ford. This was the only way for now.

The side of the mountain, we'd passed into was in the dark of the moon. I now moved blindly behind the leader, she'd narrowed the gap between us so I could almost touch her, I could hear her breath. She was sensing her way now, holding the path with her feet, dragging them to feel each change in direction. I did the same, not knowing where the edge was, how far the drop, faith alone, once again.

Then over the leaders left shoulder I saw a flicker of light, not steady, a fire probably, a small camp fire. As we neared I could see an outline of a cave entrance, inside a small group crouching around the fire, warming themselves, a large pot hung steaming. The smell of food filled the cavern, I realized I hadn't eaten for some time. The hunger in me was suddenly overwhelming. While the leader exchanged greetings with the group in a muffled conversation, my two rear guards took me by the arms and led me to a patch of level ground near the fire. Near enough to feel the comforting heat. The mountain air was brisk, I could feel it's chill now that we had stopped our climb. One of the group around the fire left and returned carrying two objects, a mat and a cover, laying them down beside me.

"If you need more for your comfort, let us know."

His eyes showed a steady concern. I was surprised at the thoughtful consideration when I must be seen as someone who was instrumental in the obvious loss of life of their comrades. Did they sense my true nature here? The fact that though I was a part of the condition, I really wasn't. My warnings in the tunnel had an obvious effect on the outcome of the battle. This concerned me. Had I overstepped my Galaxium guidelines in dealing with evolving life forms? Were these beings around me capable of developing the instinctual skills I had and had used? If they were, then my actions were appropriate, if not, then I had overstepped my boundaries and changed the natural course of events which was against Galaxium policy. A fine line, yet I felt I'd acted spontaneously, unpremeditatedly throughout the course of events.

The leader brought me out of my train of thought, standing before me with the fire light behind her. I became aware of her beauty. Young, slender with the light dancing on her feminine fullness. She nimbly stooped and sat in front of me.

"We want you to be as comfortable as possible, during your stay with us."

My surprise at this further extension of hospitality showed in my voice.

"Do you treat all your prisoners so well?"

Her eyes had softened.

"No, not at all, but we've been receiving reports of your activities and it seems you took no part in the hostilities, although you were instrumental in foiling our mission. Our leaders are interested in meeting you. Possibly tomorrow."

One of the fireside group had come over with a bowl full of whatever boiled in the pot. It smelled delicious. I ate ravenously, then covered myself and slept and dreamt.

My psychic dream projection was of a lucid nature, colorful, peaceful. I was in a loving, warm, comfortable relationship with a woman and two children. We lived in a strongly structured two story building. Huge logs and rocks supported a high ceiling. The living area below was spacious yet sparsely furnished. The children played on the dirt floor. My mate was standing seductively at the top of a flight of stairs leading to the upper chambers. I climbed up to her waiting arms. I felt the softness of her opulence. The caresses were ecstatic, the warmth of her was everywhere, touching me inside and out. Her breath was quickened with passion. I felt myself being drawn deeper and deeper into her being, losing myself in the ecstasy of her soul. What paradise, I thought yet the nagging sense that it just couldn't last forever. Then I saw it coming, a darkness, a deep blackness enveloping the forest beyond the meadow. A storm approaching so huge, so fierce, I knew we could not survive. The waiting, the fear of the unknown upcoming experience of death, losing everything I loved, everything I lived for. I closed my eyes waiting for the impact. Feeling the wind, I went deep inside myself, touching my heart essence, choosing to touch the Mahaj within and trust in its power to guide me through this process of transformation. I felt myself floating, no pain, yet a sensation in my side as if it were pierced.

Then it was over, I opened my eyes with the sense that I had died and was now in the ethereal dimension forever. No returning to the physical with all its pleasures and pains. My mate was no longer with me, I knew my children were gone. A sense of loss, yet a sense of completeness. What adventures lay ahead, now that I lived in an unlimited form. I slowly moved through a broken wall floating down to a lusciously green lawn, there I saw three coffins, my wife and children. Although it was daylight large torches burned ceremoniously around them. Should I approach? Why? They were gone, only their shells remained.

Then feeling the freedom, freedom from all my recently experienced relationships with their inherent limitations, but not feeling a loss of the love, the passion. It now lay deep inside of me. The sense of an eternal condition growing all around me, within me. Not subject to change, no chance of losing it. Mine to keep forever.

Then the joy of flight, always such a pleasure, rising higher and higher along a cliff wall, no fear of falling or hitting anything. The sense of omnipotence. Three female forms suddenly surrounded me. Flowing, white veils covering them as they accompanied me on my flight upwards, then I saw our destination.

A brilliant white castle sprawled luxuriously on the pinnacle of the mountain. A lazy river ran past nourishing the meadows and fields surrounding it. Me and my company flew slowly to the front gate. As we drew near, it swung open welcoming us. Settling gently on the ground, I was ushered inside by my company. The smell of a luscious garden met me and drew me deeper inside. There sat my mate in a glory of color on a throne adorned with growths of green and blossoms. She was holding something, as she slowly raised it, I saw the physical representation of my reality disruptor, but now it was vibrational. In a state of flux her voice had the melodious ring of bells:

"Approach my love, your inner psychic tool has come to me for transformation. In your last encounter, its limiting aspects put you in danger. Your hesitation in its use put you at risk. This hesitation was due to the fact that you understand the extreme nature of disrupting a reality. The result has a karmic influence. In its effective use, you must visualize the condition of the projection and are therefore responsible for the resulting reality. Responsible for the course of events which naturally follow, even if they are growth full. The limits of your imagination are at play here and your inner wish is to explore the unlimited nature and imagination of the Mahaj. This tool was given to you at the early stages of your development in the psychic realm by your old warrior friend, Moham. His ways of visualizing the outcome are inherent in the tool. As you know, the tool has many eyes or buttons, each offering a unique option in dealing with your challenge. Yet each option is limited by either your or Moham's imagination. Each is growing, yet lacks the perspective of entirety. This lies in the realm of the Mahaj, the unlimited creator.

You are now ready for an additional psychic tool, unlimited in its nature. Your old tool will always be a part of you, by Moham's will. It will always be a precious part of you, a divine gift indeed, given in the true sense of comradeship."

As she spoke, I saw the reality disruptor turn a deep orange, hover above her hands with all its eyes emitting a hazy light green hue. Suddenly the sky was full of my reptilian tormentors flying down to the tool, each in turn flying into one of the eyes. As each passed into the disruptor, a glance my way, a look of favor, a warmth, a respect. As the last one passed inside, the disruptor faded and I felt it once again deep inside myself. The warmth of comradeship, the sense of support in dealing with whatever challenges lay ahead.

Looking up, I saw the smiling face of Moham above my goddess's head. Again the sense of a bond, an eternal bond between friends quite different, yet similar, deep inside.

My goddess was now spinning, dancing, arms waving high above her, reaching for something. Then something began forming in the vortex of her spinning hands. It shone a pale yellow-white veiled with brilliant white sparkles. Its outline was vague, almost in the shape of an old relic weapon I'd encountered on a visit to a far-off developing planet. They called it a gun. Yet it had no trigger just one button on its top.

As she slowly stopped her divine dance, stood silently, the object formed solidly and settled gently into her outstretched hands.

"Here is your new visualization tool. It comes to you from the realm of unity. The one button represents access to a field of potency beyond choice. Your only choice will be its use or not. When activated, its influence will come from the unlimited imagination of the Mahaj. The responsibility for the outcome will no longer be yours, yet you will be conscious of its workings each step of the way. A participating observer. You will soon see its all-encompassing nature in the resolution of any challenge. Trust its power and nature and no longer hesitate in using it. Its influence will be growth full at no one's expense, yet deal effectively and quickly with any form of threats. The underlying results will be the harmonious transformation of enemies into respectful allies much like Moham's disruptor, without the limitations of choice and responsibility. A general aura of letting go into the process rather than creating and sustaining it."

As she held it high above her, I saw a flock of white birds descend from a cloud and enter the tool one by one singing melodiously, casting tiny sparkles over the tool and my goddess. Taking a step towards me, she held out the tool.

"Hold the image of this object in your mind's eye, let it sink deeply into your psyche, touch its corresponding energy form already there."

I felt the newness inside, as if my previous tool, the reality disruptor now had a companion. A sense of completion.

"You now have the ideal combination. A will projector, when you are sure you want a specific condition and access to the Mahaj's imagination in the times when you are not sure or simply want to experience a unique, unlimited reality projection. Both are now in harmony inside you. Play in the reality they form around you."

Stepping back, she again spun and danced, holding the reality transformer high above her. A pale-yellow cloud formed above and swept down absorbing the tool leaving her hands free to flow in her spinning divine dance. Above her, the cloud faded and disappeared along with the tool. A face slowly formed, steady, somewhat serious, the eyes radiated compassion and friendship. Then I recognized my old friend, Marty, he winked once and disappeared.

I woke, still feeling the inner radiance of my dream, my head felt light, spinning as if my goddess still danced inside.

My female leader was gently shaking my shoulder.

"Wake up, you must be dreaming, we're concerned that you may roll into the fire." I could see the camp was in motion, getting ready for the day. A pale light came in from the cave entrance, it must be dawn.

"Yes, I replied, "It was a fascinating dream, a vision, I'll tell you about it sometime, if you like."

Her eyes showed interest.

"Yes, we respect our dreams and others, sometime I would like to hear about it. It must have been quite an adventure."

Yes, I thought, quite an adventure, one I will never forget. The kind that affects reality on many levels, the kind that must be lived openly with respect. Allowed to seep its magic into one's reality on all levels, whichever it chooses."

As we stepped out of the cave entrance, into the morning freshness, I felt a corresponding inner freshness, an awareness. Rested from the night's sleep, but more. The energy of the dream lingered inside reminding me of its content. What was this new psychic awakening in me heralded by such a projection. What challenges lay ahead demanding my new form of armament. I could still see its form in my mind's eye dimly, yet its feeling inside was strong. A short distance from the cave, the group separated out, bid their farewells and were gone into the nearby forest. My original group now took their former positions and we continued our climb, a slighter incline now but still climbing. Occasional brilliance, then cloudy, a sense of moodiness, almost manic in its changes. I wondered if this was a forecast of the upcoming day.

As we passed an open area in the bushy terrain we kept to, probably for cover and safety, I noticed something quite strange. A small bushy shrub was blooming throughout the openness. It was a strangely familiar plant, a plant I'd grown up with on Javada. As a child I was warned to stay away from it as it was highly poisonous. Yet in later years, during my training in herbal medicine as a support system for the newest techniques in visionary healing, I learned of its beneficial aspect. If picked randomly and consumed, it was highly poisonous, however if the blooms were picked at dawn, then at high noon, then again at sunset and boiled for an hour at the height of the moon on the same day cycle, it produced a tonic of extremely high value. It's tranquillizing effect was of the highest potency, putting a patient into a deep, relaxing sleep for a period of three days. During that time of mental stillness, the patient became extremely open to healing visualization projections. I'd been very interested in this technique and studied under a master of the art known for her impressive success rate. By picturing the healing process inside the patient, then speeding it up, miraculous results became common place. Obtrusive surgery was no longer necessary. All internal repairs could be achieved by an adept in the art, within the three day rest period.

The smell of the blooms in the warmth of the morning sun was again familiar. I wondered if these people were aware of it. The leader had stopped and was gazing out over the field with a far-off look in her eyes. As I stopped beside her, I felt a sadness.

"A beautiful spot, where blooming bushes smell delicious, are there many around here", I queried. Her tone was sharp, full of an emotion I found hard to read.

"Yes, beautiful, delicious and deadly."

I was curious about her emotion.

"Deadly?"

"Yes, very deadly." Her eyes glanced my way sadly, seeing my serious attentiveness, she continued.

"I lost a younger brother to them a few years ago. He was doing some experiments with them, thinking they might be useful for healing wounds. He had cut himself and applied the plant leaves on the wounds, he died within hours, quite painfully."

I said nothing, this was not the time to venture any suggestions as to their usefulness, I felt myself wanting to hold and comfort her but could only look at her, projecting comforting energy.

Her tears showed her grief, but she quickly drew herself away from it, held up her head and looked at me.

"You are quite sensitive for a killer, I wonder about you."

I felt a warm compassion but still some reservation at complete openness.

"I feel your grief, it saddens me."

She was now cooling.

"Yes, these things happen in life, those we love are often taken from us by Cristo for his higher purpose. We must let go, whether we like it or not."

Saying this, she continued walking, now with a slight accent of heaviness remembering dear moments, feeling the space left inside by the absence.

Cristo, an interesting name for the form Marty must have been in during his short stay here. My thoughts went back to last night's dream, the joy of its flight, the sorrow of letting go, the ecstasy of the dance and the intriguing gift. It felt unlike the disruptor, this new tool had more to offer than protection. Only living with it, at play in my reality, would I see its full potential. My psyche projecting Marty's image as the bearer of the gift made this group I traveled with an integral part of it all.

CHAPTER 6

As we moved cautiously down a steep embankment, I heard a loud wail coming from somewhere near, ahead of us. My captors tightened up around me and quickly led me to a clump of growth near the base of the hill we'd just come down. I was signaled to sit with the two older women, as the leader disappeared in the direction of the wail. There was no conversation, just waiting. The sound of the wind moaning through the nearby trees, a sense of intensity.

In a short while, she was back, hastily signaling us to follow. We followed the base of the hill around some brush and entered a thick forested area. The path was overgrown and difficult. We clawed our way through, breaking out into a small opening. There, I saw a group of soldiers, some stood holding their weapons ready, while a few others were bent over something. As we got nearer, I saw it was another soldier, obviously injured, lying on his back. I could see his occasional twitches, his moans were deep. This one was in great pain. The leader went directly to the group surrounding the fallen one, bent down and placed her hand on his forehead, comfortingly. My impulse was to follow her and see what I could do but felt I would most certainly be stopped. To my surprise, the leader looked towards me and waved me to come. As I neared, her face showed anger.

"Come closer and see what your actions have done."

Leaning over the soldier, I saw several wounds, some superficial, but one very serious. The signs of internal organ damage. His twitching and general agitation was not helping.

"Will you allow me to help, I have some training in these matters." Her response was short and quick.

"There is nothing you can do, he has internal injuries requiring surgery but we don't have the tools or anesthesia. Furthermore, why should you be trusted, it was your bullets that did this."

Stepping back, I realized the futility of the situation. I knew I could help, probably even heal the soldier, but would not be trusted to do anything. A sense of helplessness.

The soldier suddenly lurched in his pain, a scream of agony, I felt his need. What was I to do? I felt a strange sense of responsibility as if I had truly done this. A sense of guilt, yet I knew better. I knew I was again getting too deep into the physical realm playing itself out here. I must remain distant and observe. That is what I was here for.

As my passionate involvement began fading, an unusual phenomenon started rising inside. The new reality transformer came clearly into my mind's eye, I saw its form clearly, shining in a pale yellow aura. I could see the one eye glowing, firstly yellowish, then darker until it glowed a deep red color, like blood. Then a drop came out of it, and fell. I felt its warmth creep slowly down to my heart as it touched the essence within, a burst of energy shot out through my whole body, my hands tingled with power. I knew what this meant. I'd been filled with healing power and it had to be released, channeled. But how?

The leader, meanwhile was comforting the soldier, holding his head on her lap stroking his forehead, a look of helplessness contorted her face, making her look very old. Then I saw something fall out from under her shirt and hung loosely between her and the soldier's face. A pale yellow aura emanated from the object which appeared somehow familiar to me.

I realized the glow was of the same hue as the aura surrounding my inner tool. A psychic connection existed here in the ethereal. As I had drawn myself away from the physical, I saw the ethereal reality existing simultaneously.

The leader suddenly turned her head to me with a look of desperation.

"This man is dying painfully, help if you can."

The psychic connection had somehow changed her emotion and opened her to the possibility which lay beyond the normal realm of the possible she knew as reality. My opening had come, I was almost shaking with the intensity of the power flow. It had to be released, now!

I hurriedly placed my hands on the psychic power points surrounding the soldier's body, almost touching him. I felt the link-up between us, ethereally, as a jolting bond. Then the flow, like a built-up pressure finally releasing itself gradually. If this much power was released too quickly it would do more damage than good. Yet I felt the entire process was in the capable hands of the Mahaj. Just the right amount was flowing and being absorbed. There was no necessity for my visualization at this point, it was all happening automatically.

Keeping my attention on my heart center, monitoring the slow ebb of the power pressure, I saw the soldier had quieted. His face showed signs of relief. His pain was being blocked, ethereally.

The leader had noticed the change, her amulet was glowing brightly, yet she could not see this. It was an ethereal phenomenon. All she saw was my unusual posture and the soldier's response.

I felt the final release slowly flowing out of me. All that remained was a warm, gentle glow, a feeling of love, divine love. A sense of doing nothing, yet having been a part of a doing beyond the limits of my knowledge. The reality transformer had shown me it's power, quite dramatically. I was right. Its power lay beyond the realm of simple protection.

Her eyes were softer, questioning.

"Whatever you've done, it seems to be helping."

I knew it was helping, quieting him, yet he needed much more. Would she co-operate? I wondered how I could explain all this.

"I've taken some courses in touch healing, its all quite experimental, but some success has been experienced,"

I knew my explanation was vague but would have to do for now. I'd also noticed that the soldier's wounds were bound by rags now soaked with blood. A high risk of infection.

I'd detected a faint pungent odor floating on the breeze from time to time. My herbal training had taught me that odors like this came from plants with a high content of an antiseptic, infection control excretion the plant used to screen the sun's rays. I noticed the odor again, following the direction of the breeze I saw a plant with broad leaves surrounding a small compact head.

"This man's wounds need fresh bindings, do you have any?"

The leader hurriedly began asking her comrades. One stepped forward taking off his shirt, offering it to her.

I quickly explained the need for cleanliness. The shirt was dirty, sweaty, full of germs yet the wounds must be bound. The plants' inner softer leaves were gathered on request and wrapped directly around the wounds, then held in place with the generosity of the soldier's gift. His night would be cold but his heart would feel the glow of his gesture.

I could see the concern of using an unknown leaf on a wound in the eyes of the leader. I sensed her thoughts on her brother's misfortune, could my knowledge be trusted? I was gambling. The plant itself was unfamiliar, yet the smell was not. I leaned over to her, looking straight into her eyes, I felt the connection.

"We have no choice, we must try. There's one other thing I want you to do now, you must trust me in this thing. I know it will be difficult, but if we don't do something more, the man will die."

Her eyes felt full of un-cried tears, my heart could feel them.

"What do you want me to do?"

I could again see the reality transformer in my mind's eye, her amulet glowing at her heart. This might just work, I thought.

"The plants, we passed, in the clearing, the plants which took your brother's life, I know how to use them to help this man. If you trust me and do as I ask, I believe we can save him."

Her doubts seemed drowned by the combined power of the transformer and her amulet. She slowly nodded her head in reluctant agreement.

After giving instructions in the gathering and preparing of the potion, I sat back to wait. The man now rested but for how long? Would we have enough time?

The day continued in its moodiness, cloudy grey-depressed, then bright sunny almost cheery. The picking of blooms was being done precisely on time, the last picking at sunset was soon approaching. The sense of doing something which had hope seemed to stir through the camp. Helplessly waiting for the inevitable was replaced with a doubting motion but still a motion towards a possibility. If this worked, they all knew, it could be shared with other units in similar situations. The sense of a mobile experimental laboratory. Everyone seemed involved, everyone except one. I'd noticed him sitting off in the shade, cleaning, polishing his weapon with a constant, disturbing look of anger. It seemed every group had one of these. The doubting, disbelieving, frustrated mind always seeing the dark, hopeless side of reality. As if carrying the venom of the group to its extreme.

In Javadian thought, each family had one which seemed most prone to carry the collective ill of the family. Often the most sensitive, quietly absorbing the ill and growing sick with it. Then when it erupted into what was seen as deviant behavior, the choice: To see the behavior as something separate from the family; to be treated; pushed away; to be categorized as sick; or to see the family as a unit; the sick one as an integral part of it. Understanding the phenomena and embracing it, each individual looking inside and seeing their contribution to the sore spot. Then approaching the healing process as a unity process, supporting, comforting, understanding, as if the family was an entity and the sick one was a part of it to be healed and made useful rather than pushed away, gotten rid of, amputated.

In Javada, family mentality had evolved to the point in this process, where the so-called sick one was seen as an opportunity for growth. It was understood that the whole could not evolve far beyond its weakest member. Like the strength of a chain being only as strong as it's weakest link. An obvious opportunity to heal the weakest link to the best interest of the unit. Then as a whole healed unit to evolve unhindered by any weakness in the service of the Mahaj.

Yet, here sat the ostracized one, fuming singularly, a bomb ready to go off. I could sense that I was at this time the object of his anger. A threat not to be taken lightly.

The shadows of evening had lengthened across the opening, the time of the final picking was approaching. The leader left,. taking two others on her final excursion to the field of blooms. She was dealing well with her inner turmoil around the blooms, confronting them head-on as the warrioress she truly was. I respected her straight-forwardness, self-control and compassion in such a difficult situation.

As the light began to dim, the patient became uneasy, his body began writhing in his pain, yet there was nothing I could do, the healing power I'd felt earlier was not there.

His comrades were doing everything possible to comfort him. It was a time of waiting. Once the potion was prepared, I could go to work.

The quieting effect of the potion would push aside his conscious mind and allow me into his deeper levels where I could do some quick mending. I would become the bridge between his inner innate psychic healing powers and the physical disruptions in his body. I hoped he would last till then. As I touched his forehead to gauge his level of fever, I felt a rough hand push me, an angry voice in my right ear.

"Stay away from him, you've done enough damage around here. I don't believe you want to help, you're just a coward, playing for time and us for fools."

The unexpected push threw me off balance, as I fell, rolled and came up with my back against a tree, I could see the angry one glaring down at me with his weapon raised. Once again I thought, what now?

As I slowly rose, I saw a face forming in my mind's eye, a sense of intensity, a fierceness, almost anger. It was Moham, my warrior friend, holding the reality disruptor, an eye glowing a livid green.

"Use it, visualize your enemy's fate and use it."

Meanwhile, my tormentor was leveling his weapon squarely on me. Just as my consciousness began moving to engage a visualization, I felt a warmth in my heart, a soft, seeping feeling of hesitation. Then the memory of my thoughts around this one. The understanding of his condition and also the glowing amulet getting brighter over his heart, the same amulet as the leader. I found myself withdrawing from the disruptor, nothing would be gained by its use here now. Like cutting off the head of the Hydra, only to be faced by many more.

As I straightened out, I felt the inner drop in union with the outer symbol around his neck. I projected myself into it as I suggested:

"Do you really think killing me will help your fallen comrade? If you do then go ahead, I'm getting tired of your company, anyway."

The combination of my ridiculous stand and the ethereal emissions seemed to be doing its job, having its effect. His face was less intense, still angry, but frustrated with the choice.

"AH!" was all he said in disgust as he raised his weapon, turned and returned to his watch point.

As my adrenalin rush slowly faded, I wondered about my inner workings around this incident. The disruptor was there, at ready, already glowing in readiness. I could have visualized a relatively unobtrusive interference with the rising reality yet chose to move with the drop of blood from the transformer now alive inside my psyche, trusting its outcome. Curious as to its full nature and the final outcome it heralded. How would I ever know if I didn't trust it and explore with courage and openness? However the risk was great and I was thankful for the presence of my old friend and his gift. It gave me a sense of surety, a sense of balance. All things working in harmony for the greater good.

The angry one, still angry, but having made his choice, now seemed to be part of the shadows, no longer dominant in my view of this physical scenario.

The bloom pickers soon returned with the final contribution to the potion. We had now only to wait for the moon to rise to its high point. I often felt this part was unscientific, I understood the science behind picking the blooms at the different stages of the sun. There would be different excretions from the plant in response to the intensity of the sun's rays. The combination of these secretions created the necessary balance in the potion, but having to prepare the broth at the height of the moon seemed like superstition, a leftover from the days of witchcraft. Beliefs in the unknown workings of forces beyond experience, always a little dark, mystical and fearful. Yet I wasn't about to take any chances at this point. There may be a scientific reason for this which simply evaded me at this time.

So we patiently waited.

The moon slowly rose to its high point amid the sounds of the night. All night creatures marking territory, hunting. Life and death, natural cycles unfolding in the shadows, out of our sight, yet quite alive within their own realms. Would life prevail here to-night or would the Mahaj claim yet another for the distant needs in the universe we knew nothing of. Simply a faith, an acceptance of ununderstandable workings, maintaining an openness to the learning process and participating with that tremendous force inherent in us all towards the perpetuation of life for as long as possible.

Always before doing this, I asked for guidance as to the universal will. Had this individual come to the end of his natural evolution in this form, was it a service to his evolving spirit to keep it here, or an interference, a hindrance, a simple waste of time, keeping him in a state of little or no use to the overall scheme. In the past there was always a sign, how would it come this time.

The time for the final preparation of the potion had come, the boiling of the blooms started over a small fire well concealed behind a circle of rocks. Dry material was used to insure no smoke drifted up to mark our location. The smell assured me that we had the right essence in these plants. I hoped I was correct, although I knew not taking the risk would end in certain death.

Just before the completion time, I moved away from the group to a knoll under the watchful eye of my now calm challenger. I sat facing the moon, waited a moment, then moved inward for my final psychic preparation. The upcoming journey into another psyche took a great deal of one's energy. It was imperative that one be completely centered, moving from the creative point of being, the place of no thought, no motive, the simple resonance of pure being. Only then could it all work.

The motion inside was slow, first there were the sounds of the night, then the emotional sense of the group, the fear, the aloneness here in the night, then my own thoughts running through the scenario of how I got here, the sense of guided motion.

The set-up of circumstance bringing me to this part of the play, if I succeeded there would be an aura of credibility cast my way, undoubtedly. Was this the underlying divine motive? The need for credibility to create a bridge. It would make sense. In conflict peace almost always starts with the bridge of credibility, then the interaction leading to open communication. Was I here for that purpose? My mind raced with all these possibilities and my options. Then a sudden realization that I was a long way from my center. I was lost in the thought realm. No resolution would come from here. I must go deeper.

Then touching it, the point of stillness, the solidity, no need to know and understand anymore, just stay here in the stillness, let everything else pass, the unimportance of it all, the fleeting nature of all that.

But this, so full, so real, so permanent. Then a flash, a momentary image of the reality transformer, barely visible yet the feeling of it. The eye glowed a deep red for an instant then nothing. The transformer was gone but now a voice. Deep, almost inaudible, yet very understandable here in the stillness of myself.

"Your talents must be used here now. The results should not concern you, they will naturally be in harmony with the entirety."

Then quietness, a feeling of completeness. The direction had come, simply, with no undue explanation, just the surety that action was in order. The success or failure was now out of my hands. The inherent nature of the reality transformer had again revealed itself. Like the Mahaj, not to be probed and understood, but to be allowed and trusted.

As I slowly returned to the physical reality, the sounds of the night, my own mental activity, the emotion, I saw the leader motioning to me. All was ready, the potion had been taken off the fire and stood steaming beside the soldier. Now with the assurance of my inner vision, I moved towards the group. No longer concerned with the rightness or wrongness of my upcoming actions, just the knowledge that action was in order and the use of my skills was needed for an outcome beyond my need to know. The group, however, did not share my assurance, I could clearly see the division of thought and commitment to the path we were all on. The soldier's condition had deteriorated to the previous point of writhing and twitching, moans of pain. I thought, "you lucky fellow", soon you'll be free of it, floating somewhere, waiting for the point of return or onwards to your unknown destination. Both much preferred conditions to your present state of agony.

I poured about 3/4 cup, enough to begin the process, handed the cup to the leader and stepped back. It was now her final decision. She was not given any time to think about what to do. The soldier lurched up to a sitting position from a pain convulsion, mouth open shrieking his pain. She quickly grabbed his head in the crook of her left arm and began pouring the potion down his open throat. The Mahaj had made the job easy for her, no time to think of her brother's unfortunate reaction, only the immediate need for her reaction which was quite effective. Little was spilled. Now to wait for the outcome. Too late to change the course of events about to ensue.

The potion was taking effect quicker than usual, the soldier's breathing became easier, regular. A look of relief was coming over his face. His eyes slowly closed. He was drifting off in the gentle warmth of the blooms relieving influence. I knew inside himself, a physical short-circuiting was taking place between his pain sensors and his conscious mind. His conscious mind was resting after the turmoil of the pain. As his mind came to rest, his body eased itself into a limp relaxation, a state conducive to the natural healing rhythms inherent in his being. His external wounds had stopped bleeding with the aid of the binding plants excretions. Externally no more could be done for him. It was time to move inside. If the wounds were not so severe, causing so much pain, the process could have been initiated with his conscious participation, but under the circumstances everything would have to be done for him. The power of my being and more would perform the task.

As the man relaxed into his relief, the leader continued holding his head in her lap comforting him. I needed his energy alone with no other psychic influences. I hoped she would understand.

"I must be alone with him now. Place something under his head and move back at least three feet."

Her eyes showed a questioning, but she quickly took off her jacket, placed it under his head and moved back.

The others followed suit and I was alone in his aura. Again placing my hands on his psychic pressure points, I reached inside myself and himself simultaneously. Feeling the connection, I went deeper. His mind was drifting in memory, out of the way, I went past it touching the emotions, now quieting, still some fear, some holding back from the pain. I saw a small child, frightened by the strangeness of all that had taken place. I visualized myself as the father reaching out, holding, comforting, assuring, feeling the warmth of home in our mutual space.

The child settled in his father's arms feeling a sudden sense of safety.

"It will be all right now, my son, just relax and trust."

Leaving the father and son, I went deeper.

Here, in the psyche, a stillness, as if nothing was happening. Nothing unusual just the natural motion of the universe. The natural patterns of life and death seen as temporal conditions, one leading to the other.

A questioning, what psychic process is unfolding for the individual here. The answer: Rest, transformation, possibly leaving, going to a new home, the pleasure of the upcoming journey. No sense of death trauma here, just a calm acceptance.

My psyche seemed to be suggesting, why not stay, are you not comfortable here?

The sense of the answer:

"Yes, comfort is the inherent nature."

However the image of being caught in a pattern, an ungrowth full pattern, a living death. The reality of the physical intrusion brought to the individual to end it, free the consciousness through death.

My psyche again suggesting:

Are there any changes which can be implemented to facilitate your needs, to aid your evolution here in this form?

The mind-form, I support, will co-operate in these matters.

The answer:

Yes, the overly self-indulgent tendencies of this mind-body must be purified. The will structure must be balanced with a process of inwardness, a conscious awakening to my presence here. Then a growth full dynamic can be initiated making this life form worthy of continuance. Otherwise death will be the better option. A freedom to start again although the tendencies will be re-born to replay themselves over and over again. If your mind-body will co-operate and initiate a self-developmental program for my host, continuance would be much more favored. Some headway in the emotional aspect has been gained. To waste this would be a loss.

I found myself suggesting an approach to my most honorable and powerful company.

On my way out, I can instill a suggestion in the mind memory banks dealing with the emotional future reality formations.

The appetite for knowledge of the inner workings can be instilled to arise in the mind-body consciousness soon after the physical healing.

I heard the voice resonate through our commonness.

"Your suggestions are acceptable, the healing has begun."

I could feel the incredibly powerful emanations carrying me out, past the emotions, past the child being left alone again but comforted ready for play, through the floating mind lost in memory. There I instilled the suggestion for balance and left.

As I came out of the mutual connection, feeling myself alone again, my hands still on the pressure points, I knew the operation was a success.

The soldier was lying peacefully, a strong yellowish hue emanated from his entire body. The feeling of comfort was everywhere.

Looking up I saw the moon, now sinking in the sky emanating the same yellowish hue. A sense of a mystical connection, me, my soldier friend and the universe watching through the eye of the moon. The Mahaj, once again manifesting his creative will through the co-operative actions of the created. How does a visualization process like this one unfold? Not through the science of the process used as a framework, but through the inner genius unfolding its unlimited wisdom spontaneously through the dancer who dares to dance the dance.

As I gently drew my hands away from the access points, I felt the disconnection like pulling my hands out of soft mud. A slight resistance, a holding, then the pop of release. I was free of the process, once again just me, yet feeling a unity. A unity that was probably there always for all things but the sense of it not always in the conscious experience. I felt this was a part of my evolution coming to a constant awareness of this. Stepping back from the soldier, I saw the pale yellow moon sink gracefully behind a distant mountain, the exclamation point at the end of this passage. I now somehow saw how the moon fit into this healing process. Through it came the mystical connection to the Mahaj, the seeing eye emitting the juice which made this tree grow. What happened in this man was not just a scientific process. The process could not work without the juice.

As the darkness again enveloped me, my thoughts went through what had just happened. The overpowering feeling that a part of me, a part of us all created our experimental reality each step of the way. Firstly affecting our emotions which in turn affect our desires, influencing our actions and thoughts creating an aspect we know as mind.

This, our identity, then playing back the cycle affecting our approach to all future realities, getting caught in pleasure patterns losing track of the underlying reality, that part of us truly in charge, holding the power of life or death. If we become so entrenched in the physical and give our complete attention to it, death must come to free us. Send us on a journey to bring us back to understanding the true nature. If only we all knew this fundamental truth, without doubt and acted in accordance, death itself might become unnecessary. Growth and spiritual evolution would take the place of aging, rigidity, pain and finally death.

Seeing this now, made my Javadian training in the systems of trust, letting go into the inner guidance systems, and moving spontaneously with its nudges the only rational approach to life.

The approach leading to the unlimited exploration of infinity rather than the helpless floundering of a sense-victim on his way to death, the final transition.

Ah!, but that overpowering inner aspect of desire, creating realities for the perpetuation of the species. Without it, a dying out of form, with it a headlong leap of faith into uncertain terrain, laden with turbulent emotions such ecstasies and such agonies. Once again, a balancing act, one coming to balance the other. Her hand was resting gently on the small of my back, her voice was soft, low.

"We don't know exactly what you did here, to-night, but the effect is good. Our comrade is quiet, and growing stronger. I'd like to know more about all this, someday." I suddenly felt tired and dirty.

"Yes, someday I will teach you, if you like."

Removing her hand, stepping back, seeing my condition.

"I would like that, but now you need to cleanse yourself and rest. Come with me."

As we passed out of the camp's circle through a small opening in the thick underbrush, I noticed a faint light on the horizon. It must be dawn, a mystical night speeding through to a new day. No wonder I was tired. I also noticed that our rearguard was no longer with us. Had I earned some trust? Enough to be alone with the leader who was just a step ahead, feeling her way along a narrow path leading down to the sound of running water.

My foot hit something, tripping, falling forwards, I reached out ahead of myself for support. The support, I found was the back of the leader. Her footing was solid and held me from falling. However in the process I found myself embracing her femininity, feeling her strength, her tension, her slow turn in my arms, now facing me, not disturbed by the closeness, smiling at me as if she'd expected this.

My embarrassment was obvious, she probably thought I'd intentionally done all this to approach intimacy. Although that was not the case, now, in her arms feeling her warmth, I welcomed her response.

"It's all right, your warmth is a welcome comfort from the cold of the night."

My hands were touching the softness of her hair, the base of her neck, then dropping gently down her back to the slenderness of her waist, resting on the fullness of her hips strangely appealing. The area structured in their fullness for bringing more into this world. I was finding myself irresistibly drawn into playing out my part of this process.

CHAPTER 6

In the dim light, I could see my now intimate leader tearing off her uniform with the fury of an animal. No stopping now, I thought, trembling with the intensity of the feelings. My coverings came off remarkably easy. This must be in harmony. I saw a glimpse, a fleeting vision of my two visionary tools intertwined in a mixture of lights, then the sight of my now naked leader holding out her arms to me. Moving forward, I felt her warmth enveloping me, drawing me closer, closer, until we were as one. Holding, touching, feeling light with the euphoria of the interaction, then sinking into the rapture of our psychic mixture.

Shrieks of pleasure woke me from a deep, dreamless sleep. The sun was high above me, warming me. The forest moss was soft but tiny spears of wood kept me aware of the natural bed, I'd rested on.

The sounds of pleasure along with water splashing came from nearby.

"Get up, sleepy head, time to wash and get on with the day."

Being a prisoner in these conditions quite suits' me, I thought.

The day passed slowly, lazily, like a moment out of the normal passage of time. This transformation from prisoner to what? Somewhat unexpected yet so welcome. A celebration, a reward for flowing in harmony without question, accepting the wisdom of the overall leading to the climax of harmonious pleasure.

It seemed that the camp accepted this turn of events readily. A few came to visit and bathe. The war seemed far away. Yet the haunting presence of weapons and readiness lurked in the air. When would it all start again? For now, I drank it all in. Pleasure beyond compare.

That night we lay on an open bed we'd prepared during the day. Soft boughs, moss, leaves like birds feathering their nest. I wondered, were we really preparing a nest like nature intended all physical beings to do. I felt my preparations on Javada, my training in Galaxium, my career in the U.I.A. how would this fit into all that?

Yet the feelings were so right, drawing me closer to this lovely creature now nestled in my arms looking up into the star-studded sky, lazily languishing in the aftermath of passion. Her voice resonated in my heart.

"Did you ever wonder, just what's out there? Is there really someone out there watching over us?"

How could I begin to explain what I knew and still wondered about?

"It is vast, isn't it?"

My vagueness passed unnoticed, she was lingering in her own thoughts.

"Cristo's teachings say there is a father out there orchestrating our lives, yet we have so much pain here, so much violence."

I could feel her tightening as her mind drifted into the conflict she was involved in. How could I relay the perfection lying behind the temporal which had evolved into such chaos here and my part in it all? It seemed like too much, unbelievable.

"In my experience, there is a universal wisdom behind all things, closer than you might imagine. For instance, the feelings we are sharing here, where do they come from?"

Her mind was leaving the painful emotional realm now coming back to us.

"From our hearts, that is where love lives and our father is love."

Her words left nothing more to be said all that was left was the expression of the love we were bathing in and express it we did, throughout the night.

CHAPTER 7

The next day began with activity, the camp was in motion, preparations were slowly made to move. The soldier's condition was stable, he still slept but was beginning to stir. The potion was not as strong as the one we processed on Javada, but the work had been done. His wounds were healing, the binding plant's secretions had effectively warded off any signal of infection. The true nature of the healing was not known, just that I had somehow been instrumental in aiding the process by touch. This suited me just fine, I preferred being left in the shadows, a high profile at this point would serve no purpose. My leader friend and I were now seen as a couple. I was her responsibility but it was clear to everyone that I had no intention of running off or doing anyone here any damage. Just a love-sick puppy following along.

The procession started moving around the high point of the sun. The day was overcast at times, darkening with occasional bursts of bright sunlight, almost blinding. The soldier was carried in a sling contrived from branches and heavy leaves. My mate and I followed close behind him and his carriers.

My curiosity spoke;

"Where are we going, can you tell me?" My mates' eyes were serious, distant.

"We must get back to our base camp for supplies, we are running low. There are also those who wish to meet you there."

I felt an uneasiness in her voice.

The climbing was slow and tedious, the heat of the day, the cumbersome load of the still-unconscious soldier, I wondered about what lay ahead. More challenging soldiers? Being drawn deeper into the physical scenario. When would it change, when would I return to the ethereal state of being. Strange, feeling such ecstasy just hours ago and now the physical torment of dragging my physical body upwards, to what?

Undoubtedly some form of trial, decisions, judgment, possibly more torment. Most interesting was the change in me. All I wanted to do was hold my mate. Surrender myself into her passion. Listen to her soft, low murmurs.

Not like the normal me, I thought, temporary insanity?

The sun was beginning to set behind the distant range of mountains as we entered the gorge, a dry river bed leading between towering cliff faces. A perfect spot for an ambush, I thought. This was obviously on everyone's mind as the procession tightened up their ranks, moving slowly, cautiously. A scout had taken a far lead sensing the terrain, watching for any signs of their enemy. My mate glanced back at me with a look of concern.

"Stay close to me in case of trouble."

I felt I had to offer the obvious.

"Why are we going through such a vulnerable passageway? Your enemy could be hidden any where around here."

I knew the answer before she gave it, I was just reaching for her attention, bathing in her turquoise eyes.

"There is no other way, we must go through to get to our base camp."

I felt a sinking feeling in my gut, I wondered if Beno's troops knew this. It seemed reasonable that they might.

The procession had all entered the vulnerable area by this time, moving quietly, looking up the cliff faces, weapons on ready. Then it came, a sharp bang followed by a dull roar, an avalanche, behind us. Looking back I could see rocks falling from the overhead cliffs, blocking any possibility of retreat. What lay ahead, I could just imagine. Then a loud voice, echoing along the cliff walls.

"You are completely surrounded, surrender at once or die."

The group had all taken cover along the base of the cliffs, what little cover there was. The whole situation seemed hopeless. Each one would either get picked off one by one or another blast creating an avalanche would bury all of us in one shot. My mate and I had ducked behind a bolder shielding us from the direction of the voice, but I was certain we had weapons trained on us from all the other directions. All efforts at resistance here were hopeless, yet I could see there was no sign of surrender. A fanatic mentality willing to die for their values, their ideals, faced, I was sure, by a similar committed group who held all the power in this situation. Well, I thought, it's time for me to crawl out from under my mates skirts and do something. I felt, the helplessness of being attached to her, the concern for her above all else. A very depowering emotion, yet I knew I must break free of this and leap with faith into the only reasonable way out. Taking my mate by her long hair pulling her close, I kissed her full lips long, relishing her tingling vibration once more possibly never again.

"You must all surrender to me, I'll personally take charge of your safety."

I had no idea whether or not this would work. I still wore my uniform, would I be recognized as an ally or an imposter? In reality I was both. Once again, no choice. The only possible way out.

My mates eyes were full again, those uncried tears.

"They do not treat their prisoners as well as we treated you. Most of us here would rather die here and now."

My voice trembled, but the conviction of my intent shone through.

"I'll use all my influence and power to safeguard your group, after all we're family now, trust me."

The overhead voice again.

"You have one minute, then you will all die."

There was no time to delay, I felt the inner surge propelling me. Snatching my mate's white bandana, I stood, stepped into the open raised it over my head and began walking in the direction of the official voice. Would I be shot? if so, by whom?

By the looks on the faces of many of the soldiers, I slowly passed, there seemed to be some trust, yet many frowned sure I was just out to save my own skin. Partially true, but I was sure I could do more good in it than out of it at this time. After all that work on the one soldier to see the whole group die seemed incomprehensible.

Then those above us, going through the formality of surrender tactics, probably relishing the idea of the upcoming turkey shoot. A perfect opportunity to release their pent-up anger over their losses.

I cleared the point scout leaning against the cliff wall looking dejected. He'd failed to detect the ambush and led everyone into what could be their final burial site. I shrugged my shoulders gesturing a life's like that sometimes, don't take it too hard. While there is life, there is still hope. Stepping slowly around a bend in the passageway, I ran head-on into a make shift roadblock of logs and rocks. It had taken some time to put this together, I thought, they knew we were coming.

The guns pointing at me from behind the blockade made me feel unsure of my next move. Should I advance or just stand here in this state of vulnerability, hands raised fluttering a woman's handkerchief?

A soldier stepped out from behind the blockade, waving me forward. This looks promising, better than a shot in the head at any rate. The look on his face was serious but not angry or threatening. His voice held authority without aggression.

"Come forward, we've been expecting you." I felt a sense of relief as I stepped around the boulders into the ring of those waiting, lowering my bandanna, I ventured.

"You've been expecting me, how did you know I was here?"

His face showed a pride of accomplishment.

"We have our ways. News of your great healing powers fell on many ears."

I felt slightly mocked but was thankful that once again, I seemed to be in the hands of benevolent captors. At this point I wasn't sure which side I was on if any. A tricky place to be in, considering my inner emotions at play.

"Who's in charge here, is it you?"

He laughed.

"Oh yes, I'm in charge of this boulder but the commander is up there waiting for you. I assume you're still on our side. We have heard some stories of the intimate care your captors gave you."

I found his jesting a relief, after the tension of not knowing what I would run into.

"I still wear Beno's uniform, my allegiance is not easily swayed. You fellows should take what you hear through the rumor mill with a grain of salt."

His grin showed me he accepted the allegiance bit but not the latter.

"You'd better head up, the commander has a decision to make here, you might be of help."

One of the soldiers took the lead, I followed, the climb was steep with loose rocks making our footing tricky. As we came to the crest of the incline, I saw what my friends below faced. A full company of soldiers lay face down aiming their weapons down on the passageway below. A shudder of the possible ran through my being.

Then I saw her, Cinda, leaning against her command vehicle, dressed in full battle gear, a formidable looking warrioress wearing a welcoming smile.

"So you made it through after all, I got a little tired waiting for you, thought I'd take things into my own hands."

My relief now was complete, there was a possibility of some reasonable resolution with Cinda in charge, at least a chance.

"Very capable hands, I might add, Moham has guided you well. You had no trouble getting through the cave and home?"

The assurance in her voice reflected her satisfaction with the outcome.

"We had a few difficulties with the small ones and father's complaining, but all are safe, thanks to you. How did you get captured, so easily?"

Getting credit for the outcome, raised my hopes.

"I was captured by Moham's will. Rhona, your spirit guide, led me right into the trap. She told me it was necessary so I allowed it to happen. What do you intend to do with them?"

I motioned towards the passageway below. Her look showed confusion over what I had said.

"Why would Moham want you captured? I don't understand. As for those below, I must deal with them severely, the soldiers want revenge. They all lost many comrades in the tunnel."

My heart sunk at her answer, it was as I'd feared.

"By accepting Moham's will and co-operating with my captors, I have learned much about them and gained some trust from them. This is an opportunity to create a bridge of communication between us. Killing them would just make them all martyrs deepening the gap between you. I know you really don't want that. I will take personal responsibility for them, if you spare their lives. I'm sure this is Moham's will."

My words, their logic, had impact, I could see that, but there was still hesitancy. How could she win her soldiers' support for this unusual approach?

I suddenly saw the artistry of the great Mahaj in this whole Set-up. Bringing me here under Marty's dimensional auric process. Placing me in a position of credibility with these followers of Moham, deepening the trust between us by the play in the tunnel giving me more influence, then showing me the transient nature of the whole play through seeing the soul play and its actual exodus, then dropping me into the lap of the followers of Cristo, my friend Marty. And now the capture of those I'd gotten to respect and love. The orchestration of all the events leading to this moment when Cinda, the one in charge, with the authority to command life or death in the situation. Would she support the limited aspect of her stately responsibility, the hard line of inflicting the will of her faction on the helpless ones below or would she move towards her teachings about the inner reality? The realm of compassion, understanding and the ways of what was known here as universal love.

I felt as if this planet had been brought to this moment by the Mahaj for the ultimate judgment. A self-judgment. Would the planet be allowed to move further into the darkness of conflict, selfishness, competition or would there be a turn around?

The moment when one decision could lead to an evolution, the quickening of the spirit, a step towards being open to the approach of Galaxium and all its developmental influences.

I knew the Mahaj could influence Cinda by touching her in some demonstrative manner affecting her decision or allow her mind to stay practical and do the stately appropriate thing, making an example of the hopeless ones who in turn would accept their fate as martyrs.

In my eyes it was all in the hands of the Mahaj. Did he want this planet to become a part of Galaxium? If so, all was possible. A herd of unicorns could fly down from the heavens and change the course of events instantaneously, yet my experience was that choice was the underlying factor, the constancy throughout the universe. The turning to the subtle teachings must be voluntary, yet I had often seen "A Divine Nudge" come at times like these. The soft nose of an invisible unicorn pushing gently, making the difference for one on the edge.

Here we all were, definitely on the edge. The soldiers peering over the edge, their weapons trained on those they saw as the enemy, yet inside each, a wondering, why all this, what if that was us below and well it could be. Those below, on the edge of life and death willing to accept their fate and pass beyond their edge of conscious reality into the unknown.

Cinda on the edge of becoming a victorious heroine to her people deepening the conflict or taking a step into the unknown, uncertain direction of a peacemaker.

I could see Cinda's dilemma, her head was bent forward, pondering, searching for the right decision. How could I give her the nudge. I felt I had done all I could. I'd been brought to this point, offered my service as a bridge, now must watch the course of history unfold before me.

As Cinda raised her head, I could see the deep lines in her forehead, the look of cold determination, the resolve.

I was sure she'd decided to do the politically astute thing, I understood. It was now the time for a divine intervention or all would be lost. My friends below, any chance for peace?

My senses were suddenly full of a feeling, a thrill almost shocking in its suddenness. I saw the image of my reality transformer with a shining feather waving out of the one eye-key passing through my mind's eye.

Then, there she was, Rhona, flying down from an overhead cloud, shrieking, passing over Cinda's head, over the soldiers and down into the ravine.

Cinda, moved to the edge, I followed. Both looking over, we could see my friends below, huddled, waiting for the onslaught and Rhona positioned on a tree limb directly in the line of fire. A perch of sacrifice, a divine picture indeed. Cinda could see it all now. I could feel her mind absorbing the sign. She knew she really had no choice. To move against something so small, yet so large in its symbolism. To kill now would be to kill a part of herself, a precious part of herself and she saw all this clearly.

She turned and looked into my eyes with the same tear-filled eyes as my mate below. How similar the two of you, I thought.

The look said I know what I must do now but what do I do with all these fingers squeezing down on their triggers, tightening and those below who are not surrendering. I now felt I had permission to move. The divine nudge had come, Cinda had responded. It was time for a resolution to this standoff. I took the microphone out of the hands of the official standing by Cinda and handed it to her.

"Cinda, explain to your men, that in return for my contribution in the tunnel, my safeguarding you and your family, I ask for the lives of those below. I'm sure Beno would grant me this. I'll go down and convince them to surrender with the understanding that they will not be mistreated but treated as emissaries of peace. They will surrender their weapons but be allowed to stay as a group under my personal supervision."

To my surprise, Cinda put down the microphone and waved in two soldiers positioned back of the front line. Pointing at me as she spoke to the two men.

"I'm going to grant our security man here, his request for his unusual contribution in the tunnel. It was his sense of observation that warned us of the attack and kept us from being completely surprised. Tell your men not to fire, allow him time to go down and make the arrangements."

Cinda had made good use of her authority, little said or explained, just the inference of do it or face the consequences. Each commander would have to see to it by keeping his men on their leash. Emotional indulgence would not be tolerated. I saw the wisdom of this type of military authority in this type of situation.

As I moved down the hill, past the barrier, I wondered how my friends here would respond. They really have no choice, trust me or die. Yet martyrdom was an inherent nature among this group. Would they see the opportunity being presented here by the Mahaj? A step towards stability. Only through stability could each individual grow in the psychic sense. As I passed slowly through the group I saw little had changed, some were surprised to see me back among them, others weren't. I could see my time with them had made some inroads gained some trust. As I approached my mate huddled behind her boulder, I felt the inner tug, the common place between us. How quickly these bonds form and hold tenaciously through all circumstances. I had to admit to myself that my actions here were not purely service to the Mahaj. There was my personal feeling and concern for her and hers. I felt that somehow our love-bond existed for the higher purpose of bringing the warring factions together. Love, the key opening the door to communication and finally resolution. Our embrace was fierce, a mixture of relief and uncertainty. I hurriedly explained the situation and again asked for her trust. She assured me that she would trust and follow me, many others probably would, but some were not so trusting and would rather end it right here in a hail of bullets.

I decided it was time to step forward and test the situation by trial. Taking my mate's hand, I stepped out into the open and walked over to the soldier I'd worked on. He was awake and sitting up, healing well, was he healed enough to walk with us? Feeling that he was the key to trust here, I asked.

"Will you come up with us?"

I wondered if he knew what had taken place, had his comrades filled him in?

"Yes, I was told about what you did for me, I will trust you."

Standing up shakily, he placed an arm around me, the other around my mate. The three of us slowly moved towards the barrier past each soldier still gripping their weapons. As we passed each, I sensed a letting go. First a reluctance, then the acceptance of the condition. The sight of the three of us supporting one another, weary of the fight, struggling forward towards the unknown was eliciting a loosening of the grip. Control was ebbing into a trusting acceptance in the face of overwhelming odds. Reluctant acceptance, but still acceptance.

As we came to the crest of the incline, I saw Cinda had made preparations for our arrival. She'd created a semi-circle with her carrier trucks open backs, our obvious transport. Soldiers lined our approach, there to demonstrate the authority, however not flaunting it. Their weapons were on ready but not pointing at us. I took this as a sign of respect. Here as well, a reluctant acceptance of the condition. Not particularly liking this new turn of events but accepting it as the will of their authority.

Looking back, I saw that most of our group was coming up, unarmed but not all, some were still down there holding on to their ideals. I wondered who? How would I deal with them?

Cinda stood in the center of the semi-circle, waiting with her two officers who'd obviously carried out her orders effectively. There was little sign of hostility in the eyes of our captors. I wondered if they had ever been this close to their enemy without the emotional heat of battle raging inside each of them.

CHAPTER 7

By this time, the soldier, my mate and I supported, was growing weak. We were almost dragging him. Cinda waved in two women dressed in white, medics, who gently took our burden, lay him on a carrier and carried him to a specially marked vehicle, outside the area we were entering. Cinda stepped forward, greeting us formally.

"Have all your people get into these trucks, they will all be taken to our mountain camp, fed and given quarters to rest." She had said this directly to my mate, now moving her gaze to me.

"You can go with them if you like, I must deal with the one's below."

By the look on her face, I felt her mode of dealing with them would be quick and severe. An opportunity for some release for her soldiers.

"No, I'll stay, I might be of more use here."

Turning to my mate.

"I'm sure you'll all be fine, I'll see you at camp soon."

Her look showed no fear, some concern.

"We'll be fine, but those remaining, they will not co-operate. The one you had a run-in with, is now in charge, He can be quite irrational."

As she finished speaking, I heard a loud burst of gunfire. It came from the ravine below. The two officers began shouting orders, a small group stayed with us while the rest ran to the edge, weapons on ready, pointing down to the trapped yet unyielding. Touching Cinda's shoulder.

"Give me one more chance with them, they're stubborn but I'd like to try."

Her face was stern, almost lifeless, her reply had the ring of finality.

"They are too unyielding, even if you convinced them to surrender due to the odds, they would be a constant source of agitation and aggravation. Better I deal with them, here and now."

As her words sunk deep into my mind, I saw the wisdom in what she said. This fanatic element would indeed always be at odds with her faction. Yet like the head of the Hydra, cut these off, martyr them and they would only grow back in greater numbers, becoming symbols for others with similar mentality. Used as role models for the modes of behavior in releasing their personal issues around anger and frustration.

"You know there are many others like them. By killing these few, the many remaining will be fueled. Their influence will be strengthened. Those who are now neutral, developing an appetite for peace, will be angered and move closer to the ways of thinking of those few below, away from the ways of these who are trusting me and you."

I could see her face softening; she recognized the truth of what I had said. I knew now that she was a peacemaker at heart, yet her position demanded a harsher attitude, a dilemma indeed.

Meanwhile the sounds of gunfire below had intensified. The soldiers above had not fired, just waiting for the order. If they unleashed, the battle would soon be over.

Rhona suddenly appeared, flailing her wings cresting the ridge, hovering overhead for a moment then flying away from us along the roadway. She no longer stood in the way. Was this a sign, were the trapped mice below destined for slaughter?

I could not accept the necessity; the courageous spirits below could be invaluable if placed in the right positions, trained in using their courage for peaceful efforts. I'd seen this transformation many times. It was a simple matter of re-aligning their force of commitment. Each must be brought to an understanding of a higher ideal, persuaded to commit themselves with the same fervor as they now held for this conflict. Yet not such a simple matter, in fact, seemingly impossible, here and now.

The situation reminded me of a psychic exploration I'd been involved in during my Javadian warrior training revolving around the issue of fear. We were all asked to go deep inside ourselves and find the place where fear existed. On my inward journey I faced my younger years when small threats appeared so large. The traumas of hopelessness leaving retreat as the only option. Hiding deep inside, putting up walls barricading myself in a cave, huddling there in terror of attack. As I approached the cave entrance, now an adult, knowing this trembling, terrified child inside was really me, a deep part of me, afraid. How do I deal with this child? The child was armed, dangerous, cornered. Not wanting to be approached yet lonely and not enjoying his self-made prison. I couldn't just walk in and say.

"Come on, trust me, all I want to do is play with you." I just wouldn't be allowed that close. I decided to build a little fire outside the cave, cook some deliciously smelling food and wait. Then I pulled out a musical instrument, played and sang a sweet, haunting lullaby my mother used to sing to me.

As I sang, I saw the wild-eyed ragged, dirty little boy peering at me around the edge of the cave entrance. I slowly put down the instrument, stirred the food, took a small piece out and held it offering. The hungry little boy just looked but wouldn't come out. A sense of such an inner battle, wanting to come out and enjoy the offerings, yet too terrified. I poured a small bit unto a plate and cautiously stepped towards the cave entrance. The little one shrieked and ran back inside, hidden out of sight. I knew that trust was the key, in times of terror, trust was the only life raft one could hold onto, until the storm passed. Fear like a storm always passed, just a matter of time.

Placing the food at the entrance, I went back to the warmth of the campfire, ate, continued playing and singing softly. I could see the young one carefully come to the cave entrance, watching me, take the food and devour it in one big gulp. Now nourished, he sat on his haunches listening. I sang lower, lower until he couldn't hear me at that distance anymore. The warmth of the fire beckoned. Then one small step out of his safety zone. In that one small step of faith, I felt an incredibly powerful inner release. Every journey starts with that one step. I now felt my soul reach out and take the little child upon a cloud of assurance, bringing him nearer, nearer to the fire, the warmth, home.

The food was eaten, the fire roared, the singing and dancing, the embrace of integration. I can still see the broad smile of trust and love on the dirty little face of my own limitations.

How could I use my understanding of this situation to bring .it to such a resolution. This condition was an external manifestation in this society of the same process I'd witnessed in my inner exploration. They were parts of the whole. The distrusting, trapped, dangerous, yet small, afraid and helpless.

What would the adult do here and now? The gunfire below continued, an occasional lull, then the chatter, the trapped child would not give in. I knew Cinda could not wait much longer. Her credibility as a commander was at stake. Her level-headedness had allowed me to bring out the flexible, rational majority but now the irrational would have to be dealt with. She looked at me again with that stony, distant gaze of a commandeering warrioress knowing what she had to do to fulfill her duties to her state, right or wrong.

"Your prisoners are ready to leave, go with them. I can't be responsible for their safety if you are not with them."

I knew she was saying this to get me out of the way, there just was no more I could do here now. Cinda would have to make the final decision and bear the weight of the outcome.

"May Moham guide you through this day, his will be yours."

Turning towards the waiting trucks, I could see my mate waving to me. The feeling that this was where I belonged for now, away from this confrontation. Rhona sat on a tall tree down the road, watching, signaling the way out. There was a sadness in my heart, not so much for the fanatic personalities below facing their self-imposed judgments, but for the innocent frightened child in each one of them. Yet I knew that their guide Cristo would be waiting in the ethereal to comfort them. To warm them by his fire, feed them with his grace, take them to their next stage in the on-going play of evolution.

How easily I was beginning to move between the physical - emotional aspect of reality and the ethereal plane, the place of oversight, seeing the wholeness of reality and how everything fit into the overall scheme of things.

As my sight moved into the ethereal, I looked back towards the ravine. At first there was nothing, then the faint image of a being forming, hovering over the area below. Arms spread wide, welcoming, the reverence of permanence emanating down to the trapped, the condemned.

Then I saw Cinda nod to her two officers. The blast of gunfire from above, the finishing touch had begun. As the barrage continued, I saw the ethereal form turn a brilliant white, blindingly bright surrounded by a pale-yellow hue. Then the drops of blood forming on his out-stretched hands dripping down to the dying below. Forms were rising like mists up to their waiting master. As they touched his hovering feet, the same phenomenon I'd witnessed in the tunnel. Each form would sparkle in their heart area. The glow about them would intensify. The being would lay back in relief and satisfaction. A sense of completion, home at last. Then the sparkle intensifying to the same brilliance as the master, a flash and they were gone as if absorbed into the feet of the master, their gateway to the universe.

Then an image in my mind's eye of the reality transformer, a stream of blood pouring from the eye and the voice.

"Go now, you've done what had to be done here. Your focus must now go to maintaining and enlarging the bridge between these two groups. Your relationship with Cinda and your mate is the key. Turn it with consciousness, open the door which will eventually lead to unity. Only as a unified planetary force can this place be approached for integration into Galaxium and the conscious service of the Mahaj. Ask your mate where I used to spend time alone, it is still a special place, held in reverence by my followers. You will know when to come, I will be waiting."

I found myself slowly drifting back to the physical dimension, again feeling my form, my emotions, my draw back towards my mate. Turning from the sounds of gunfire, Cinda carrying out her duties and the death, I walked slowly to the waiting trucks and the welcoming arms of my mate. I had my direction, its unfolding would be spontaneous as it always was. All that had to be done was to keep the focus, knowing this place was being prepared for approach by Galaxium. But when? How would this slaughter, this martyrdom affect the climate on this planet? Would it speed or hinder the approach to the bargaining table, where integration could begin. Only under a unified planetary administration with all working towards the same goal could approach be feasible. I felt, it was now all in the hands of the Mahaj and my two friends whom through their differences were somehow responsible for the condition. The changes would have to start with them and filter down to their followers and then reality.

The officer in charge met me at the first truck, offering me a ride in the command vehicle.

"Beno, has sent word that he would like to see you as soon as possible. You can go ahead of the rest of us, if you like."

I felt my place was with my ward now. It was their safety and comfort that concerned me, not the official workings of government. The results of their policies had left a bad taste in my mouth. A taste which might linger for some time.

"Thank you but I'll ride with the prisoners. Let Beno know, I'll see him when we all arrive."

The ride was hot and dusty. Everyone sat quietly, resigned to their fate, wondering if they'd made the right choice. Had they stayed with their comrades, they would be free now, in the hands of Cristo. Somehow they ended up here, uncertain of the future, trusting an enemy who seemed to have some concern for their well-being. He even chose to ride here with them rather than triumphantly going ahead to be rewarded. I knew my choice was right, here around me sat my hope for a bridge. Beings who witnessed the incident back there and could give an accurate portrayal of it all unlike the myths which would undoubtedly develop through the rumor mill. Then there was my mate, softly leaning into me, letting go of her responsibilities for now, simply trusting.

Our arrival was quite uneventful, a few armed guards, no formalities. Everyone was shown to their quarters which were quite adequate. Officers quarters, quite comfortable with a common gathering area. Cinda was obviously complying with my wish that these people be treated as peace emissaries rather than prisoners. I was sure anyone could slip away unnoticed if they decided to, it was being left to me to deal with this possibility. After we'd all been fed, again quite well in comparison to the lean offerings on the past trek, I asked for a gathering. I wanted to address the group.

The weight of the day lay heavy on each one solemnly sitting around the camp fire. The night was starry and still. Only the occasional sound of a pot being washed. I was sure my tiredness showed in my voice.

"I appreciate your co-operation up to this point. I hope each of you will be comfortable here for now and not decide to leave prematurely. I would like to start discussions between you and Beno's administration tonight. If you could draw up an outline of what you think can be done to down scale the conflict, it would help me in my meeting with Beno. Try to move past your distrust and open to the possibility of compromise. I will ask the same from him. Hopefully we can come to some common platform which you can take back to your people for consideration."

The group, now free of the extreme views of the few left behind, seemed ready to do their part. A list of grievances and suggestions was quickly formulated and given to me. I was now ready for my meeting with Beno.

As I left the warmth of the campfire, I felt a need to be alone. Sitting on a patch near the bush line, my gaze went up to the segment of the sky, the direction of Javada. A loneliness, a desire for the familiar, the peacefulness where violence knew no place. No longer living in the hearts of the Javadians, it knew no place to rise in the external reality. Yet here I felt its potential potency. Inner conflicts manifesting in the collective external society bringing individual's and groups head to head in strife.

Through the meditative systems of transcending the physical, entering the ethereal dimension, I could call on Marty to end it all here and now and take me back home, where this all started, but I knew I could not do that now. My place was here in the struggle. The Javadian peace would have to wait. All the inroads here had been made; I was the center of a flow of trust. The creative aspect of the Mahaj could now move through and around me to create an environment of receptivity where the feelings of peace, comradeship, a planetary wholeness could rise and dispel the agitation of conflict.

I rose and stepped towards the lights of the command center, a dark fortress quietly waiting emitting a feeling of power, forceful power, the kind of power which lay in the hands of a privileged few unwilling to voluntarily let it go, yet knowing that the rising resistance to their rule would eventually overwhelm them, strip them of everything they held precious.

My job was to find a compromise. A place where each side could find enough comfort to justify the sacrifice of their extremes. As I drew near, I spotted Cinda's command vehicle standing in front of the main entrance. She'd come back quicker than I'd expected, probably contentedly resting after the day's adventure. Was she jubilant about her victory, celebrating with her father? Having eliminated a small part of the extreme faction must have delighted the power structure waiting inside. I wondered how, in this moment of apparent triumph, my move towards peace through compromise would be met. The victorious were not known for generosity. Arrogant self-righteousness was the norm. However, I felt hopeful inside. Somehow my approach would be supported by the Mahaj, I was confident of this. All indicators pointed to this being the appropriate time.

As I passed the vehicle, I glimpsed a form slumped over the steering wheel, looking closer I could see it was Cinda.

"You got back quickly, was the outcome satisfactory?"

I felt a sharpness in my voice. Her reply was surprising.

"No, it was not."

My concern was not overly genuine.

"What's wrong? did you lose many?"

Her eyes were full, not releasing but full.

"No not many, just one."

I found my reply uncomforting.

"One is a small price, compared to the cost of your enemy."

Her hand waved to the back of the vehicle.

"It is a great loss to me, look and see."

I saw her tears now as I moved to the back of the vehicle wondering who could cause such distress. Lifting the back tarp, looking inside, I saw a small form covered by a white sheet glowing in the semi-darkness. Removing it carefully I saw her, Rhona, lifeless. No longer shrieking her divine message. Gone. I understood the grief. The cost to Cinda was high indeed. Losing her bird spirit guide was probably the highest price that could have been inflicted upon her at this time. Her connection to Moham had been severed.

I saw the balance of the play unfolding. The responsibility at least partially, lay on the shoulders of the one making the final nod at the ravine. The final release of the death machine. In return, a price to be paid. A balance of pain, one external, the other internal. Still both in the same realm, pain.

Placing the sheet back over Rhona's body, fixing the back tarp, I turned back to Cinda.

"Rhona is fine now. Free to fly on the winds of the universe, in the shelter of Moham's eye, you must feel happy for her."

I knew she was not but seeing it from Rhona's perspective might lighten her pain.

"I feel sad for the loss, but her freedom is conciliation. She was very dear to me in both forms. Now I've lost her twice."

A sudden gust of wind brought a haunting echo of sobs, as if I was hearing the sobs of those who had lost their loved ones this afternoon at the ravine now combining with Cinda's sobs in the night air over her loss.

The preciousness of life lay heavy on us now. It's premature loss, like a fruit picked too soon was a waste. Not allowed to mature into its inherent potential, robbed of the experience, its ultimate destiny. But the price of our actions always lay heavy on us, reminding us of our unity. Pain inflicted was always pain received. If only all life would simultaneously see this, the infliction of anything other than kindness and understanding would become extinct.

Cinda had stepped out of the vehicle approached me with slumped shoulders, came close and lay her head up against my chest. Her sobs were the release she needed now. Encircling her with my arms, I held her feeling the flow of care emanate from my center, encircling, bathing, comforting. It was not a time for talk, the logic of it all could wait. It was a time for raw emotions, pent-up feelings coming out around this whole event, releasing the toxins of the day possibly even more. Toxins of a life. Then a fresh start. Learning from the misfortunes, building on the foundations of our inner understandings. Her tear-reddened eyes looked deeply into me.

"You are very comforting for someone doing your work. You puzzle me. There is something hidden about you." My evasiveness was automatic.

"There is something hidden in us all, look deeply and you may find it." I could see, she wasn't sure what I meant.

"Yes, will you reveal it to me sometime?"

I was sure, I would, someday. But now it was time to see the power center. Deal, head-on with my challenge waiting inside.

"All will be revealed soon. Now I need your support in there." I was drawing our attention back, motioning towards the doorway, her responsibilities of state, the very thing which brought about all this grief. Her voice was re-assuring.

"You already have it. I've spoken to my father about what you are trying to do, he seems to understand, but the rest of them, I don't know." My query was to forearm me as much as possible.

"Who, in there, is most extreme?"

Her answer was sharp and unhesitating.

"General Miko and a few other's who follow his directions. I'll show him to you."

I felt the necessity to re-group myself after the emotional interaction.

"Would you go in ahead of me, tell your father I'm here? I need a moment to myself."

She turned and started walking towards the heavy doorway, then looking back over her shoulder almost seductively.

"Would you come up the mountain to my special place tonight to send Rhona off? I would like your company."

My tiredness seemed to leave, I felt slightly split. Cinda and my mate waiting.

"We'll see how things go inside. It's been a long day."

She continued, opened the door, went through and was gone. I stood alone in the chill of the night air wondering. I felt drawn to Cinda, drawn from the very beginning before the tunnel, yet the circumstances were unfolding in their own pattern. Were my feelings for both these women simultaneously inappropriate? Or was this again, Mahaj's way to nourish the beginning of communication between the opposing factions. There was no way to be sure, just follow my inner self, my feelings within the aura of respect and support. I climbed inside Cinda's vehicle, sat and gazed out again towards Javada asking inwardly for guidance through the upcoming interaction.

There was a sudden shudder through the vehicle as if a quake had run through the area, then the haunting echo of a cry, a bird cry from the forest nearby, deep and dark like our deep unconscious. Rising in our lives, creating and destroying patterns at will. I felt a corresponding shudder and cry from within.

Closing my eyes I focused on the area. The image formed slowly, hazily. A great bird-like creature emitting an orange-yellow hue, one eye gleaming in the deep unfathomingly deep, dark inside. Yet the darkness had a feel of comfort, solidity, immovable in its resolve. Here is where my strength would come from in my dealings tonight. A reservoir of immense power, unlimited in scope, funnelling itself through the bird-creature covering the entirety of my inner vision. The eye of the creature suddenly glared at me, not in anger but in intense attentiveness. Ripples of red mixing with the clear blue of a midday sky, much like Cinda's eyes tonight. Then the voice filling me, overflowing in me.

"Your path has brought you here for an influence in the course of the evolution of this place, but there is more. Your life and evolution will also be affected by what happens here. Co-operate with your feelings to the two now a part of you. They will each give you something you will cherish the rest of your life. You, in turn, will nourish them and all those here with your connections inside yourself and out. Don't concern yourself with the social limitations, they are easily re-framed when you move with the universal creative forces in harmony with your innermost will. The power system you are approaching tonight is a temporal condition, see it for what it is. Play your part with integrity and leave the outcome in the capable hands of the Mahaj. All will be as it should be, Trust."

The inner vision slowly faded, leaving a feeling of surety, security. An appetite to dance the dance once again, spontaneously for the joy of the moment not the future of the outcome.

Stepping out of Cinda's vehicle, saluting the lifeless form in the back, I turned toward the heavy door ahead, thinking what incredible beings we are when we manifest from within. The previous feelings of sadness were gone. How could one be sad in the face of such grandeur. It all fit so well. I wondered how I forgot this so often falling into the confusion of self-rule. Only to be lifted into the light of surety over and over again. Quite a ride up and down the roller-coaster of life.

CHAPTER 8

Opening the door, stepping inside, it felt like a different world. The silence of the night now gone, superseded by the busy beings in communication, each absorbed in their own world of thoughts, images, convictions, appetites, communicating. A self-importance emanated from the individuals and their particular group. What an illusion, I thought, in contrast to the immense silent grandeur of the universe going about its workings.

Beno was leaving his group at the far end of the room, not palatial, but regal in its simplicity, moving quickly towards me. His walk projected a conviction, at ease with his authority but taking nothing for granted. As I moved towards him, I felt the attention of the room move towards us. As we neared the center of the hall, I saw a small smile forming, a welcoming sign. Then the arms outstretched, surprisingly welcoming, I thought as I stepped into the bear hug. The embrace was brief but genuine. It felt hauntingly familiar. Almost like Moham's hug, still felt after the separation. I could hear the applause beginning at a far corner of the hall, slowly spreading, finally encircling us completely. We were certainly the center of attention, a very good sign. Stepping back, still holding my arms in his large hands.

"Welcome back, security man, we'd thought we lost you for a while there. Come have a drink with us."

The offer made me realize, my approach to negotiation tonight would have to be subtle. It would all be in the timing. As we stepped into Beno's group, I felt a warm arm slip around my waist and link into my left arm. It was Cinda.

"Father, I see you've finally found me a man."

The group chuckled at her forwardness, I jested.

"Man enough for you! I wonder if such a being exists in the universe."

Beno took his turn.

"Well, there better be, I want at least one grandson."

The group was now laughingly nodding their approval, projecting their adult knowingness on the attractive young couple. Humor, I thought, an incredible tool when used wisely. Cinda, reached her hand up around my neck, pulling me down for a playful embrace. Her mouth nibbled at my ear.

"General Miko is the large man directly opposite you, the one not laughing."

Beno placed his hands on both of us.

"It would please me to reward you with my gregarious daughter but I understand you have already been granted your wish."

I felt this was a good time to bring the attention on focus, yet maintain the humour.

"My wish is to see this situation resolved favorably so that you and yours can live in peace and prosper. I thank you for treating our guests as well as they treated me. This is a step in the right direction. However your daughter's embrace would definitely be among the highest ranked wishes, if I had another." The group teasingly uttered, "oooh!"

General Miko abruptly interjected.

"Let us not forget, they are our prisoners, not guests."

I knew by his aggressive gesture and glare, I would have to deal with him head-on. His strategy would be to somehow discredit me, but for now I held the favor of the room. Beno diplomatically stepped in.

"We will deal with this matter, shortly, for now I would appreciate you keeping my daughter company, you seem to cheer her, she was quite distraught earlier. But now she's her old flirtatious self."

I thought it was a good time for a little negotiation, smilingly.

"My services do not come cheap. Bathing in Cinda's beauty is almost enough, but I would like to ask for another favor."

Beno put on his official look, twinkling.

"If it is in my power?"

Handing him the document of grievances and suggestions.

"Please look these over with an open mind, I would like to send our guests (throwing a challenging gaze at general Miko) back tonight with your counter stance."

The general aggressively stepped forward, glaringly.

"We don't negotiate with rebels."

I knew I had to deal with him now. He was laying territory like top dog. If I accepted his authority my efforts here would be futile. Directly.

"How many were lost in the tunnel?"

His answer was arrogant and evasive.

"Not many, our forces were superior."

Beno stepped in again, placing his hand on my shoulder.

"The losses were high and would have been much higher had it not been for your attentiveness."

The general saw the support and stepped back. Beno continued.

"I will look this over with my advisors, meanwhile take Cinda over to that table and help yourself."

He had pointed out a table full of food and drink. A most pleasing array. My tone was warm.

"Yes, thank you, I am hungry and your hospitality is much appreciated."

Cinda ceremoniously led me towards the feast, glancing up.

"I don't think the general likes you very much, be careful."

Glancing back to the group, I could see the general whispering to one of his aides. I didn't like the feel of it.

The wine was rich and full. The feast was delicious. There was no famine here. I found myself holding back a little. I didn't want to be full, slow, tired, digesting, if the challenge did come.

The music slowed to a romantic theme. Cinda playfully stretched out her arms.

"Take me, security man, on a dance among the stars, if you dare." The challenge was not hard to face. The warrioress, no longer wore her harsh battle gear. Soft garments clung to her femininity. Slipping my arm around her waist, drawing her firmly to me, we smoothly floated onto the dance floor. Her motions followed mine easily, responsively. A dance of synchronicity. Slow, feeling each other's auras intermingling. The brush of my leg between her thighs, a momentary holding, then release. A slight blush at the intimacy then the rudeness of interruption. The man had caught me by surprise in my moment of extreme distraction. His push sent me reeling backwards. His voice was raspy as he reached to a surprised Cinda.

"Let me show you what a real man feels like."

Her response was lightening fast, precise.

"Let me show you how an arrogant pig bleeds."

The blade in her hand seemed to appear from thin air. A flash of steel, an arm split wide open from wrist to elbow. The gushing blood, the man's look of amazement at the speed of his defeat.

My response was automatic. I knew this man had been sent by General Miko to embarrass and discredit me. I held back my angry impulse. Instead, placing my thumb on a pressure point around his left shoulder, I snatched a towel from a passing waiter and quickly bound the wound. Looking into his dilated eyes.

"Tell the sender, I've received and understand the message." Two of the man's comrades came running over and quickly hustled him out the back door. The interruption was brief, so brief that I was sure many didn't even notice it. I could feel Cinda still tight from the encounter.

"The commander was right, you are very capable in these matters." Her reply had a ring of disapproval.

"And you are too kind."

Beno came striding over to us with a serious look on his face.

"General Miko has overstepped his boundaries doing this, but he's gaining support among our extreme. It's made him quite arrogant in his stance. Nevertheless this is going a little too far. Your restraint was appropriate and appreciated, yours however, my dear, was a little extreme."

I could see he was actually proud of his daughter's capabilities but a little concerned with her volatile manner of expression, he continued.

"She's very much like her mother, fiery temper, a will of her own."

Yes, her mother, I wondered.

"I have not met her, where is she now?"

Sadness passed over his face.

"She's no longer with us. Her greatest joy was riding unescorted in the hills. One day her horse stepped on a land mine." Placing his arm around Cinda's shoulder.

"We've missed her a great deal."

At the risk of being disrespectful I ventured.

"Everyone in this conflict is losing a great deal. The most precious, often times. You have my sympathies."

His look of sadness was lightening.

"I am fortunate, she left me with many precious memories and a precious gem of a daughter."

The deeply felt hug between them told me all I needed to know of their closeness. "I hope this step towards communication leads to some stability. I would hate to see you lose any more." I could see my point was understood, continuing.

"Have you studied the proposals?" He turned to me with full eyes.

"Yes, I have. Much of it is unacceptable at this time, but some of it is negotiable. The section about a self-rule can be considered, details about tax sharing would have to be worked out. Unlike General Miko and his supporters, I would like to work towards stability. After what happened here tonight, I can't be absolutely sure of the safety of your friends, our guests as you say."

My feelings around security agreed.

"I think it's important that we send them back with your intentions tonight. Cinda and I can escort them to the boundary but in my opinion your personal word on all this to them now would be most appropriate."

His co-operation was almost surprising.

"I will go and speak with them with my most trusted advisor. His wisdom has been invaluable to me. Would you work with him in our efforts? We are all quite safe here, as safe as can be expected considering the recent upscale of action along the perimeter tonight."

My concerns over this afternoon's incident were correct. The extreme faction has been fueled by today's sacrifice. The rumor mill has a way of exaggerating incidents like this. It's imperative that we balance it by sending our guests back with your message and their accounts of the incident as soon as possible.

Beno was looking at me, piercingly.

"You're unusually wise for a young squirt. I think you'll have quite a future here with us."

Cinda took my arm again.

"Leave his future in my hands, you know the power of a good woman's guidance. We'll have to start with a haircut and some nicer clothes."

I became aware of my ragged look, the old uniform, half-worn out shoes from the mountain trek.

"Ah, but you see the clear, shining heart inside. The heart growing fonder of you by the moment."

Beno was enjoying the flirtation.

"Oh yes, the power of a good woman a great molding influence, I know."

His momentary look into his memory, then coming back.

"Go and tell our guests, I will come and speak with them shortly. Cinda, come with me, we'll show you a safe route to the boundary."

As the heavy door closed behind me shutting out the inner buzz, the silence of the night enveloped me. How I'd grown to enjoy its solidity, the feel of the shadows. Moving silently among them, seeing everything in the light but staying hidden, a shade of the darkness. As a child afraid of the dark, now feeling embraced and protected by it. How change came even on the inside. Change, the one constant, always manifesting everywhere, yet so resisted by those attached to their comfort zones. Now the silence of the night, more appetizing to me than the celebrations I'd just left. Here like an animal, I felt the surge of the hunt.

As I moved towards the guest quarters, I wondered, why was I feeling this instinctual animalistic essence coursing through me. Everything seemed to be going fine and yet this intensity. Then coming around the edge of one of the buildings, still silently in the shadow, I understood. The group around the fire had been surrounded by three heavily armed soldiers, pointing their weapons at them, keeping them in a tightly bound circle. They were no longer being treated as guests, more like General Miko's vision of prisoners. As I scanned the group I saw no damage at this point, but my mate was missing. Then a muffled cry from a building on the edge of the courtyard, I knew it was her.

I felt a faintness, an emotional drop inside, then a surge of adrenalin. A form appeared in my mind's eye. A Javadian cat-like creature which roamed the mountain ranges. Silent and deadly. Its strike was impossible to detect until it was too late. Black, a creature of the shadows. I felt its power, its stealth,its unmercylessness, the power was carrying me from shadow to shadow gaining speed and momentum. Then a flying leap at the door standing between me and what lay waiting inside. I knew the door was solid, locked, immovable, yet I was unstoppable, moved by the fury of the creature of the night. As my feet hit the door, I knew it would submit to the power. A momentary resistance then hinges flying off the door frame. Logic would say they were rusty but I was not feeling logical. I was an irrational creature in the heat of the hunt. Only death could stop me now, there was no fear of it. A welcome friend always waiting in the shadows like me. I heard his voice.

"Treat me, you have the right."

The door hit the floor with me on it, continuing the momentum, I rolled knowing there would be someone waiting at the end of it. There he was surprise on his face at the suddenness of my appearance. I knew there was no time to access the situation. My hands instinctively took him by the back of the head, my hands ripped into his hair, turning him, my closed fist rammed its way into the base of his spine. As he fell, I scanned the room and saw two others. One was holding someone, it was my mate. I saw the bandaged arm holding her underclothes. The rage inside exploded. It felt like centuries of pent-up anger releasing, flowing through the patterns of Javadian training now in motion. The momentum carrying me into the room lost little in my first encounter. Another roll and I was on him. I heard a sound from inside, the sound of a cat with its ears laid flat back, warning. It was too late for warnings. The one holding my mate had thrown her aside, reached for his weapon and was leveling it on me as I hit the bandaged one. As he kicked at me, I took him into the roll, bringing his wounded arm around his back, spinning, letting the other's bullet finds its mark, me or this animal in my grip. The sound of the blast, the splat as it hit him in the chest. Feeling his body going limp, my shield was dropping away. As I straightened out, I saw three things happening simultaneously, the gun pointing at me, the trigger finger tightening, a foot flying out from the left of my vision, a dark shrieking bird, flying past me on the right of my vision. Then the blast knocked aside slightly by the kicking foot of my mate, I felt the bullet sing past my right ear. But now the bird had sunk its talons into the man's eyes, wings flailing, pulling at them, then pulling free with one eye in each talon flying back towards the door.

Looking back, I saw her, once again in battle gear with the falcon bird sitting on her left shoulder, holding the two eyes in her right hand, a smile of achievement on her lush mouth.

"Well, security man, you can move when adequately inspired."

Cinda was looking at my semi-nude mate moving towards me. Her body felt cold, trembling, withdrawn. Cinda offered her cloak for warmth and cover.

"These pigs have gotten their just rewards, my father is dealing with the ones outside. Come with me to my room, a hot bath and some clothes."

As their eyes met in the moment, I knew a friendship had come into being. A deep friendship which transcended worldly differences. She continued.

"Let me make you a necklace out of these lustful pigs' eyes."

As she held out her prize offering, I felt fortunate to have her as a friend and not an enemy. I was sure I'd try my best to keep it so, for more reasons than one.

I could hear Beno's voice giving orders angrily. Stepping outside, I saw the former armed guard had been disarmed and stood waiting. Beno, meanwhile was speaking with our guests, reassuring them. I felt this show of support might even deepen the commitment to communications, eventually peace.

Finding a quiet, dark place under a tree spreading itself over a section of the courtyard, I sat and began gathering myself. Letting go of the recent fury closing my eyes seeking the inner tranquility, finding it, bathing.

Then the images of the Milky Leader and the Beige Leader forming. The Milky Leader was smiling happy with my spontaneous movements, my use of visionary power and the outcome. But the beige-heart aura leader was shaking her head, holding her heart, I could almost hear the words from her mind.

"A little extreme, my dear."

I had to agree, on one hand, what had to be done, was done quickly, decisively, but I had been drawn deeply into the illusory emotional realm. Was I getting too involved? Had I lost track of the true ethereal nature of the reality here? Where had all that pent-up anger come from, releasing itself with such a fury? Was this an overkill with the offsetting balancing aspect coming? The spontaneous nature of the incident comforted me. There is no karma in spontaneity, only in premeditated action.

However, would I have been as extreme if it hadn't been my mate in the hands of the violators? Probably not. A condition to be aware of. I opened my eyes in time to see the three violators being brought out by Beno's guards. One covered with a sheet, shot dead by his comrade, limping badly from the pressure point blow to his back. He would heal soon enough. The last one blind, holding the holes where his eyes used to be. A high price for his indiscretion.

As I started to rise from my rest spot, a dark shadowy object slipped into my peripheral vision. Coming into view, I saw a small, black cat slipping silently past me. As it passed in front of me, a glance, the eyes, yellowish, calm, satisfied, smiling, as if signaling a sense of accord. I felt the inner power of my visionary cat, a unity, oneness. The sense of contentment which comes in the completion of a task. I knew all that had happened was in accord with a higher, hidden purpose. Possibly the union in the moment of intensity between my mate and Cinda. What would it grow into? I remembered the voice before entering the meeting hall, heralding a union between the three of us. Now it was manifesting around me. Movement in an unknown direction in harmony with unknown forces creating a still unknown outcome. Faith in the guidance systems, courage in the motion, acceptance in the outcome. I could see the divine formula unfolding. The cat had now slipped into the silence of the night. My inner vision dimmed and faded away. I could see Beno had completed his discussions with the group. There seemed to be a diplomatic friendship in the air. Some handshake, guarded looks of approval, suspicions gradually ebbing into hopefulness.

Cinda's command vehicle suddenly came sliding around one of the buildings, grinding to a stop in front of the group. My mate stepped out of the passenger's door, now dressed in comfortable battle fatigues, her hair bound loosely behind her with a tanned leather cloak hanging over her shoulders. Cinda had been very generous.

Beno quickly stepped to the driver's door and opened it. Cinda stepped out, now dressed in a form-fitting suit. Not a uniform, more like an exploring tourist on an adventurous tour of the hills.

As I approached the group, a dusty in obscure truck pulled up behind Cinda's vehicle carrying two forms. The passenger stepped out holding an official looking package and moved quickly to Beno's side. His hair was grey, solid in form, and calm in disposition. I assumed he was the trusted advisor Beno had previously mentioned. The three spoke quietly, intently, then turned and walked back to the group. There were some introductions, formalities, and the package was handed ceremoniously to my mate. I could sense the aura of haste in the air, a determination, the power of conviction.

My mate saw me first, coming out of the shadows. She quickly left the group and came to me. Her voice was once again solid, balanced.

"Thank you for risking yourself like that for me. I'll never forget what I saw. You were not like one of us, more like an animal, I mean you felt like a wild animal, not just the motions, but the feeling."

Her eyes radiated warmth, I drank it in feeling its stilling effect. My voice trembled slightly.

"I don't relish doing all that, but it was necessary. I'm glad you were not harmed in any real way."

I knew the trauma of it all would linger but soon move deep into the unconscious. A healing would have to be addressed in time, but for now no more could be done. Her embrace was complete, physically melting, psychically enveloping, mentally reassuring. Her eyes beamed her love, her words pierced my heart.

"I care a great deal for you. You will always be precious to me, but I know our lives will lead us in different directions. Please stay in touch, somehow."

My intention was genuine.

"I will, to the best of my ability."

She was leaning back in my arms, now smiling.

"Yes, your ability, that will be enough for me. I guess we should leave, your friend Beno seems a little worried about things around here."

The group had entered the back of the truck, Beno's advisor was back in the passenger seat ready, Beno and Cinda were coming towards us. Beno's look was serious but calmly contented. His voice was low, authorative.

"Well, my friend, you've really got yourself in it now, haven't you?" I knew he was referring to the conflict.

"Yes, I guess I have, but surrounded by such beautiful, capable allies, I feel almost invincible." His seriousness softened. He was looking at my mate and his daughter.

"Take good care of your allies, they may be our hope for the future." I could see he sensed what I already knew. A bond was forming between them. A friendly alliance which could grow into the societies, almost like a role model, an example of the possible.

Cinda stepped up to my mate and linked her arm.

"Would you mind driving, security man, my friend and I have a necklace to make on our short journey? I could see this gesture might be the most important part of the journey.

"It would be my pleasure driving through these hills with my two favorite ladies."

Laughingly, Beno added.

"Keep your eyes on the road, I know it won't be easy, but you are a disciplined fellow, aren't you?"

The bear hug was again hauntingly familiar, now almost fatherly in its intimacy. Was Moham playing games with me? Possibly! I could almost see his broad warrior's grin. His words.

"Quite a game, if you don't get caught." I knew I was close. All these powerful influences, friendship, duty, affection, adventure, life and death, love.

Quite a volatile package yet the essence of the ethereal, lying silently in the darkness behind it all.

As I drove away from the compound, I could see Beno's salute in the mirror. Concern was on his drawn face, but an acceptance of the condition. This was his life and his daughter's. It didn't come into being overnight, but grew around him. Now he had to play out his part, still primarily responsible for his people but now extending himself to the unknown rebellious faction growing stronger as well as his own opposing faction within his own administration. A sensitive point in the balancing of power. I felt sure he would deal with it all with integrity. Still, that haunting familiarity. Were my two ethereal friends playing with me, pulling strings magically and if so, why? Just a game? Or was there a deeper underlying reason for it all. If this was all just an illusion, then why were my emotions so involved? From deep primordial fury to exhilarating feelings of love and protectiveness. The gentle inner caress of friendship and allegiance. I knew if I let it be it would all be made clear in time.

I could see the dimmed lights of the group's truck following close behind as we wound our way up the almost undetectable trail towards an unknown drop off point. Unknown to me, but Cinda had it all in her mind. Her periodic directions kept me on track, turning with little warning, switchbacks, steep inclines necessitating dropping into lower gears slowing us to a crawl. Then headlong bursts down ravines more suited for mountain goats. Through it all Cinda and my mate played with their artistic endeavor in the small light cast by our dash board. The gesture and their focus was the thing. Occasional girlish giggles erupted from their hushed chatter. I was sure now the friendship was ingrained deep enough to withstand the inevitable trials ahead.

The sacrifice of the violator's eyes did not seem overly extreme in view of the possible outcome. Then it was done, finished. Cinda gleefully held up the creation. I could see the two glistening eyes in the dark of the night almost like the eyes of the shadowy cat back at the compound. Now lifeless, staring but emitting another sense, another feeling. Cinda ceremoniously wrapped the leather tong with its beads and eyes around my mates neck. It was tightly formed and fit well.

"Let these lustful eyes be a warning to those of similar intent. I've made the clip weaker than the leather so you can't be choked with it. It will break before that."

The delicate concern touched my mate deeply.

"I will wear it when I meet with the leader of our movement, my brother, and tell him of your kindness."

This new turn of events surprised me. An influential brother who might appreciate the gesture. Just another foot in the door.

Mahaj's way of letting me know, the work was being done, synchronistically on many levels. My part was a small contribution to the wholeness of it all.

Their hug was short, each a little embarrassed with the quickness of this interaction. A closeness coming into being without warning, yet the hovering eminence of the separation, soon.

Cinda's hand touched my shoulder.

"Pull over here, I'll take over, we're getting close to the boundary, shut off all the lights."

As we stopped, Cinda jumped out of the vehicle, ran back, gave a few directions and was back in the driver's seat before I had time to settle into my place. My mate gently slid close and lay her head on my shoulder. Each of us knew, our time for separation was near. The future was uncertain, but we each had our road to follow. She slowly turned under my outstretched arm.

"Cinda and I have arranged a meeting place in two days. That should be enough time to hammer out some details. Will you be there?" I really had no idea where I would be, here on this planet or back to where? Was Marty finished here, would we be leaving, like ghosts as if we had never come? I suddenly remembered the voice over the ravine.

"I almost forgot to ask you something. When Cristo lived on this planet, he had a special place he went to meditate. Do you know where it is?" Her face went into deep thought.

"Yes, I remember my mother telling me of a plateau on a mountain in this range where he would go, always alone. Some thought he communicated with his God there, others thought alien beings came to him because of its flatness and isolation. It is now considered a sacred place. No one goes there, believing it is protected for the time of his return. Many do gather periodically at the base of the mountain to worship, but she never did take me there. She said she would when I was ready. I'm sure she called the place Sunea or Sona."

Cinda suggested.

CHAPTER 8

"I know of a mountain area called the peaks of Sonia. It's isolated but not far from here, in fact, the place I want to take Rhona is near it."

Cinda's vehicle had come to the crest of the hill we were climbing. In the darkness, I could see a dark valley below. She instructed my mate.

"There is a narrow trail. Our forces have been instructed to let your group through but still take care as those of General Miko's ilk are everywhere. We're not absolutely sure of their reaction to all this. My father is taking precautions but one can never be absolutely sure."

As we gathered at the head of the trail leading downwards, the valley below seemed dark, dangerous, unknown in its terrain. I was sending my mate down into it with reluctance inside, yet there was no choice. The dark would have to be encountered, traversed and passed through to facilitate the process now underway.

Cinda and my mate were now holding each other's hands, standing back for a moment gazing into each other's eyes, as if they were windows into each other's souls communicating in another dimension. I wondered what they chattered about on the journey. They're deep, dark secret for now.

Then the embrace of farewell, hurried as the group was already starting down the incline, silently in a single file, feeling their way. The kiss, lingering, then the drawing away. Her eyes spoke.

"Farewell, my love, until the next time." The tremor in me as I felt the separation.

"Yes, until the next time."

Then she was gone, over the edge, into the abyss waiting below.

Turning, I could see Cinda had already gotten into her command vehicle and was waving me in. The transport truck was turning, pulling back down the trail in the direction we had come from. The grey-haired advisor was looking at me, a look of uncertainty. Destiny had brought us together, yet circumstances were such that we had not time to even touch, physically or mentally. Yet psychically, I sensed an ally, a seasoned warrior on the diplomatic front I would encounter again.

As I slid into the passenger seat, Cinda reached over touching the side of my head reassuringly.

"I'm sure she will be just fine, I've given her a powerful protective omen. But you, security man, constantly amaze me with your willingness to be vulnerable."

I felt a slight lump forming in my throat in response to all this genuine emotion.

"I'm glad the two of you hit it off so well, like a couple of peace doves."

The warrioress beside me didn't particularly like the image I had just summoned as she slammed the vehicle into gear and headed towards a dim shadowy mountain range ahead.

As we sped on towards the shadowy range ahead, I wondered, how she kept the vehicle on track. There was little light, we were still running dark as if she expected danger on this side of the boundary. I jested in an effort to change the thick feeling between us now.

"Fancy meeting you here, do you come here often?"

Her eyes darted my way.

"Rhona and I used to come here for a part of my training, you'll soon see.

There was no humor in her now.

I felt the heaviness of the day settling on both of us. Settling back into my seat, I queried.

"Did Rhona teach you to handle your falcon so effectively?"

Her voice softened a little, seeing my efforts at lightening things up.

Rhona always had an uncanny way with the birds. She communicated with them mentally. I've practiced the technique but still lack her poise.

As we reached the edge of the foothills, I saw the moon rising over a distant ridge, a yellowish haze through a thin film of clouds hovering around the peak. By its light, I could see a narrow path going up the side of the hill towards the mountain ahead. Pointing towards it.

"Is that where we're taking Rhona?"

Her reply was curt.

"You'll soon see, it's not far now."

I sensed an uneasiness.

"Is there anything particularly wrong, you seem very withdrawn?"

Her answer was almost apologetic.

"No, nothing particular. I do have something to tell you and I'm not sure how you'll react."

My curiosity was obvious.

"What is it?"

We'd reached the bottom of the trail, pulling behind a small clump of brush for shelter, Cinda stopped abruptly and turned to me.

"Later, now we have a climb ahead."

Taking a small bag, she moved quietly to the back of the vehicle, opened it and placed the white sheet with its contents into it, slung it over her shoulder and headed towards the trail. Almost too spontaneously, I jibbed.

"No food or drink, are we going to eat Rhona?"

Her reply set me back a little.

"Don't push me too far, security man, I may like you, but I've suddenly developed a taste for making necklaces."

I suddenly felt very appreciative of my ability to see here in this physical dimension, I followed silently.

The trail up was sharp but not overly difficult due to the light cast by the fullness of the moon. Cinda's voluptuous form was always in view stimulating many of my senses.

"Ah" I thought, the nature of desire, the more it is fed, the stronger it gets.

Cinda, as if reading my mind, seductively glanced back striking a pose accentuating her feminine fullness.

"Follow my dance among the stars if you dare." I remembered how our first dance ended and wondered if I was ready for a replay.

"Lead the way, I'm fool enough to follow."

Coming to the top of the incline, I could see a narrow high passageway between the towering rock formations. I thought I heard the distant sound of drums. Cinda stopped and held out her hand.

"This is a tricky passage, you'll have to stay close to me. I used to play here as a child and later with Rhona, so I know it well."

Taking my hands, she placed them on each side of her waist.

"Follow directly behind me, like this."

I had no complaints with the procedure but I knew I would have a difficult time keeping my focus on the trail.

"Can I just let go into you and trust?"

Her closeness and look were reassuring.

"It looks like you have no choice, I do warn you that I always get what I want."

I wondered what her wants were.

"I hope your not planning to eat me."

She stopped abruptly, I felt the heat of her body against me as I ran into her back.

Turning her head.

"I'm sure you'll enjoy being consumed."

My mind slipped back to my mate, a wave of guilt tightened me.

"Your beauty is intoxicating but we have someone else to consider."

Her laugh took me by surprise.

"We've talked it all over and decided to share you, like a common love toy."

I wasn't sure I liked this projection.

"A couple of children enjoying a toy for a while, then casting it aside when they got bored with the play? What about the toy?"

Her eyes were glistening with the duel, she knew she was winning.

"I guess, you'll just have to be a very entertaining toy. You'll enjoy our playrooms."

I had no doubt I would.

"Is that what all that hushed chatter was about?"

She was pulling away now, continuing her progress, swaying her hips for my obvious pleasure.

"Yes, we talked about you. Her feelings for you are very strong and so are mine."

My head reeled with the vision of having two incredibly beautiful creatures interested in such a generous arrangement. Playing with the flirtatious fantasy.

"Which one shall I marry?"

Her reply sounded matter of course.

"Both, but me first, tonight."

My curiosity as to our destination was getting stronger and I was sure I was hearing drums ahead. My hands had slipped down to her full swaying hips, they seemed to move in harmony with the distant beckoning sound. The heat I was feeling inside was almost unbearable. Her glance back, told me she knew.

"Wait, my dear, enjoy all the subtle preliminaries. A good meal must be eaten slowly in stages, I know you're not exactly starved."

She obviously knew about the precious few days in the mountains. My feelings of guilt were subsiding but I wondered as to the wisdom of it all. I was being drawn into a paradise of feelings and emotions. Could I stay somewhat detached and objective or would I get lost? How would I feel when Marty called me back and away? An inner voice said enjoy your moments, here and now, that is really all you ever have. Trust that your next moment will be even more enchanting.

Suddenly we were through the dark passageway, coming out on a high trail ridge dropping off into a deep valley. The moon illuminated the entirety in its pale yellow hue. The sound of the drums was now quite audible coming from below. I could also see a flicker of flame from the far side of the valley. I reluctantly let go of my guidance system, fighting off my impulse to pull it closer, envelop it, but now I could see the trail and my preliminary taste of the meal would keep me going anticipating the orgy of tastes lying ahead.

Cinda moved ahead a few paces and turned. Her hair glistening in the moonlight, her eyes a flame with the interplay.

"Well, do you like it?" I knew she was referring to the whole package.

"Oh yes, I feel like I've stepped on a space shuttle to paradise."

Her seductive smile fueled my fantasy.

"So you approve of the arrangement?"

I realized she was quite serious about what I thought might have been just a flirtatious game.

"Why do I feel somewhat manipulated? Are there underlying motives here deeper than just passion. I know I'm a fairly good looking fellow, but this. It's almost too much!"

Her look became serious.

"Yes, there are. You have won the respect and trust of my father as well as many others. As my husband your authority would be as a prince far exceeding that of General Miko.

This would give you the power to influence our policies and facilitate the formation of this bridge of communication we've started. Our sources also tell us that you have become quite a myth among the rebels. Your unusual abilities displayed in the tunnel and on the trail seems to have caught their attention. You already have an intimate connection which I'm sure will blossom as well. I'm willing to try and stay emotionally detached to some degree in order to facilitate this alliance between the three of us. This is what I had to tell you."

A moment passed as the proposal slowly sank into me, gazing at me, then throwing up her arms impatiently.

"Well, do you accept?" I knew the power of commitment. If I agreed, the flow of the universe would begin to move to facilitate the condition. I felt I should project myself into the possibility slowly, testing its level of harmony with all other factors. Anyway I was enjoying the seduction, the appetizers and I wasn't yet starved but getting hungrier by the minute as I sipped on the ambrosia of Cinda's beauty, physical, mental and psychic. The sudden burst of drums from below gave me the needed distraction. Cinda sensed my hesitancy, her face showed signs of slight rejection but her warrior mind maintained its balance.

"Come, let's go down. You can give me your answer later. I guess it's a lot to think about for a little brain like yours."

I detected a definite tinge of anger in her voice.

I followed her down a winding path towards the flicker below. I'd expected a small fire in a cave, hidden from view for the funeral pyre. Instead we were headed for a blaze easily seen for miles. Who was down there so confident that their valley was safe from aggressive intrusion. I would soon know as the fire grew larger, the drums louder.

As the path leveled out at the bottom of the incline, Cinda moved quicker putting some distance between us. I could still see her form ahead intent on its destination. I heard her voice reassuring.

"They know we're coming, there is no danger. I know them all well."

I settled back into an easy gate and reflected. How this planet was teaching me the subtle movements between the physical and ethereal realities manifesting simultaneously. So many times now, I've touched the transcendent, unlimited space inside myself and out, lived in its stable emotional feeling, its permanence, then so quickly gotten drawn back into the physical, temporal condition with its fluctuating emotional nature. Now here I was so involved that I felt I might be approaching the borderline of over-involvement in the affairs of this place. Actually altering the natural evolution of the beings here with my attachments and their corresponding emotional ramifications. Yet I felt this is what was meant to be happening here, right now. My participation seemed to be melting into what was unfolding naturally anyway. Supporting, even aiding the path towards a higher consciousness, a more harmonious way of being.

But this love triangle, it challenged my thought forms around the physical, emotional love relationships between individuals. I knew the unlimited nature of love but monogamy was the thought pattern of conduct in my upbringing. Now this standard was being challenged. It seemed that almost all my existing patterns were being shown as limitations to be seen as challenges to be overcome. All I could do was trust in my inner guidance systems and how they moved with the external, constantly changing realms of reality. Then there was Marty, Moham and the Mahaj, all moving things around to facilitate the unknown outcome. I sensed it was all structured in a motion preparing this place for integration into Galaxium. Centralizing the power system with all these factions at play would be no easy task. Yet I knew with all these powers gathered here moving in harmony towards a common goal. Nothing could stand in the way of success. So all I had to do was stay awake, relax and let go into the unfolding condition even its temporal aspect and my relationship to it.

CHAPTER 9

Cinda had entered a circle of tall, temporal structures surrounding a blazing fire. I could see many brown skinned, semi-dressed females moving towards her. They all came together in a small, tight circle and spoke in low murmurs. One took her bag and headed for one of the smaller structures while the others led Cinda to a longer dome-shaped building closer to the slow moving river glistening in the moonlight.

I wondered where I was supposed to go. Was I being left to roam this strange place on my own? There was a small group of males gathered near the fire, crouched, speaking to each other in muffled tones. I began feeling like an outsider, not quite a part of this, yet here nonetheless.

As I moved leisurely towards the fire, I saw a flap covering the entrance to one of the structure fly open. A stream of nude males came out one by one hastily heading towards the nearby river. They were shining wet in the moonlight. Their appetite for the river seemed overwhelming, each plunging headlong into its waiting essence. Sounds of relief erupted everywhere. The splashing, gleeful laughter filled the night air. The gentle wind swept past me bringing a wave of scented, hot air. The whole scheme seemed familiar. A part of my meditative training on Javada had a ritual similar to this. The young warriors would gather in airtight lodges with specially designed fire units heating the interior to almost unbearable temperatures. It was a sort of contest among the young men. Those who had attained depth in their meditative processes could stay in the space longer than those just beginning their inward disciplines. The inward withdrawal made the temperature bearable and actually facilitated the vision quest part of the process. Many would stay in so long that they would lose consciousness and have to be carried out. They would be made comfortable and allowed to sleep and dream. Their dreams often affected the rest of their lives. Divine messages, lucid dream sequences, actual out-of-body experiences were common place.

I wondered, was this a similar event? If so, this was a sacred spiritual place Cinda had brought me to. I would probably soon know. A ceremoniously dressed male was approaching me holding a long object with smoke coming out one end. His expression was friendly, welcoming.

"Come join us around the fire, the great spirit watching over our valley welcomes you."

I could feel the gaze of the others near the fire beckoning. There was no hesitancy inside me, as I moved co-operatively towards the heat of the flames. Sitting down with the others, the pipe was passed around, each taking in a deep inhalation.

Holding the pipe close, I saw an array of forms carved deeply into the wood. Animals, birds and half human-bird animals in a flow from the smoking end to the mouth piece. These people apparently worshiped their great spirit through a ritualistic interaction with nature. I took a deep puff, the smoke tasted sweet but caught in my throat. Choking, I passed the pipe along noticing a general look of approval among the group of men, deeply weathered and thin, but well-muscled. The look of hunters and gatherers.

The one who had welcomed me came up behind me, leaned over and whispered in my left ear.

"Our Shaman waits for you in our sweat lodge, his welcome will begin the ceremonies but first you will have the opportunity to learn more about us and possibly yourself."

As I rose, he took my shoulders and slowly pushed me towards the lifted flap of the building the young nude men had come out of. Moving towards the opening, I noticed a young man coming out with a pile of rocks and another going in with a different pile. This must be their way of heating the area, a constant interchanges of hot rocks from the blazing fire, I'd just left. As I moved through the opening, my guide closed the flap and I felt the intense heat inside. It was pitch black except for the deep glow of the hot rocks. Positioning myself near them, taking off all my clothes, I settled into my meditative sweat posture. Closing my eyes, following my breath into the coolness of my inner cave, I relaxed and felt the caress of the hot moist air.

Then a deep, raspy voice.

"You are adept at this practice, that is good. Cinda has chosen well, our spirit is content with you. You are wondering about us. We have lived peacefully in this valley for a long time. Our ways have brought us in harmony with our natural surroundings and give us all we need. We know that those who have much but lack inner wisdom have little. Those who have little but wish for more, suffer. Only those of us who have little and have learned to be content with what is given us by the Great Spirit prosper inwardly and outwardly. As you see, our vision is simple but we are never in any danger unlike those who live outside the protection of our valley."

As I sat, listening, sweating, a vision grew inside. I saw the people happily going about their daily activities. Safe within the psycho-physical creation their collective had formed. Each one transferring their individual psychic power into a common image of reality.

The Turquoise Leader on Javada had taught me the power of Reality-Affectation through the use of fantasy and visionary ritual. The conscious awareness of the phenomena was designed to free us from being victim to social group projected images which tend to stifle our inner creative genius. Yet these beings had either consciously or unconsciously created a safe place in which to evolve in the center of the turmoil all around them.

The voice brought me back again.

"We know you understand us and we want to give you a gift, an experience. Place a wish, a question, possibly an uncertainty in your mind, then relax." The process was familiar, I'd reached into collective psyches at other times and experienced their catalytic effects on my own inner visionary process. This seemed like a perfect opportunity to explore the nature of my relationship with my two female friends and its harmony or disharmony with my own psychic evolution as well as the events unfolding on the political stage.

The Being with the voice was chanting in a low ceremonious tone, occasionally throwing a sweet-smelling herb on the fire. As it dimly glowed, I saw a deeply lined face, old, yet full of vigor. Then darkness.

I felt his presence enveloping me, assuringly urging me inward. A drowsiness, an inner coolness keeping me comfortable, my body drenched with sweat. A sudden surge of fear, going deeper to the stillness, then melting, floating away.

I was walking down a forest path with a sense of being surrounded by danger, possibly someone stalking me. Glancing around I saw the deep green of the forest, but no one there. Continuing, coming to a turnaround with two paths leading deeper, I felt drawn to the one on the right. As I moved along I could see an opening ahead, a cliff, the feeling of being cornered with no retreat, yet ahead a drop of unknown depth. Summoning my inner faith I moved ahead a few steps, the sudden urge to fly, a feeling that I could. Taking a few quick steps, leaping into the air, I found myself floating, then I realized I had wings, I was half man and half bird, yet I was still me. Spreading myself, catching the wind and clearing the cliff's edge, I flew high and free. What an inspirational feeling, unbound, totally unfettered. My soul, free to explore. Then surfing on the wind, warm, permeating, feeling its power move through my very essence. A sob of joy, the feeling of home, high and safe.

Then ahead of me a high wall and the thought. I've just left everything I know behind and I don't know where I'm going, but the wind is still blowing me away, away from all my securities. Turning my flight into the wind, I began the struggle to return. Yet the struggle seemed very easy, I had immense power in my bird-like body. Just before the cliff I saw a small village to my right, gliding over it I saw Cinda and my mate walking arm in arm waving up at me. I felt no need to descend, all was as it should be, my friends were happy, safe, and I was in flight. My most precious experience.

As I approached the cliff I saw my two other friends, Marty and Moham beckoning to me. They stood together like sentinels, assuring me of my safety. I felt drawn to them despite the ecstatic joy of the flight. The sense of importance in their company filled me. I knew their words would dispel all uncertainty and bring resolution.

As my bird-like feet touched the land, I felt myself sinking deep inside to the place where joy and unhappiness were not. The place of stillness, ananda, a state far beyond joy. The tingle of infinity, the place I was beginning to know as home, eternal home.

Moham, emitting a glorious array of deep colors, passionate colors, held up his left hand and spoke.

"Welcome back, I see you still have the power to exercise your will. It was a strong wind taking you away."

Marty stood bathed in gentler, lighter auric colors. The colors of acceptance. His right hand raised.

"Why didn't you just keep going? You will never know what lies on the other side of the wall of your own self-inflicted limitations."

I remembered the feelings of insecurity at the wall. Where would I sleep? What would I eat? The general lack of faith. Not completely trusting the permeating wind blowing through my soul, carrying me. Then the exhilaration of another sort on my flight back. The sense of power, the ability to go where I wanted experience fulfillment of my desires, my way. The powers of both processes etched deeply in, my consciousness. The abandoned flight of surrender in the universal winds. The inner surge of determining my own destiny, commitment, determination and the power, to see it through to the end.

Here, standing before me, the external symbols, the outwardly manifested personas of my inner processes. The divine scale between will-oriented action and surrender. Me, standing between them, feeling the radiance of their presence. Was I supposed to choose or find a balance between the two extremes? It appeared that my question was about to be answered. What started as a dot beyond the clouds got larger and larger until it seemed to fill the sky above us. A great bird emanating hues of light from all aspects of the color spectrum settled gracefully behind my two friends, spread its great wings around them and spoke.

"You have seen the nature of the dualistic external reality. While there is a you experiencing it, the choice will be there. Your dance will be the expression of the mingling of your two friends, essences within you. Bring them into harmony there and peace will come to pass here. You know from your flight experience that letting go into the delights being presented here now will be ecstatic. Be confident in your power to return to this place with your two friends and allies. You won't get lost. Trust your inner guidance and enjoy."

The vision began to fade, dimmer, blurred then I could hear the raspy old voice chanting, calling me back. A soft hand at the base of my spine.

"Come back to us security man, we still need you."

As I returned to the darkness of the sweat lodge, I felt Cinda's bare skin pressed against my left side. Her hand running up and down my spine coaxing me back to the physical dimension. A most pleasing dimension, here and now.

The Shaman threw something on the rocks, it sizzled and glowed sending out a wave of piercingly, pungent steam. The blast of heat and smell drew me back completely. His voice signaled the end of the experience.

"You have seen a great deal, a great deal more than most. Live in the wisdom of your vision. May the two of you prosper in each other's radiance."

As his words faded, he rose and threw a handful of herbs on the fire. I could see him leaving in the light of its glow. The smell was exotic, full as a garden of blooming

Picdalias. In its light I saw my most beautiful Cinda, glistening wet, tantalizingly nude, a playful smile on the fullness of her mouth.

"Kiss me, you fool."

I gave a long-lingering sweaty embrace ending with a quick, withdrawing toss of her hair. It stung my skin like a thousand tiny whips. Her question would not be denied twice.

"Well, do you agree now?"

My answer came directly from my flight vision. I saw the image of my two friends nodding their approval and the great bird looking down at us solemnly with his great wings slightly raised in a divine benediction.

"Yes, if you will still have me."

Her answer was in action, rising.

"Feel like a swim, hot stuff?"

Standing at the doorway, holding open the covering flap, illuminated by the blazing fire in the background, my new bride beckoned. I felt the heat of the moment, inside and out. Surrender was so easy in this situation, if only it was so easy in all others. The drums outside had suddenly resumed, their fury was matched by the passionate surge of my hormone-laden blood. The time was here for play and love. Sweeping past her, I again felt her hair, now smoothly brushing across my chest, arms and back. The coolness of the night air felt refreshing, awakening. The race to the waiting river, Cinda a few steps ahead, leading the way. Her incredible beauty, the power in her limbs, I saw a flash of my unicorn, my horned flying unicorn in the meadow reaching for the stars. I remembered her challenge.

"Come, dance with me among the stars if you dare."

I also remembered the warning.

"Fools rush in, where angels fear to thread."

Yet now I knew angels had no fear, only faith and courage to leap into the unknown.

I leapt headlong into the coolness of the river's water, swam deep, rising to the surface into the waiting arms of my lover. Our union was as frantic as the beat of drums resonating through every fibre of our beings. As we emerged at the shoreline, stumbling, dazed by the exhilaration of our union, a group of women met us with a flowing luminous robe. Wrapping it around Cinda's chilled body, they joyfully danced around her singing, leading her away from me to the structure they'd previously taken her to. A group of smiling, pleased males surrounded me, slapping my nude body until the sting took away all feelings of the cold. The pipe carrier stepped out of the shadows, beckoning.

"Come, we have a hot drink and your wedding robes ready for you."

As we entered the structure positioned on the other side of the fire from Cinda's structure, my guide turned to me.

"We would all like to hear about your sweat vision, our Shaman seems overjoyed at the result, he has gone to his place of seclusion to meditate on it."

The herbal drink was hot in temperature and in its spicing. I could feel its warmth creeping through my entire body with a tingling after affect, lingering. I spoke to the eager listeners gathered about my fears, flight and the great bird spirit and his message. When I finished, all were still, some nodded, some seemed lost in their own thoughts and images. They all seemed to know that I was sharing a most intimate part of myself with them in trust. Their attitude in return was respectful and attentive.

Dressed in my warm, colorful ceremonial robe, I was again led back to the fire. The drums were being beaten low, steady. There was a hush in the still night air, a waiting. From the other side of the fire, I could see Cinda, surrounded by her group coming out of her structure being led to our meeting place. In the flickering light of the dancing fire bursts, I could see our destination. A flowery seat large enough for two, made from twigs and branches surrounded by mothers with their children. The children were quietly laying up against their mothers in various positions obviously a little tired after a full day. I was surprised they were still awake. As we arrived at the seat simultaneously, our respective groups withdrew, leaving us standing face to face amongst the mothers and children. Cinda was glowing with the radiance of potentiality, reaching out her hands to me.

"Come!My husband, sit with me. Let us bathe in our future."

I knew, as I sat down beside her that she had every intent to fulfill her father's wish for a grandchild. There was no hesitation in me, although children were not a part of my self-image until now. I found it a gentle, warm vision. I remembered my dream of my love, children, the storm, the flight, standing before my goddess and receiving her gift. It seemed that all this was a part of the dream. A physical reflection of my psyche's projection. I wondered whether the destructive storm ending it was imminent. I seemed willing to take the risk. The risk of emotional devastation at the end knowing the ethereal reality would always be there to fall back into and be carried up into the clear meadows of the transcendent realms.

As we sat, I felt the eagerness in my new mate's energy body. A being, fully developed and ready for her contribution to the propagational process. Here I was committed to my part in the play, just as eager, yet aware of my other commitments. A sudden sense of the growing number of commitments I was taking on. How would they all unfold and be dealt with?

I knew my concern was unnecessary, I was in motion, in harmony with the unfolding pattern being woven by the Mahaj. In that moment, I saw my place beyond cause and effect. Although my commitments and actions all had effect, my inspirations and deeply felt motivations came from the deeper realm ruled by the Mahaj. In this place, cause and effect melted into a unity of time and space where all was now. A feeling of it beyond my ability to comprehend. All I could do was accept this sense. A safe, secure place to lay my restless mind and all its wanderings, allowing it to release its dilemmas around control and responsibility.

The mothers with all their children had formed a line and were passing before us, each family presenting a gift. Ornately wrapped offerings to be explored later. Then they were gone and we sat alone. Cinda's hand lay on my thigh, her eyes watery with emotion. Her voice soft and low.

"Tonight we will create someone very special, I know it. I am at the height of my cycle and your seed is strong."

My head reeled with it all. First the vision and now this. Fatherhood, imminent fatherhood. I felt it too. As I embraced the already visualized mother of my child, I whispered.

"You will be the most beautiful, sensitive mother of them all."

There was a sudden moving off to our left, out of the shadows dressed in various forms of nature; animals, birds, insects and even reptiles; were the men of the tribe. The fighters and hunters, all displaying their vigor. Dancing, chanting and yelling. A most tumultuous array. Such a contrast to the serenity and calm strength of the mothers, the resting place of potentiality waiting for the inspiration to create new forms of life. These were the bearers of the seed. Agitated, searching for a place to rest. The catalyst necessary for motherhood to manifest. They descended upon us like a horde of locusts demanding our attention. The leader, a slim yet well-muscled, agile, fierce young warrior whirled before us. His dance, leaps and rolls were in league with the Milky Leader's abilities. It was his energy that carried the seed of the group. A whirling leap, falling directly in front of us, stretching out his right hand and touching Cinda's foot and stretched out his left hand and touched mine.

A living symbol of the passing of the seed through the tribes' conduit. The strongest and most agile summoning the very best in me. I could see the union of the three of us in the ethereal forming like a pink cloud around us, pulsating with the vigor of the moment. The Shaman parted the group of men gathered in front of us, stepped between the stretched out legs of the young man at our feet, stood on his back rippled with muscles like steel and held out his offering; an ornately carved scepter. The group fell silent, just as he spoke.

"May your union be fruitful. We offer our power and protection for your use, we are sure you will use it wisely."

I could feel the psychic power within both Cinda and myself simultaneously reach out and take the power sceptre from his outstretched hands. A deeper reddish hue enveloped us. In it I felt Cinda's love, my eagerness and the Shaman's wisdom.

The young man lurched upwards with the Shaman holding on to him as if he were riding a horse kicking him onward back to the fire. The group of men followed, now even more frantic, their incantations and forcefulness filled the night air. I felt the urge to join them and express my vigor and pleasure in the dance but knew my place was here with my love holding the tribe's offering, the visualization of protective power, the power that kept this place secure and safe. I sensed the immense potentiality of this, something to be shared with the outside world. Our union, the power of it, was the hope, the permeating underlying hope.

Then, as if orchestrated by the Great Spirit of this land, the dance stopped, the drums ceased their seemingly endless beat, the fury was replaced by the stillness, the subtle sounds of the river and the calls of the distant birds. Feeling Cinda's softness next to me, close almost a part of me, the power of the dance surging through my loins, I knew my seed was fully empowered, ready. My arm tightened around Cinda's shoulders, as I leaned into her. My voice intense with passion.

"May the vigor of this dance, bring you every pleasure you've ever dreamt of."

My point was fully understood as my wife leaned her fullness into me breathing out her reply.

"Oh yes, I'm sure it will in your most capable hands."

Taking my arm from around her shoulder she placed the scepter in both my hands.

"Rule me and mine with the vigor of this night. We all trust you."

As the impact of her words sank into me I felt yet another commitment rising in me. A commitment not just to my bride but to these people, so expressive in this moment of life, love and passion.

The Mahaj is certainly filling my plate to overflowing. The meal of a lifetime and the appetite to match, I thought.

A shimmering mist had silently moved into the camp from the river. A ghostly haze moving of its own volition, its own direction, covering, then revealing by its spontaneous coming and going. Then like the mist, a row of young females dressed in transparent silky white cloth came out of Cinda's former structure and approached us slowly, noiselessly as if they were walking on it. The dark skinned young female leading the group carried something in her outstretched hands. It glistened in the moonlight. As she moved it sent out sparkles, like tiny moonbeams reflected off its irregular surface. Cinda offered.

"They're bringing us their most precious gem, the Truth Stone. It is believed to have the power to bring the past and future both into the present for one with the insight."

An older woman followed the younger group carrying Cinda's bag with Rhona's remains. I noticed the men were moving, bringing large pieces of wood and throwing them on the blaze. The light grew in intensity reflecting off the gem. Its sharp corners amplifying the beams of light both from the moon and the increasing fire. Cinda stood and reached out her hands, the gem was gently placed in them. The group formed a semi-circle and sat facing us, waiting. Cinda turned to me with a far-off look in her eyes.

"Hold it with me. Let our souls mingle and create a vision for us to share."

I stood and reached out my hands. She stepped forward and placed her hands holding the gem inside mine. I felt the heat moving up my arms, into my body, my heart region. As it touched my inner abode, the seat of the soul, I felt its radiance and power. A tingling feeling, a dizziness, a sense of drowsiness and then a spinning fall into myself and out through the gem with Cinda intertwined, flowing around me. Our souls leaving, flying, playing among the stars, touching intimate out-of-reach places from the past and the future, all in this moment of soul flight. How long we played and explored, I'll never know, yet it seemed like only an instant. The illusion of time, now standing still. Then the vision.

Walking arm in arm in a garden of color. Heavenly scents filled my senses, laughter filled the air, laughter for no reason. Not the taunting humor at someone's expense but the spontaneous eruptions of heart felt humor expressed in the joy of the moment for its own sake. Then a little curly haired boy running towards us.

"Mommy, Daddy, I saw you coming, come and see what Freeda has found."

As we followed, I saw an elderly grey-haired woman bending over a pond pointing at something. As she turned I recognized her. It was an old friend, a Javadian teacher, smiling her welcome. My heart felt full, so full holding back the tears was impossible.

I woke with my head in Cinda's lap looking up at the stars. Her hand was gently stroking my brow. Her voice showed some concern.

"Nice flight, my dear, but then you left. Where did you go?"

My answer was unthought.

"Into our future, its most pleasing. I'll tell you about it sometime, or better yet, I'll show you with our lives in time."

As I stood, I could see the fire had reached a fierceness, lighting everything around it into clear visibility. The tribe had all gathered around it, the women in a semi-circle on one side, the men on the other. A haunting chant rose up over the crackle of the fire. Everyone had linked arms and where swaying slowly, periodically raising their arms to the heavens in unison. Cinda reached down, picked up her bag and looked to me.

"It is time for the final farewell, will you join me in this?"

I felt this was a part of her life, I had not shared. I would allow her psyche freedom to go through this separation ritual unhindered by my involvement.

"No, you must do this on your own, I'll be here waiting."

I sat on our love seat, watching her move towards the inferno. The group opened a space, letting her inside their circle. I suddenly felt a protective concern. An emotion of attachment, not willing to lose her now. The pang of jealousy, having to let go and share her with her ritual and her people.

How quickly these inner bonds develop and grow. One moment I'm a free Javadian, Galaxium U.I.A. agent roaming the known universe, ready to explore the unknown alone with only the Mahaj as my guide and companion, then suddenly the sense of union with another. The inner wish to maintain the connection at all costs. Yet, knowing deep down this connection was of form, temporal in it's very nature. Temporal as the dead bird about to be consumed in the fires of eternity. Rhona was no longer here except in the minds and hearts of those gathered to bid their farewells.

Cinda had taken the white sheet with its contents out of her bag and was holding it high above her head, offering it to the heavens. I wondered if Rhona, as she was now, could perceive this moment. Was her consciousness lingering, taking in the remembrance or was she gone, totally immersed in her new experiences with Moham and the Mahaj or did she lie peacefully in the universal sea in eternal rest.

Unconsciously, my hand moved and touched something cold and sharp. Looking around I saw the Truth Stone where Cinda had left it, in a hollow of the seat. It fit so well I assumed the place had been carved for just this purpose. As I gazed into the coolness of its pale blue hue, I saw something forming. As it became distinct, I saw two forms sitting at each side of a small pool of water gazing into it. Above them the great bird spirit from my sweat vision, hovered, gently soaring on the wind, back and forth looking down at the two. One of the figures was Moham, the other I assumed was Rhona. As I looked closer, I could see what it was they were watching. There in the pool, from an oversight perspective, the camp, the fire, the tribe's circle and Cinda.

Again, I began feeling the dizziness but drew my attention away back here to Cinda and the fire. Had I seen the future or was it all happening now in different dimensions. My thoughts were interrupted by the change around the fire.

The group circle had all leaned forward, their hands almost touching the ground, the chanting had deepened and was increasing in its tempo. Then with one simultaneous yell, all leaped up and forward reaching their arms upward. Rhona's remains flew out of Cinda's hands onto the blazing fire, burned for a moment and then were gone. Just sparks and ashes now in the gust of wind coming off the river.

The moment of reverence was over. The drums began beating with a heightened fury, the young native girls encircled Cinda bowing, touching her wedding garment. The young men came bounding towards them, encircling, whirling in their frantic dance. A strange mixture of parting, greeting and starting afresh. A farewell to an old friend, the greeting of new friends and a beginning of a union of two souls. A full evening.

As I watched, I felt lulled, almost drugged by the rhythm, the cascading energy levels moving in some unearthly connection with my now alive and well emotional structure. There was little ethereal objectivity left in me, overwhelmed by the influx of sensory stimuli creating inner waves of instability. So this was individual love, love between distinct psyches each on their universal program route coming together, mingling, losing parts of their evolution, into a common place. The danger of getting so drawn into the common, losing one's own center becoming one with the new entity created through mutual agreement.

My Javadian orientation in these matters stood like a gargoyle at the gate to these intimacies. Beware, many have perished in the heat of this burning sun. The sun of desire, propelled by the hunger instilled in all form to re-create, re-populate at all costs. When bathing in the warmth of these cosmic rays, one must exercise the inner disciplines for balance. The emotions I was feeling around the issues of possessiveness leading to the emotional insecurity of loss of this precious, yet dangerous connection were beginning to spin my head as I watched my Cinda whirling, dancing with her female entourage. From my seat I could see their near-naked forms writhing in the pleasure of the dance, as the roaring fire behind them illuminated each curvature, each undulation, each expression as it manifested before me.

Then the men, as if unleashed by some strange, powerful erotic force swarmed over them with their frantic passion. Each spontaneously choosing his mate, separating her out from the group, pulling her away, coaxing her into an arena of privacy only steps from the view of the others.Yet the illusion of being hidden, alone.

Cinda, lost in her own dance, seemed oblivious to the nuance; the loss of her surrounding companions now being slowly and methodically undressed before me. I could feel my heart quickening with each surge, each vicarious experience unfolding before and inside me. Then the young warrior who had connected us and the Shaman in the ritual of vigor appeared from the shadows. Gliding up behind the now entranced Cinda pulsating to the beat of the drums, taking her by the waist, encircling her with his eagerness. I ,now knew the danger heralded by my Javadian instructors. Fury filled my heart, faintness, a compelling urge to strike, to destroy the intruder. An inner flash of my reality disruptor, destroy him, my training shining through.

Wait, you are over reacting. Then a flash of my reality transformer, accept, it is time to move, get involved and allow the Mahaj to recreate the situation through your participation.

Standing, moving without hesitation, yet containing my fury, not knowing what I would do upon contact. The drums beat furiously, the fire blazed hot, a war-like chant rose up from the intertwining couples. Now Cinda was almost nude, not resisting the current passing through the fires of the night. Feelings of passion and rejection raged through me. A violent, dangerous current, unbalanced in its essence carrying me into the heart of its fire. I could see the young warrior's hands were near but not touching Cinda's vulnerability, yet methodically baring her before my approach.

Then suddenly, everything stopped, the drums, the writhing couples. The young warrior stepped aside, grinning at me, the couples stood looking, waiting. Cinda turned to me, a challenging look in her eyes, a smile of achievement, I understood. The feelings inside eased. I realized the play as it unfolded was the last gift from the group. The gift of furious passion almost violent in its essence.

Cinda's arms were now outstretched to me, the warriors were all laughing and clapping. The now nude females again gathered behind Cinda, rhythmically swaying to the resumed, mellowed drum beat. Cinda's brown skin glistened wet in the moonlight. Drops of perspiration gleamed like diamonds in the dancing firelight, her voice hoarse.

"Well, my husband, are you enjoying the dance you have dared to dance with me?"

My answer was frantically desperate.

"I've accepted your challenge, your dance, now it must end in our bed."

As we embraced, I felt the weariness of the night, the need for the end, a longing for completion. Everyone gathered around us urging us to join them in the culmination, the dance being beat out by the drums for the silent ears of the night.

We separated and danced, each in our own experience yet feeling the other from a distance, a distance for the perceptions of the body but not for the senses of the soul. That connection had somehow deepened through the fury of the recent past. My response had obviously pleased Cinda, she seemed to be floating on the waves of my reaction. I thought she probably felt secure in the fact of my need for her, my display of emotion was the ethereal bond she would wear inside herself despite what might happen in the days to come.

The dance ended with an encirclement, as Cinda and I enveloped each other, the group pressed close. A body to body warmth crept through the collective organism. A nutritious pulsating entity holding us all in its ethereal grip. The drums were silent, the group was silent, the night was still except for the universal sound ringing in each of our beings. Then a gentle stirring, a separation, the men pulling me away, the women pulling Cinda away. I felt myself being hoisted up high above the heads of the strong young men holding me, carried towards the river, gently put down at the shoreline beside a waiting wife linking her arm to mine.

Before us lay a small boat bobbing in the moonlight. Three men with oars and a rudder sat waiting. A flowery cushioned seat welcomed us into its reclining comfort. We lay back, taken noiselessly up the river. Behind us, I could hear a song. A gentle, multi-leveled chorus bidding its farewell. Ahead, the dancing ripples of the river, sparkles of moonbeams greeting us.

CHAPTER 10

It was a truly magical journey, past open fields, through dark forest areas pressing in close, ending at the base of a mountain. A waterfall and a small structure, our wedding-night hideaway. The passion was intense releasing the fury of the fire, the force carrying the gift, the seed to its new home. Then the lingering warmth of love bathing us in its breath. A gentle, caressing breath moving through our souls, touching us at the very essence of our beings. An ethereal linkage which seemed familiar, as if we had done all this before, then separated to evolve to this point. Coming back to once again touch, caress and sleep the slumber of contented completion in each others arms, each other's auras. Dreaming universal intimacies, soul eruptions, flying on the winds of bliss coming back to waken in each other's arms to the sounds of the morning, the waterfall, nature busily going about its routine seemingly oblivious to our rapturous condition.

Everything in our hideaway was perfectly laid out. Fresh clothes, a delicious array of fruit from the nearby jungle, fish from the river, fowl from the plains. Sweetness surpassed only by the lips of my lover, whose kiss was quickly becoming obsessively dominant on the scale of conscious pleasures. Our conversations were scant, brief. It was the pleasure of each other's touch, the erotic flare-ups of passion, the gentleness of the ebb-tide that filled our senses. No more was needed or desired.

At mid day, the heat drove us bounding like deer to the waterfall, the swirling cleansing waters at its base. A tropical paradise with its aqua-green essence, cooling our fever, cleansing our auras, leaving us fresh and clear, as if re-born. A feeling of cool transcendence, yet still full of the heat of the night waiting to flare up at the slightest touch to the blaze of the funeral pyre consuming its offering, us, mingling with the other in the newness of our unity, our oneness. How easy it seemed to let go into it, despite the awareness of its dangers, the limitation of temporal form moving to its inevitable end, the pyre fire. We loved, dozed, then slept and dreamt. The dream was full of familiar forms, beings from Javada, allies from Galaxium, new friends from the night's fire. The Shaman waving the scepter of power casting sparks in the dim evening hue. Cinda and the curly-haired little boy playing at the river's edge. My surging inner feelings of fullness welling up tears of joy.

Then the intrusion, the specter the red dot in the sky growing larger, larger until it filled it from horizon to horizon. The mechanical buzz of its immense presence. The heat growing with intensity almost unbearable, the sense of inevitable, impending doom. No time to reach Cinda and my son. Remembering my inner nature, my true identity, closing my eyes and reaching into myself, feeling its coolness drawing me away from the heat, the doom, alone but safe. Knowing all form was ending, all that was left was me in the arms, the ever-present embrace of the Mahaj.

I woke to the sound of my wife's gentle breathing, a lone bird singing its evening song, the wind breathing, beckoning in the nearby forest. I felt the immense relief, the sense that this moment was to be experienced fully, as it would never be here again as it was right now. I left my sleeping bride in our hideaway, walking past the river into the shade of the forest, along a path, its narrowness drawing me into itself, upwards to a waiting meadow. The overwhelming need to express my love, my appreciation for the gifts, the blessings. My bride being the peak of the blessed mountain. Picking a bloom with her shining eyes, smiling face in my minds eye, I felt another sense. The sense of wanting to acknowledge the ultimate blesser, not just the individual blessings. Not being of specific, individual form how would I do this?

As I pondered, a process began to arise. My hands began finding almost invisible growths in the meadow, along the forests edge, around the dry rocks. As if propelled to me, into my eager hands picking a bouquet for my love, in form and beyond. A sense of unity through it all, beyond conflict or choice, the simple expression to it all. Yet being of form, the gift would be laid in the lap of my bride.

That night, at the river's edge, beside a small camp fire, I told Cinda about myself, all of it. I still remember her wide, absorbing eyes, believing the unbelievable. The gift, picked and given from my inner essence for hers and the unifying force behind us all, brought us both to this moment, this point of receptivity. My words were not pre-thought, the flow had its own direction. The stories of my youth, my teachings, my processes, the ways of my world now hers left her somewhat dazed, full of so much more than expected. In return, Cinda shared her fears, hopes and dreams, The experiences of her life bringing her to this point of openness, where all this was made possible.

All of it left us feeling:

"Where do we go from here, back to what, forward to where?"

The answer came only too soon in the form of a messenger on a boat pulling his canoe up in front of our fire. The greetings were hurried, the message was clear. Our honeymoon was over, Cinda must leave for her meeting with my rebel mate. I felt my place was here for now, to wait and reflect. The immensity of duty weighted heavy on us as our separation left an incredible emptiness. Watching the canoe disappear into the mists of the night, the coldness, the tearing feeling of being ripped apart, a part of me, a precious part of me, leaving, then gone. Aloneness, in the dark of the night. A sense of vulnerability. Again the wonderment of it all. The psychic growing together so quickly through the intimacy of our union. The rift, separation, being felt so deeply. The resistance, the anger, the sense of possessiveness, not wanting to share my beloved. The heart wrenching, weeping at the loss, not knowing if she would return or was she being taken away from me forever. Then the deep inner surge of comfort. The place where separation does not touch the eternal link. The flow of faith in the illusory future, the glow of acceptance. The understanding of my place in all of this. The mode of service, surfacing, giving it all meaning. Meaning beyond the limits of my understanding.

I slept in our bed alone. How different being a Javadian again. A U.I.A. agent riding on the wings of service. Serving the highest order of Galaxium under the watchful eye of the Mahaj.

I woke to a sound outside, a scraping like a boat touching the edge of the shore. Then the sound of footsteps outside my door. I felt no inner sense of danger, just a curiosity. The door opened, silhouetted against the night sky stood one of the brown-skinned native females.

"Cinda has sent us to keep you company while she is gone." Before I could respond, two others followed her into my chambers carrying several containers, placing them at the foot of the bed, then moving to each side, surrounding me, sitting. The leader gently placed her hand along the left side of my neck with her fingertips touching my left ear and whispered.

"We are here for your pleasure."

I could feel the heat of the fire radiating from their near nakedness. My head spun with the scents from the foot of the bed. My voice trembled.

"I am still full of Cinda's pleasure."

The three giggled, one offered as she moved close on my other side.

"Lie back, relax, it will be our pleasure to please you."

I felt caught in my allegiance, my conditioned way of thinking, yet too tired to resist. I lay back, allowing. Their hands were soft, strong, as they found each muscle needing attention. The oil filled my senses. Their low humming song filled the room. I felt myself relaxing, sinking deeply into myself. Then drifting off into a deep, dreamless sleep. A dark, warm place where life lay dormant, waiting to be awakened by the light of day.

The light came streaming in through an opening high in my chambers waking me. My three companions lay around me sleeping, breathing deeply. The naked array of beauty spread out before me was rousing me beyond my comfort. Slipping silently out from under their touch, feeling the need for the coolness of the waterfall, I headed for the river. The water felt exhilaratingly fresh, waking me fully. The warmth of the sun dried me. I felt loved from all directions, unconditionally.

I wondered how the meeting between my two love mates was proceeding. Here I was a part of the process, yet once again like a pampered monarch softly hidden away in this valley of peace while they were both out there exposed to the dangers of the conflict. Would our efforts bear fruit? Would a bridge be formed for the much needed flow of communication, sincere communication? This morning, a dim sense of doubt resonated inside. Why?

Possibly just so much so quickly and now the sense of separation.

As I approached my hideaway, I could see my companions had awakened and were busily preparing food. The smell drifted to me on the dry, penetrating breeze of the morning. My hungers were being fed, yet growing moment by moment. The blessing of an appetite worthy of the meal spread out before me. I ate, played, rested, swam. My companions were delightfully full of youthful innocence. Their openness and honesty was enriching to my soul. I feasted on their attentive presence.

Towards evening, I felt drawn back up to the meadow where I'd spent the day before picking my offering. Finding a comfortable knoll, I sat facing a distant mountain ridge and wondered about Marty. I felt no need to approach him ethereally. A melancholy had come over me, it seemed so long ago. Coming here, getting involved in this far off place, its politics, intrigues, loves. As I closed my eyes, looking inwards, I felt the immense change. When I had arrived, I was full of the exhilaration, solidity of moving through time and space with Marty in the ever-responsive ethereal plane. The place where imagination took form instantaneously. Now, here I was identifying with my physical persona, playing out relationships with my dynamic surroundings and feeling a part of it not separate as before.

My objectivity had slowly given way to a passionate involvement. It felt good but my transcendent Javadian part felt hesitant. There were many times in the recent past when I'd gotten completely drawn into this limited scenario and only by chance remembered my true nature. Not of this place yet here nonetheless. I remembered Marty's instructions.

"Play it by ear." Well, I'd certainly done that and gotten a lot more than my ears involved. Could I detach and fly away comfortably? Feeling the way I felt now? Yet I knew these emotional states were temporal, fleeting in nature, so real in their grandeur when here but so small and distant when past.

Now I was in the middle of their surges, hungering, feasting, contentedly digesting, resting, waiting for the next offering, the next feast. But what about that deep innermost part of me? That subtle place which dimmed away so easily when confronted with the exhilaration of all this external stimuli drawing me into itself. Going deeper, I reached into the stillness, felt the presence always there waiting to be acknowledged. Then the voice:

"You have been trained to always come home, here, when all else loses its sparkle. Enjoy the sparkles of illusion, that is why they exist. Your temporary absorption will teach you much, deepen you. When you turn back as you have just done, I will be waiting to welcome you, heal you. Know this beyond all else. Settle into the ease of the knowing. This will maintain your balance. The emotions will all pass, this here will not. Welcome to eternity."

As the presence of the voice dimmed away I felt the surges of its emotional wake. Sobs of joy emanated from the very depths of my soul. How good it felt to be so loved and cared for from the very depths of my soul. The voice was always so accepting, so re-assuring, so omni present. Always waiting to be acknowledged, so ready to respond. Yes, so gentle in its inobtrusive nature. Yet so strong, undaunted in its resolve. The counsel was always so appropriate to the conditions of the moment. Omni potent in its waves surging through me and everything around me. The transformative effect of its touch always amazed me. My mood had now changed from its previous melancholy to a steadiness, a confidence, a strength. Coming out into my physical environment I felt the evening stillness, the dry warmth of the ground still emitting its days absorption of the hot sun. A time of transition when the creatures of the day were toning down their daily activities preparing for the nights rest while the creatures of the night stirred, gearing up for their explorations of the dark. The hunt, the constant search for nourishment. The cycle of life with its built-in unconscious patterns surfacing in each individual part of the whole. Me, sitting on my Knoll watching, wondering how much of the process I was still unaware of. How my activities affected the whole or how the whole moved through and around me to affect me and my evolution. Questions which needed no answer. Only the living experience would bring its own answer. I felt no need for the hunt, all I needed was being laid out methodically before me here in this protected valley of peace.

Then I saw a shadow moving in the gathering dim of the evening at the forest's edge. The eyes, light blue, gleaming out at me, scanning me, accessing. Was I food or was I danger? Little room for the middle ground of peership. The rules of the wild, consume or be consumed. Much like the population of the planet outside this valley. Severely competitive in its nature, feeling survival was dependent on that edge, the edge of individual ability to manage one's surroundings. Little knowing that the ultimate management was finding the voice within and then listening to its directions which come from an all-encompassing perspective, a perception of the whole and how everything fit whether the sentient being was conscious of it or not. Being conscious of it made it easier to move in harmony, walk through the doors of opportunity when they opened, the patience to wait contentedly when they stayed closed knowing the time was not right for motion. Using the time instead to move deeper inside to the source of it all. Building the reservoir of power to be accessed at that moment of motion.

Then the unleashing of the force not limited to the individual but expressing the will of the whole. The light blue eyes of the hunter moving, watching, waiting for that moment unconscious of the dynamics surrounding him yet instinctually playing out his part. I felt the creature was a reflection of me at this point in time. Seeing, glimpsing the nature of the play, co-operating patiently. Building strength, conserving power for the moment of the strike. I could feel it coming yet still not here.

Then he was gone, back into the comfort of the forest, a part of the shadows. The Mahaj had sent him to deliver his message. I felt it penetrating my consciousness. A sense of peace, dynamic powerful peace waiting for the motion, the coming motion, almost looking forward to its exhilarating nature, knowing the building up a happening now was just as important, possibly more so, than the actual moment of the strike. The need to wait peacefully, not in agitation that was the secret. No, just conserving strength, but through the power of the vision building a power point, a reservoir to draw on, unleash when the power from within and out put it all together and made me conscious that this was the time, the hunter and the prey synchronistically arising in the moment.

The darkness had fallen all around me, like a warm wool blanket enveloping me wholly. Feeling a strange drowsiness, I lay back on the warm ground, closed my eyes and dozed. Drifting through space, then just beneath me I saw the rings of Javada beckoning. Passing through each, I felt the familiarity, the scanning. Then touching down on the warm ground, feeling the embrace of home, hearing the song birds, the hum of the insects, smelling the blooming Pickdalias. A sigh of relief, home at last. The voice.

"Welcome home, my son."

I woke with a start, looking up into the star-studded darkness, the sense of familiarity was still with me, as if I was home. Was this place now my home, was there no real separation?

As I gazed off, a cluster of stars drew my attention. It seemed familiar, the configuration resonated deeply. Then I saw it, Javada, at its center emitting an auric hue, Beige. The hue of the courageous heart, the emotional center. How appropriate, I thought. This is the flavor of my experience right here, right now. My body and my heart were dominant in all the experiences unfolding. Little time was being spent in the transcendent ethereal realms. The fullness in my heart felt in union with the hue emanation. Javada had spoken. Harmony was the message. All felt well, at home and here.

Starting down the hill, back to my companions, I heard the low, muffled drumming. Peaceful, no longer full of the previous fury. The sound drifted lazily through the night air, each beat resonated deeply in my heart center. I felt my heart beat in complete union with the beat of the drums. As if the drummers were propelling their song through the night air in rhythmic time to the blood in my veins being propelled through my body by the resident within my heart. The feeling of the unity. Uncanny in its familiarity, incomprehensible yet so simple in its intuitive, experiential essence. Javada had cast a spell on the night for me. I knew it as a certainty in the moment. I moved with it in a sense of reverence, appreciation almost in awe of the grandeur of the vision.

Openness had reaped its reward. I could not have visualized the experience. However, it now lay in the familiar realm of the known. The sense of more reverberated through my being. As if something had been sent through the separation of space and now lay as a seed in my heart, in my soul, waiting for the nourishing sun of the Mahaj to bring it to life. All I had to do was stay aware, awake to its presence and move spontaneously with it when it came alive, trust it, love it, for love was the dominant emotion of this realm.

As I came out of the forest path onto a ridge overlooking the encampment below, I saw a story unfolding before me. My three companions sat around a small fire flickering in the darkness, a beacon in the night drawing me home. I could almost smell the smoke, the food cooking over it, nourishment. Unlike the creature, the hunter, my meal was ready, waiting. I felt fortunate. Then off in the distance I could see a small dark object on the river moving quickly towards my camp. I felt an inner surge, not fear, just an exhilaration. An awakening feeling, the hunter aware the prey was about to rise within his strike realm. Then as my gaze flowed back to the camp I looked higher to the top of the distant mountain. A form hovered high, almost out of the reach of my sight. I wondered, was it a bird, but so far away a bird would be invisible. My meadow unicorn, it must be her showing herself, an omen, an ally. As my gaze lowered, I saw him standing on a hill looking over the encampment at me. A great milky white stallion, tossing his mane in the wind. Yet I felt no wind here, on my side of the river. I could feel his power, ready to fly with the wind, yet he stood still watching me, waiting.

As the dot on the river grew larger, nearer, I felt an irresistible draw back to my camp. Was there a danger, I felt none yet the need to be in the camp when the approaching object arrived? Feeling the power of the far-off stallion coursing through my veins, I moved slowly at first feeling my way down. Then with a burst of abandonment, I ran bounding from shadow to shadow knowing I would land on solid footing only to bound again into the unknown terrain, unseen yet felt intuitively.

My companions around the fire had somehow sensed my energy, their drums resonated furiously through the night heightening my vigor, giving my race fervor. The feeling that the time had come to move, not think or plan just move, allowing the will of the moment to manifest in its own way.

Reaching the edge of the encampment, I saw a long, narrow boat with at least eight dark figures powering it. Their backs bent into their paddling, a sense of hurry, a need to reach their destination quickly. In the front I could see a slight figure dressed darkly, straining forward. I felt the familiarity, without seeing I knew it was my new bride returning, but why such intensity?

My three companions had seen us all converging on the fire, ended their song of the drum with a furious cascade and stood quietly, silent sentinels guarding the heart of the night, the fire. As I reached their company, Cinda leapt from the boat and ran towards us. As we embraced, I felt the surge of re-connection. The wholeness after the separation. The melting together.

Beneath it all, I also felt the urgency, the sense of something being wrong. A worried pulling back and looking deeply into her watery eyes. I queried.

"Welcome back, my love. Is something wrong?"

My question opened the floodgates, her sobs were deep, her words almost ununderstandable.

"It's my father, he's been poisoned."

I knew words were unnecessary now, comfort was needed. I held her feeling her grief, the tears in each of us flowed, mingled. The emotion slowly passed, a weariness after the explosion. I found my voice deep, angry.

"Who has done this?"

Her eyes made the answer unnecessary.

"You know, there is only one who can be responsible."

Looking inside myself, I knew she was right but somehow I did not feel a hopelessness, to the contrary, a sense of urgency. The question.

"Is your father gone?"

"No."

Her voice rose higher, with some hope.

"But our physicians say there is no hope, no antidote they know of, its just a matter of time."

I knew I must get involved now. There might be something from my Javadian sciences that would serve, I had to try.

"Where is he now?"

Her gesture showed a resignation yet I did not feel that. Her voice grew stern.

"He lies in a coma at a camp not far in that direction. He was there to meet with the rebels, Mirabel, your mate was coming with her brother. There was hope, a good chance for some headway. This will have an adverse effect. General Miko's extremists are spreading the rumor that it was the rebels who poisoned him. I know they lie. But time is short, the physicians have given him less than two hours."

Her tears fell down my bare left arm, down to my hand along my little finger and off onto the ground. My Javadian teachings in psycho-physical phenomenon came clearly into my consciousness. Her tears had flowed down the finger representing the ground, the solid physical embodiment of the universe. A face flashed in my mind's eye, a Javadian healer, her eyes radiating power, wisdom.

Her voice gently whispered.

"Go to his body, you will know what to do, stay aware, look up, your carrier awaits. His speed will get you there on time. Take your love with you. She will show the way but allow your carrier his freedom. His is dependent on your trust, your release. Go now! Use the Javadian Beast Soul Probe, your carrier will be receptive."

My vision felt blurred from the intensity of the experience, clearing my eyes, I looked upwards and there he was, my great milky white stallion, tossing his mane eagerly in the wind, I heard his impatient neigh.

Holding the imaging key in my mind's eye, I sent a psychic message to him asking for his help. Projecting the emotional need of the moment, the necessity for speed, almost apologetically for the intrusion on his space. I felt his great surging heart opening, absorbing, then the response, the motion, he was coming, flying over the loose rocks in abandonment like I had done, coming down from my hill. Hitting the river with a graceful leap, racing past the stunned paddlers and coming to a sliding stop before us. His regal eyes looked into mine, I felt his exhilaration, his willingness. My hand reached out, stroking his head, down his muscled neck, through his coarse mane, getting a grip on it and swinging quickly up onto his broad back. I felt Cinda unconsciously reaching up, the grip around my outstretched arm leaping upwards with my support, behind me, closing herself firmly around my back.

Without hesitation, our carrier leapt into the river, his power flowing through us. I could hear Cinda's moan as she felt it too. The surging beast beneath us, alive, rippling muscles carrying their instinctual messages through him and through us.

I felt the cool, sting of the wind and his mane against my face, the sweaty heat of his body and the strong softness of my beloved enveloping me. The sense of power and vulnerability rising together, mingling their essence around and in us.

I knew our carrier knew the short way to our destination, the passageway into the secret valley, I trusted, no need for interference. A simple knowing. As if we were all one, committed and determined with nothing standing in our way. We sped past the encampment of our wedding night, I was sure I saw the Shaman standing at its edge holding the scepter of power high above him with the young agile warrior beside him. The one he rode back to the fire on that unforgettable night. Now here we were riding back on our stallion, back to the fires of conflict, our duties, playing out our parts in the unfolding winds of destiny. The passageway lay dead ahead, a dark aperture waiting to usher us into another world, a world full of the strife this valley had evolved past. Would the essence of its power, which we were both now full of, be enough to stabilize the conflicting condition. I felt sure it would, a sense of power and sureness filled me as our stallion made his final stride towards the path, he could not enter. His place was here, on his hill, roaming the valley, expressing its spirit in his own uniquely powerful way.

As we slipped off his back onto the rocky base of the path, I felt our psyches disengaging, a sense of saying good-bye to an old friend, someone I'd known much longer than the brief journey we'd just experienced. As I once again gazed into his large, regal eyes, I knew we would meet again. I thanked his courageous heart for his service, gave his mane a final stroke and turned to the next step. Time was short, a hurriedness permeated the feeling of the night. As we started up the incline, I heard the neigh, the clatter of hooves on loose rocks, looking back I saw our carrier disappearing into the dim of the night, mane and tail flying in abandonment. A milky white haze in motion, I thought I saw a glimpse of the Milky Aura Leader's smiling face in the faint cloud of dust drifting on the night wind. I could still feel the power of the beast inside. The probe had gone deep, made a connection not yet fully disengaged, a gift propelling me through the passageway to the waiting vehicle hidden behind the same bush. Cinda was close behind breathing deep and hard, straining to not fall behind. Her strength was equal to the challenge.

Cinda had cleared her emotions through the surge of our night's rush on the back of our beast. She once again felt like the warrioress entering the tunnel so long ago, as she started the engine, slammed it into gear and accelerated into the dark of the surrounding hills. I closed my eyes trusting her abilities, feeling a warm confidence in my heart. I drank deeply knowing its wisdom was alive, guiding us, protecting us, a force unsurpassed by any other in our surroundings, in our future. The exhilaration of motion I'd felt coming in the meadow was now here. The time to move with faith, no thought, instinctual as the stallion on his run of service.

Opening my eyes, I saw the flicker of lights ahead, the encampment stretched out before us, I was surprised at how quickly we'd made the trip. I expected a much longer one, but little should surprise me, here in the heat of the moment. I felt Cinda's question before she asked it.

"Will your Javadian abilities be enough to help my father?"

My answer was spontaneous, from the depths of the heart space I'd just come out of.

"I feel very hopeful, however the outcome will be in the hands of the Mahaj. I've told you how my trust is the key in the implementation of our ways. Your father's will to live, I feel, will be the final influence. This situation is his perfect opportunity to leave if he so wishes. We'll just have to convince him to stick around and experience the result of the seed we've just sown."

Reaching out, I gently touched her womb, now rippling tight with the exertion of the ride. Her voice, now full of hope.

"Oh yes, I would like him to be here for that, my husband. Please do what you can, I will pray for the both of you, I love so much."

As we sped past the perimeter guards I felt and saw looks of concern and compassion on the faces behind their salutes. I realized we'd entered a hastily formed encampment by the temporal structures around us. Cinda ground the vehicle to a sliding stop in front of a group dressed in white waiting, with looks of despondency. A sense of hopeless resignation lay heavy in the air. I was sure we'd made it on time despite the look and feel of the gathered.

An older, grey haired nurse solemnly walked towards us, leaned over to Cinda. Her voice trembled.

"I'm sorry, your father is gone. There just was no chance, nothing we could do."

Cinda's head fell forward against the steering column, her sob tore deep into me. I just felt this could not be so. My sense of hopefulness was still with me. My feelings, so strong, had never been so wrong, or were they?

The healer's whisper again.

"Go to him, now. It's not too late."

I jumped quickly out the door leaving Cinda in her moment of grief, no time for the comforting, racing past the group in white into the flimsy building, I ran headlong into Beno's grey haired advisor. His eyes dully expressed his loss and concern. His voice nervously high.

"This is a terrible thing. Not just personally but for all the people. The mantle of power was not transferred by will to Cinda. The position of rulership is now up for grabs. General Miko and his followers are already making their move. They might very well succeed."

I vaguely understood the situation. The general and his followers had been methodically instilling doubt in the peace-making moves, Beno's administration had initiated. I was sure many of the more gullible were becoming undecided, fearful and now with the possibility that their popular leader had been assassinated by the rebels, the general's message held even more appeal. Striking back with force had a reassuring ring to it. The appeal to fear and power were realms the general and extremists could play in very proficiently. I had no time to discuss the issues. With urgency in my voice.

"Where is he?"

A gesture to a far corner of the long hall showed a form covered with a white sheet, surrounded by an array of disconnected medical technology. As I moved quickly to the area, I felt a strong ethereal presence, it felt strangely content. I remembered Beno's hug, much like Moham's, the uncanny similarity, the feeling of strange affection transferring itself through the embrace. Pulling back the cover sheet, I saw Beno's face, calm, settled, at peace, the look of eternal sleep. The look in harmony with my perception of the ethereal presence in the whole area. My hands tingled with a strange electrical pulsation. Not like the warm, healing flow I felt with the soldier in the field, but lighter, higher, the sense of the turquoise aura. The transcendent ethereal plane beyond pleasure and pain. The realm of stillness, contented completion. The healer's whisper.

"Left hand at the back of his neck, right hand on his solar plexus, just below his lower rib cage. Close your eyes and breath into your hands. Open yourself and flow."

I could feel myself being drawn away, away from my physical form into the coolness of Turquoise. The tingling in my hands leaving, going into the still warm body. The sense of a circle, my heart, soul and mind uniting with another. The other peaceful, still, resting, waiting. Then a flash. A brilliance, slowly dimming into a hue of blue. The sense of a great wave carrying me, laying back into it, trusting. Lost in it, yet not fearful. Just lost in it's power and direction. No idea of where it was going but knowing I couldn't find my way back. No choice but to trust.

Then the wave subsiding, a falling sensation. Falling through feelings inside myself but also outside myself. Reflections of each other, supporting each other. Down into a warm aqua blue pool of warmth, not solid, just vibrational, yet felt as form, subtle form. Where was I? There was peace yet unresolved. Not the totally contented peace I felt in my own flight arrival and rest in the universal sea of the Mahaj. This was not my place, I had entered the realm and experience of another, Beno's soul probably. I felt him all around me and more.

Then before me, a form, almost unperceivable, hovering. I knew it was the essence of Beno manifesting for contact. A step beyond the feeling interaction into the realm where cognitive interaction could take place. The voice felt like Beno's but sounded more like the gong of large bells.

"Welcome, my son. I didn't expect your company but I'm glad you're here. I would have liked to embrace you as my new son, my Cinda's new protector, but I find myself here instead. Not alone, Cinda's mother was here to greet me. It feels so good to be together again. Moham is a kind lord. We are both so glad you will care for our sweet little girl. The separation is easier knowing she will have the company and support. My service is done back there, now it is all up to the two of you. The importance of it all has dimmed for me. I see so much more. But we know you understand. Help Cinda to understand as well. We will be watching."

My inner response was a mixture of feelings, thoughts, understandings. Here he was complete, home at last with his old lover, embraced. I just wanted to leave him in his rapture yet the sense of the greater good, the need for his presence and an orderly transference of power in time. My feelings of family, intimate, lasting throughout all difficulties, always there despite differences, embracing one another in support, always united against external threat.

Above all else, an understanding that the supreme will would work out my dilemma through and around me. I simply had the responsibility of opening to it.

Then the healer's whisper.

"You've been brought here for a purpose, explain the situation and allow the psychic presence you now bath in, decide, then simply co-operate. I'll be here with you each step of the way."

I found my thoughts resonating through the ethereal essence to the hovering form not spoken, just transferred direct.

I explained the need for an orderly transfer of power, our experiences and gifts received in the valley of our wedding, the imminent coming of Galaxium in the near future and my part in it all. I felt my message was understood, absorbed, a feeling of hesitancy. I knew one last appeal must be made on a personal, intimate level.

I added.

"I would like to get to know you in the physical dimension, very much. A seed has been sown in the Valley of Peace, a special seed, someone very special will arise from it. He will be a joy for you to experience, both of you. As the special ways of Galaxium and Javada move into the workings of this planet, all this will be possible. Now that the two of you have intermingled here, in the ethereal, both will feel and experience all of it as one. Javadian psychic technology can make it as if both of you walk together for the time you choose to remain. It will be your decision to let us know when you want to return to this realm. There is a great deal of growth potential in the physical after this experience. You now know your destiny and can relax into the remaining time spent balancing the aggressive nature of those threatening the stability in its seed stage. Ask Moham in your way for guidance in this. I will respect his counsel and your decision, father. By the way, Javadians never say goodbye to their parents, only,

"Till we meet again."

The hovering form grew still, darker in color, a sense of pondering, then a steady undulation rippled through it from its top. As the ripples subsided, the form grew more distinct. A pale orange hue glowed through it and two distinct faces formed. One was Beno smiling, the other slighter, female, barely visible, more of the ethereal now. The feeling of warmth, deep love emanated from them and enveloped me. I felt their completion. The thought,

"Till we meet again."

Then, a swirling array of colors, a formlessness, hues blending one into the other. A building crescendo, the sound of millions of insects flying in unison. Then a flash, a brilliance and the clear image of Moham, my old warrior friend standing dressed in battle gear glowing a deep red within the brilliant white. His finger, little finger representing ground, solid form, ran quickly across the familiar scar on his neck. Behind and to his left stood my Javadian healer, lips pursed as if whispering. His voice had the light ring of irritation.

"You Javadians certainly seem to enjoy meddling in my affairs."

Then the roar of his laughter as he glanced back at the healer, then me.

"Actually I enjoy the company. Makes me feel appreciated. You've certainly gotten absorbed in your new world down there, haven't you?"

As I gazed into his light and felt his power, I realized just how absorbed I'd become. My voice carried a tinge of self-conscious guilt.

"Well, you've put together quite an intriguing scenario for me to get involved in. Congratulations, I take off my hat to your unlimited imagination."

I made a sweeping gesture of respectful acknowledgment as if I had a hat even a distinct enough form to wear one. But anything was possible here in the ethereal, even a sense of humor. His roar of laughter had now subsided to a chuckle as he spoke.

"I knew you wouldn't settle for any less. You've gotten yourself into quite a pickle here though. You know by coming here through Beno's poisoned body, you may absorb too much of the poison to process. That will be the end of your little game. Quite painful too."

I hadn't thought of the danger, I knew this type of healing did open me to the regular healer's risk through osmosis, but the events had all moved so quickly, there seemed no choice. My thoughts went out to my host.

"Well, you might have yourself a permanent guest after all. I'm sure I'll enjoy our debates." His thought returned instantaneously.

"Don't worry about it, I've sent a little friend to help you out. I hope she doesn't frighten you. Look to your little finger when you get back there. Meanwhile, all this emotional attachment to your new family, you've lost track of the facts here. Everything happening is in harmony with our combined will. Your Mahaj is on the move. The planet has been accepted for integration. Your Marty and I are co-operating to help the process along. Beno's old approach would only stand in the way. The extremists will bring things to a boil and your challenge will be clear. Your bridge has already formed. Concentrate your attentions on the forces behind your two mates. Sometimes a common danger brings about the necessary unity by making it a simple matter of survival. Giving you the actual details would only take the fun out of it all. Explore, enjoy, your blessings will be many, as if you could stand much more. Like any conduit, expand yourself and more will come, as much as your openness allows."

The playful twinkle in his eyes showed his joy in the play, the divine play. I felt him deep inside my heart once again, then with a swirl he was gone back to his worlds, but a part still here inside me. Available when needed. I glanced towards my Javadian healer growing dimmer, shrugging her shoulders in acceptance, then disappearing into a turquoise haze.

The wave carrying me back up high on its crest, spinning, whirling. Then a sense of nausea, sickness, the poison was taking hold. As I came into form, my hands still in place, I felt something sliding down my left arm under my shirt. I felt dizzy, about to fall. Then I saw it, a small snake moved down my hand to my little finger, along it to Beno's neck. I felt its bite piercing through my finger into Beno's neck, it drank deeply, a mixture of my blood and Beno's. Looking into it's eyes, I heard.

"It was my poison used to do this, now I have it back. My power will now be with you by Moham's will, use it wisely."

The eyes gleamed a faint green as it disengaged and slipped quickly back up my arm. I felt it settle, coiled in my armpit. I accepted it as my ally, considering the challenges which lay ahead.

The symptoms of the poison, the dizziness, nausea disappeared instantaneously leaving a warm glow in its wake. In fact, I felt a surging pulse in the lower parts of my body, especially in my genital areas, the lower chakra, the center of the propagational process. I saw the divine artistry of the picture. In Javadian symbology the serpent represented the coiled sexual energy at the base of the spine, resting, waiting for the opportunity to rise and express it's power. The expression was in both the physical and energy body of the being. The power of the serpent flowing through the physical was motion, sexual and in the arena of the milky aura. The flow of power through the energy body went up the spine through each chakra nourishing, enriching, finally moving through the crown chakra uniting with the psyche in the ethereal plane. This was the goal of each mystic on Javada. To bring about the awakening of the serpent and allow it's movement to it's ultimate destiny.

I felt the motion wanting to express itself through me both physically and psychically. Images of my two loves weaved themselves through my thoughts. A sense of readiness, arousal wanting to touch, caress, release the seed of perpetuation. Play out the physical propagational process in this life. Ready to use the power of the serpent through the motions of the milky aura teachings. Spontaneous motion in harmony with the synchronistic unfolding of the Mahaj's will here on this planet.

At the same time, feeling the uncoiling within my energy body moving gently upwards, entering each inner center of energy, each chakra, welcomed, embraced, almost eagerly drawing it into itself. The waves of ecstasy, the completion, the nourishing after glow. Then the release, full of the mingling, the farewell, the continuance of the journey upwards. Coming to the next center, the knock, the opening door, the outstretched arms, the falling together in rapture, the fury of the union, the ecstasy of the completion, the peace of contented unity. What an incredible journey, what an incredible life.

CHAPTER 11

The motion at the doorway brought me back to the physical reality completely. I realized Beno's advisor must have been watching me all along. I was sure there wasn't much to see, just me holding Beno in a strange way. What really transpired was invisible in this realm but who knows what physical reactions were going on here while I was there. Where did my serpent come from logically speaking I knew where it really came from but the events of the physical realm must also have their corresponding motion?

Drawing back from Beno's body, placing the sheet back over him, posturing myself in the mode of grief and farewell while really feeling a joy for his new home, new dimensional reality, I turned and walked slowly back to Beno's old companion. I disguised the real feelings in my voice.

"For the short period of time, I knew him, I found him a true friend. Did you know him a long time?"

My question was answered curtly.

"Yes, a long time. We served our country together for over forty years."

A questioning look came into his eyes.

"What were you doing with him?"

I wasn't sure what he meant.

"Do you mean as his security man?"

His answer still had the ring of shortness.

"No, I know about all that, I mean just now, over there."

I wondered what had caught his attention.

"Just saying my farewells."

His piercing eyes showed me his disbelief.

"I've been a reader of people a long time and somehow you just don't fit. I don't know what it is but I sense you're not telling us everything about yourself."

I knew by the sincerity of his remarks that I would eventually tell him all, but not just yet.

"Security has a way of making one a little more secretive than others. That may be what you sense." He was not satisfied.

"Then there's what I saw around you over there. Like lights, faint lights and almost visible forms."

Shaking his head in disbelief.

"Maybe I'm just overcome, a little crazy with all this pressure. With the mantle of power up for grabs and General Miko on the move, I just don't know what will happen. We could end up in a blood bath. More seem to be swinging to his way of thinking by the moment. If it continues, I can't be sure of Cinda's safety and the rebel group who have just arrived to discuss Beno's proposals. It looks like you've got your job cut out for you, I don't envy you, your responsibilities.

Somehow, I feel you are capable enough to handle it." I was a little overwhelmed by his sincerity and concern.

My voice showed more emotion than I liked.

"I thank you for your supportive presence. Your counsel will be invaluable in the days to come. I hope we can work together as well as you and Beno. I'm sure he would have liked it that way."

He seemed to have released his wondering about the phenomena he'd witnessed.

"I believe you have all our best interests in mind, you can count on my support. I love Cinda like my own daughter but I fear for her safety. The madness erupting around us right now has no limits."

His words didn't surprise me. I knew that when the Mahaj began approach, the heightening effect was often disruptive. The increasing light challenging the darkness of ignorance, but the darkness not letting go of it's foothold easily. However, I knew the madness did have it's limits. The power of the Mahaj would find a way of settling it, bringing order back to the chaos. When each individual felt their place in the collective, the sense of belonging to the larger family. I found my voice soothing.

"These times will pass, I'm sure you know that. You must have witnessed many cycles during your years of service. Do you think I should take Cinda to a safe place and wait or should we make our move for the position Beno held, now."

I already knew the answer but wanted his counsel and involvement.

His forehead showed the deep lines of years of pondering similar issues. His answer I felt, was well thought out.

"I think it would be unwise to face the people right now. They are full of Miko's venom. Some still feel his extreme posture is dangerous but many feel the risk, though great is worth trying. Many of us can work behind the scenes to prepare the way for Cinda's entry but now seems premature. Do you know a safe place?"

My thoughts went to the protected Valley of Peace.

"Yes, I do. No one will know where she will be but me. I will stay in touch with her supporters through you alone."

My trust was met with affection. His handshake was firm, his other hand on my shoulder was almost fatherly.

"Good, I will work hard for both of you. My remaining days in service will be dedicated to seeing Cinda rule our people in peace with you at her side. She will need your strength and support."

I had the uncanny feeling that Beno was speaking to me through his old friend and ally. The ethereal had the power to do this. As I thought this I saw a faint red glow emanating from Beno's area of the room. My companion also saw it. My eyes assured him that he was not going crazy, just a little tired, maybe.

I suddenly had a tingling sensation, a powerful draw inside. Closing my eyes as if in a form of prayer, I saw a swirling brilliance beyond the spectrum of color beckoning me deeper. I followed the voice, so solid, so permeating, greeting me.

"The time has come for you to take a name, you will soon be asked. It is their way to form images around you, perpetuate your identity in their minds. Names have a powerful influence on your psychic projections so it is wise to choose a harmonious one. Sometime ago on a planet similar to this one in its stage of development there lived one who held similar attitudes, similar visions of reality. However the psychic sciences available to him were not as extensive as yours here now. His time was spent in service and exploration bringing him personally to a point of evolution in which I could take him. He now lives and explores with your unborn son close to me, very close to me. His name was Leon. Take the name, he welcomes you to it. He is sure you will do it honor."

I felt the power and essence of another coming into me. Strong, distant, almost imperceivable in its subtlety yet definitely felt as a supportive emotional presence. I welcomed it as I saw the swirling brilliance fade. As I opened my eyes I saw my companion gazing at me openly, solidly. His voice held sincere feelings.

"You certainly are a humble fellow for one with your background. I hope your God watches over us all in the times to come. By the way, I don't even know your name?"

"I am known as Meda."

His hand was extended in openness waiting for my response. I again saw the incredible, immense all-present essence of the Mahaj. The timelessness, no past, no future unknown. All here in his eye waiting for the openness, just the openness to receive the flow of his all-pervasive wisdom. I took his hand, held it firmly yet gently. My voice felt deeper, as if I was suddenly older, more grounded.

"Leon, you may call me Leon."

The glint in his eyes, showed me an inner humor, a memory surfacing.

"Yes, I knew a Leon once. He was a gentle fellow, almost too gentle. I expected you to have a harder name like Miko or Bob, but then I was surprised by our friends General Meisha and General Kwan Yen. Strong men with kind sounding names. I'm getting too old to make any sense of it, but it is my pleasure to know you, Leon."

My grin and nod showed a similar pleasure.

As we linked arms, stepped out into the night, I saw a group gathered in the center of the compound. A fierce looking array of warriors, a sense of readiness, willingness to move, express their emotion. As we stood, illuminated by the light from inside Beno's resting place, I felt the intensity of the feelings in the one approaching. It was Cinda full of sorrow, concern and anger.

Her voice trembled with the intensity.

"Is he really gone. Couldn't you do anything?"

I felt I must justify myself to her, the feeling of incompetence, guilt, helplessness filled the air. My grounded voice felt comforting from within myself. Meda had stepped aside to offer us privacy.

"It is Moham's will that Beno not come back, but it was also Beno's choice to stay with your mother. I saw them both, they welcomed me into your family and asked me to help you understand. They are very happy and content in their reunion, looking forward to their explorations together unbound by any physical limitations. They want you to be happy for them, let go and live your life knowing they are watching, enjoying your pleasures with you. They are looking forward to witnessing the result of the seed we've planted in the valley. Please believe me I speak the truth."

The stunned look on her face concerned me, would she believe me?

Her eyes filled with tears. She moved into my waiting arms. Her voice was that of a little girl not the fierce warrioress whose battle gear pressed harshly against my chest.

"I do believe you, my husband. After all you have told me about yourself, I cannot doubt you. But my anger is too harsh to contain, you might feel it, it's not personal."

As she drew away, I saw the little girl for an instant, then the fierceness, the harshness of an angry warrioress determined to wreak revenge, illogical revenge.

As I looked sternly in her eyes, I knew now my task of balancing my young bride. A resting time, learning the ways of the Mahaj, tempering the surge of emotion, so dangerous in its abandoned potential.

My voice was gentle yet forceful.

"I have considered Meda's counsel and agree. Your father trusted his guidance and I'm sure would like you to as well. Speak with him, try to open to his experienced wisdom."

I reached out my left arm, beckoning Meda, asking.

"Would you take Cinda inside for her moment of farewell?"

I knew the rest would unfold for them as it had for us. I was confident Cinda would release her anger and absorb his counsel. As I watched the two of them, moving inside through the doorway, Meda's reassuring arm around Cinda's slumped shoulders, again fatherly, I felt the essence once again in the room. The peace and contentment lingered gently in the ethereal realm reaching out its settledness, drawing them in.

Turning to the group, I saw two familiar forms dressed in battle gear moving briskly towards me. It was General Kwan Yen and General Meisha. General Meisha limped slightly while I could see General Kwan Yen was missing a right arm. Kwan Yen reached me first, almost joviality in his voice.

"Good to see you again, I'd shake your hand, but, as you can see, the price of war seems to be getting higher all the time. I see your still all here. I smiled reassuringly."

"Yes, I've been spared that kind of challenge. Did that happen in the tunnel?" His eyes went dim.

"Yes, but it would have been much worse without your warning. We held our own quite well, I thought. Your commander was not so lucky, he died right down there with so many others."

Meisha joined us reaching out his welcoming handshake.

"Welcome back, I could not be at Beno's party for you, I understand General Miko extended quite a welcome. I hear he doesn't like you very much after all that."

I remembered the three, the dead one, the blinded one, the first. With an edge in my voice.

"The general is certainly uninhibited about stepping beyond his boundaries."

The two nodded. General Kwan Yen offered.

"We are ready to make an assault on his encampment. He has many supporters but we do have a chance if we strike hard and fast."

I could see the results of such an action even if successful. I offered.

"Even if we succeeded, the people might see us in a light even darker than General Miko and his supporters. This could have an immensely unfavorable effect on Cinda's chances in the future and could throw the whole country into civil war."

As I saw the two seriously considering my words, a high terrain vehicle sped towards us. Two forms sat in front with a small armed group behind them, watching, ready for conflict. As they grew closer I recognized my rebel mate, Mirabel with a slightly older male driving. My heart surged at her sight. Mixed feelings of relief, warmth and concern for her reaction to my marriage.

As the vehicle slid to an abrupt stop in front of the three of us, I saw another speed into the compound, make a sliding spin and speed off in the direction it had come from. Mirabel had opened her door and slid out quickly glancing back at the vehicle speeding away. Her eyes were aflame, even the eyes around her neck seemed to glow a deep red, her voice was high with excitement.

"Greetings, my friend, why did you receive us with such a welcome?"

I questioned.

"Welcome, what do you mean? I haven't had a chance to greet you, yet."

Her hand motioned in the direction of the fading tail lights.

"That, the soldiers in that vehicle fired on us and pursued us on our tour of the area. We were assured, that a little exploration was acceptable."

Kwan Yen stepped forward.

"Those were General Miko's men, I think we may all be in trouble, I'll make some inquiries."

He moved off to the gathered group at the center of the compound. I felt the tension in the area, my serpent friend I'd named "Alleisha" stirred in her resting place.

I turned my attention back to Mirabel, opening my arms with a feeling of concerned protectiveness. She hesitated for a moment, I could feel her fury passing slowly. Then, opening her arms she came to me. I felt the familiarity of her form, her warmth, her hair against my cheek, the fullness of her femininity pressed close. Pulling away and looking into her sternness now slowly softening, my voice was again grounded, deeper than usual.

"You and yours are safe here for now. My two General friends will stand between you and our somewhat crazed, over ambitious General Miko. We must depart as soon as possible. However there is something I must do first." Her eyes and voice flickered a spark of humor.

"Still as secretive as ever. Something must be done about all this. We have considered Beno's proposals and found ground for compromise. Now, with this turn of events, what are we to do?"

I knew my vagueness was little consolation.

"Unfortunately Cinda cannot take over from her father just yet. The ground will have to be prepared carefully for that. You will have to fall back to the old pattern for now and respond according to the extent of the aggression unleashed upon you and yours. I'll work as quickly as possible to bring about a balance. It is Cinda's destiny to rule, but for now we'll have to hide her and wait."

Mirabel's eyes shone with comradeship.

"I owe Cinda a great deal."

She touched the necklace around her neck, continuing.

"She can come back with me if she wishes. We will protect her and you."

My answer was quick and to the point.

"I appreciate your generous offer but that would only intensify the conflict. The general would say that she was your prisoner and launch a campaign of liberation. Just what he'd like to do with the support of the people. I'm sure Cinda would end up dead and the general a sad dictator. Not too sad, I'm sure."

She understood my point.

"Where will you take her?"

My secrecy was again the issue.

"I have a safe place, I will take you there someday, when things are a little more settled."

The driver of her vehicle had stepped out and moved cautiously towards us. Mirabel extended her left arm in welcome.

"Come and meet my old lover."

Her face went slightly red with embarrassment turning to me with a look of childish unease.

"I don't even know your name, I guess we didn't do too much talking. Do you know mine?"

I struck a comical pose.

"Oh yes, my dear Mirabel, it is a pleasure to formally meet you, they call me Leon."

She played back into the game, turning to the man, now before us.

"Leon, I would like you to meet my brother, Elijah."

I reached out my hand.

"My pleasure, Elijah."

Elijah hesitated, his stern, cool eyes accessing me. Then reaching forward quickly, took it firmly, almost aggressively.

"My sister has told me a great deal about you. You have quite a reputation among us. I, however, judge according to my experience."

His coolness was understandable. Before him stood his sister's lover, who'd just married his enemy's daughter. Surrounded by enemy forces who'd already breached their promise of safety.

My voice was authorative but warm.

"I hope our experience of one another is mutually beneficial. I've assured your sister of your safety while I still live and I intend to stick around for a while yet."

The touch of humor seemed to soften Elijah's stance.

"Well, I respect my sister's judgments. I will grant you the benefit of a doubt, but I'm not quite ready to take you fishing, if you know what I mean."

I enjoyed his not so subtle humor.

Feeling Aleisha's stir again.

"Oh well, someday I would like to do that. However, right now I have a big fish in mind. More like a shark, in fact. How would you deal with that kind of fish?"

His eyes gleamed with the heat of the interaction.

"I'd catch him with a tasty little snack, then gaff him between the eyes."

His eyes had moved to Mirabel's necklace moving back to me.

"I owe you one. I'm looking forward to returning the favor."

I felt the genuineness of his remark, there was a sense of deep affection between the two and I was being given a taste of it.

Kwan Yen was suddenly beside me, his eyes full of concern. His voice reflected his nervousness.

"We seem to have a bit of a problem here. General Miko has surrounded the encampment and has issued a request to hand over our friends here. He also wants General Meisha's and my troops to join him. I fear for all of your safety. My troops and Meisha's will engage them, if you like."

The sincere allegiance of the one standing at attention before me willing to fight his own for our safety touched me deeply. I reached out and held him by the shoulders.

"No, not just yet. Where is the general right now?"

"My intelligence informs me that he's addressing a small group of business men in a town just over that hill. His arm pointed in the direction the vehicle following Mirabel had gone."

Releasing my hold on his shoulders, I stepped back and spoke to all three, feeling Aleisha's impatience.

"I have a little business of my own to take care of, it shouldn't take too long. I don't think the surrounding forces will attack, but if they do, do what you must."

General Meisha had returned and heard my remarks. He offered.

"I have a small unit of specially trained men who can help you with your business, if you like."

My feeling was that Aleisha and I were enough force to deal with this situation.

"Thank you for the offer, but I must do this alone. Dispatch your unit to safeguard our visitors, that is more important. I will return soon."

I felt a bond, an ethereal, emotional bond here in the night. A tight, intertwined force holding the real power to be unleashed at the appropriate time in the future, but now it was my time to move.

As I moved away from the group towards the town over the hill, I saw Cinda and Meda come out into the night. The light behind them glowed a deep orange. There was a peace emanating around and through them. I knew Cinda had accepted Meda's counsel and would co-operate.

As I moved quickly towards the distant hill, standing dark, ominous on the horizon, I wondered where and how many surrounded us and just how I would get through them to my waiting prey. I felt Aleisha's stir, then the slip down my arm to her favorite perch on my little finger. Her eyes gleamed green in the night, I could hear her thoughts.

"Go to the base of your spine, where I live inside of you. Keep your attention there for awhile and you will have your answer."

She quietly slipped back up my arm to her resting place. Warm, comfortable. I had gotten used to her there and felt it as a comforting, supportive presence. I knew that somehow she would be the key to success tonight.

As I moved my attention inward according to her directions, I felt a stirring, then a glow at the base of my spine. The energy felt powerful, coiled, ready to move, strike if necessary. My body began to tingle with its surges. This was the source of motion power, I knew it. I'd felt it before but not as consciously as now. Knowing it was Aleisha's presence within guiding me through the dark. Then the glow rising up through each center until my body felt alive, vigorous, unstoppable. The image of a long, powerful snake came into my mind's eye. I felt myself crouching, going lower, closer to the ground, finally down on my belly, slithering like a serpent hunting for his meal. My sight became clear, everything glowed with a faint greenish hue. I could see everything outlined as if it were bathed in green sunlight. In front of me, I saw a soldier crouched, holding his weapon, watching, waiting for any motion. My motions were silent, just the slight rustle of dead leaves from time to time, then I was past him, completely unobserved. Little did he know how close he had been to death, a quick transition in the dark of the night. Little did we know, each of us, how close our old friend death passed in all the dark nights of our lives. There was no need to take this one however, he posed no obstacle, I had passed the perimeter guard, the most sensitive observant. The rest would be easier. I continued marveling how comfortable the ground felt, caressing my arms, legs, belly in the passing, feeling the small stones tickle me, the twigs playfully poking me, probing me forward to my night's destiny.

A camps fire, small but distinct in the dark surrounded by soldiers huddling from the cold. I felt no cold, my blood felt colder than the air. My emotions steady, cool, relaxed. Determined to do my job whatever it was. I knew I would be confronting the forces now encircling and threatening my friends, allies and lovers.

But how would I bring some resolution to the immediate stand off?

Then, there I was at the crest of the hill, looking down at its lights. I sensed a joviality, a celebration, as if the beings below were so sure of their victory. So sure that their ambitions, their ways would perpetuate, grow in influence. Little did they know the powers which they unconsciously faced.

The Mahaj moving into their lives through everyone and everything chosen to bring about the necessary changes, the unification. I almost laughed out loud in the night at the picture. How brazenly we strut in the light of our own foolishness, our own limitations, not knowing what lies in wait in the dark of the night.

As I reached the edge of the town, I felt myself changing back to my normal sense of being. Standing erect in the shadows, but still feeling the power of the serpent flickering through my chakras. Ready for the strike.

Then I saw an open door, dark inside, no one around, but open. Why? The Mahaj was drawing me inside, I knew there was something there for me. Something I needed. As I passed inside, I saw clothes hanging everywhere. It was a clothing store offering me a disguise. The clothes were all finely tailored business suits, hats, dress shoes shining bright in the dim street lights. My hands guided to just the right size and color, felt quick, energized by my stealthy journey. I dressed quickly and stepped out into the night, closing the door behind me. The store had served its purpose.

I moved cautiously but relaxed in my new image, a determined businessman intent on protecting the opportunist way of life. Success, growth, prosperity at all costs. A voice moving spontaneously in a range from low murmurs to a high piercing yell drew me in the direction of a hall illuminated in the night. The hall was surrounded by an array of troops. One stepped towards my approach.

"You are late sir, do you have your pass?"

I did not expect to be confronted so directly. No words came to mind. I felt caught. Aleisha stirred, began moving down my arm, ready. The inner serpent, Aleisha's counterpart glowed bright in its resting place. Then a dark, slender figure stepped between us wearing an officer's uniform.

"Welcome Mr. Neron, we've been waiting for you, follow me."

The soldier stepped respectfully aside allowing us to pass into the waiting aura of the hall. The speaker seemed to hesitate for a moment, then continued. The officer turned to me, gazed deeply into my curious eyes, pursed his lips and whispered.

"Meisha."

I was glad General Meisha did not listen to my request to the letter. His elite force was a welcome support. I wondered how many more lingered in my surroundings. As I took my seat, he quickly moved through the gathering to the base of the stage, taking a position of authority, whispering orders to others gathered there. Security men, I could see by their movements, their darting eyes, looking for anything abnormal. Men willing to step between the threat and their ward, sacrifice themselves in the line of duty.

As I settled into my comfortable seat, my gaze moved through the room. The clothes I'd intuitively chosen fit right into the group. All well dressed, tailored to the T. Emitting an aura of influential power, respectful of each other's property, eager to broaden their field of ambition.

Everyone's attention was on the elaborate stage raised at the end of the hall, an elderly woman had walked on the stage from an opening at its back and took her place in front of the voice amplifying mechanism at stage center. A hush fell over the room as she began speaking. She spoke about the pleasure she and her husband had during their visit to another part of the planet as emissaries. How she felt this particular portion was ripe for the pickings. Not having a strong central government, an aggressive approach both militarily and economically would be virtually unchallenged. The group responded enthusiastically, cheering the prospect for expansion of their interests.

I began to perceive a hue rising from both the stage and the group, a light greenish hue similar to Aleisha's eyes. Aleisha meanwhile lay comfortably coiled in her resting place, seemingly undisturbed, waiting.

The group buzzed like bees in the aftermath of the speaker, each reaching around them excitedly exchanging information. My neighbor reached out his hand, I took it. It felt soft, lifeless, wet and clammy. His voice shook with nervous uncertainty.

"My name is Mr. Webb, she knows how to speak, doesn't she?"

My response was cordial under the circumstances.

"Yes, she makes her point quite well, my name is Mr. Neron."

I did not feel any nourishing energy from Mr. Webb and moved my attention back to the stage, almost rudely, but I felt this was normal among this group. I was right, he immediately turned and engaged his neighbor on the other side. Surface interaction, I thought, but what can be expected from shallowly beings dedicating their lives to self-gain through acquisition and control. I was beginning to feel the discomfort of my own judgemental frame of mind. I was certain that I was picking up on the aura, the presence in the room.

Another woman appeared at stage center and began speaking. She spoke warmly, compassionately about a disease which was sweeping the planet leaving death in its wake. It spared no one, striking randomly even the children. Her arm swung to her left and a child came to her. The child began speaking about the future and the fact she was infected and would probably die soon. The emotion burst out everywhere in the room. Tears flowed freely. A group cathartic release swept through the collective psyche. I felt its surge in my heart. These beings on stage were sincere, yet here they were in the center of the psychic force heading the affairs of the planet in a direction away from the necessary unity in which Galaxium and the Mahaj could bring a level of technology eliminating diseases of this sort overnight.

I suddenly saw the subtle emotional hypnotic programming behind the scenes. The group was being emotionally prepared, softened up from inside by the sincerity of these two. As they finished and left the stage I felt the group was ready, open to be molded, ready to receive the message of the night.

General Miko strode on stage with the certainty of someone on a mission. Someone believing fully in his commitments, no doubt in his abilities, a surety emanating out to the emotionally prepared gathering. His voice rang out with the authority of one who had commanded many into battle, guiding their motions, feeling a responsibility for their actions. The group shone back a deep respect. Here stood before them someone who had by accepting the values propelling each of them reached the pinnacle of success. Rising from the very bottom of their social order to command and protect, an honor bestowed on few. He spoke about his successful campaigns, about the increasing threat to the stability of the social order mutually supported by the gathered. The need to put a quick end to the irritation rising around them and expand their interests globally. The group drank it all in like an ambrosia, sweet to their ears, nourishing to their ambitious hungers.

I was impressed by his spontaneous oratory skills, not reading from any notes, just speaking from his inner self. I was amazed that the inner self would move so lucidly through one with such an aggressive approach to reality. Yet here he was lucidly presenting an almost irresistible portrayal of his vision and how it would benefit everyone, even the less fortunate, giving them opportunity to rise above their present limited life styles to heights of achievement comparable to his own. The sense of excitement, exhilaration, hope in the future permeated the aura of the hall.

The one signal of disharmony I became aware of was the rigidity and jerky manner his hands and body expressed themselves. Shooting out greenish flashes of energy, mesmerizing, entrancing, intent on control. The technique of a subtle fascist. His voice did not carry the usual aggressive nature of the fascist, but the motions, jerkily delivering their controlling psychic energy, made his intent obvious to me. I was watching a sorcerer manifesting his art before me. I wondered if his psychic abilities were developed high enough to perceive me. I made efforts to screen my psychic emanations, stay invisible, it seemed to work. He continued on to a furious crescendo changing the mood from the previous emotional openness to a committed aggressive, almost angry posture. The group was left with no alternative but to support his program if they wanted their needs met and enhanced.

I tipped my hat to his eloquence. Here was one I would prefer as an ally if his vision and commitments were reformed, realigned towards the growth full evolution of each individual psyche rather than the interests of the elite.

The general strode off the stage with the same motions of surety, commitment, a look of pleasure on his face. He knew he had struck a cord with his audience.

Everyone was standing, cheering, clapping, feeling the exhilaration of unifying their energies in one direction. I knew this type of transference of individual power into a collective focus added up to a great deal more than the sum of its parts. Here was a psychic force collected, available to be used through the art of visualization to achieve otherwise insurmountable goals. I shuddered inwardly at what this visualization would be and how it might affect those I'd grown to love and respect. I sensed the possibility of another valley of martyrdom. Nothing would be gained and so much lost to me personally. The entirety, the collective would absorb and process the occurrence yet there would be a diminishing in it. I knew I was here armed with my tools and my Aleisha to somehow resolve this confrontation, or at least affect, possibly neutralize, balance the force now unfolding.

As the general stepped off the stage into a waiting circle of security men holding back his eager admirers, I saw a thin, hardened man with gaunt, piercing eyes come through the circle, take the general by the arm and lead him to a guarded doorway. I quickly left my seat, stepped out the main entrance and headed around the building in the direction of their exit. Just as I stepped around the corner of the building I could see the general and his host slip into a dark, long limousine, the large, red tail lights flashed and they pulled away into the night.

Aleisha stirred, I saw a flash of my reality transformer with a feather, the color of Rhona's tail feathers waving through its eye in my mind's eye. Then the rearing image of my milky white carrier stallion. I knew all my forces were aligned for the challenge but how was I to follow?

The vehicle was moving away quickly into the dark of the night. As my eyes scanned the area, across the street along the side of the building, I saw a faint white object ahead of me. I felt its draw. It was a small motorized two-wheeled carrier. Again feeling the inner surge of the serpent, almost flying to it, slipping on it, intuitively finding the starter button and I was off at full speed in the direction of the departing vehicle. I could still see the faint glow of its two red eyes occasionally flashing bright, then dimming, moving up a long hill out of town.

The pursuit was smooth, the faint glow of my carriers head lamp lit my path sufficiently, yet not bright enough to be detected from ahead. I kept a safe distance knowing inwardly that a sign would come when to stop and proceed on foot. As I rounded a bend, the road stretched ahead of me, but I no longer saw my beckoning red eyes. They'd disappeared. I felt the flurry from the side of the road. A small night bird, startled, flew up in front of me, momentarily flashing in the light of my headlamp. Was this my sign? I felt it was. I stopped and pulled my carrier off the road into the thickets at its side.

Stepping out onto the roadside, I saw and heard nothing, just the slight stirring of a night breeze through the trees and the long grass. I remembered a small pouch on the side of my carrier, going back to it, reaching inside, I found a small metallic object with two glass eye pieces. It was a vision amplifying tool. Coming back onto the road I looked up the road with it.

There, a distance beyond my normal vision lay a roadway leading off the main road. Two large white pillars with a gate between them. I could see a faint, dark figure leaning against one of the pillars. As I moved my view up the road I saw a faint glow along the tree line. Possibly a dwelling, this must be where the general had gone. I had no other option, my feelings indicated he was up there relaxing after his nights success. But who was his companion, there was an ominous essence to this one. Somehow familiar, yet unreadable. The sense of power, secretive power, the power behind the visible workings, possibly.

As I moved back to the carrier, to replace my vision aide, I felt Aleshia slip down my arm and come out on her special perch, my ground finger. Her eyes gleamed green in the night, I heard her thought.

"Use the other mechanical tool to guide you up to your destination, save my power for later, you will need all of it."

She disappeared to her resting place. I reached back into the pouch, finding another object. Replacing the vision amplifier, I pulled out the other object. It was a pair of glasses, somewhat bulky, but well-fitting. As I looked through them, the dark night lit up with a faint green hue. I could clearly see the terrain, the rocks, bushes, obstacles and the way past them. I climbed quietly, slowly towards the dim light. The closer I got the stronger my inner feeling of secretive power, the power behind the visible workings, always there in every power structure based on acquisition and control. The hidden ones exerting influence on the visible mechanical aspects of rulership. This was the real challenge to the movements of the Mahaj. The ingrained concerns whose vested interests worked to maintain the status quo and expand, not give up anything for the greater good. Ambition not for individual comfort, that was already there in excess, just the ambition for more power, more influence, more opportunity to rule over more under its influence.

A grim picture, grim feeling tone and yet this was my destination. To face it, allow the Mahaj to flow through my actions and do what was necessary. The power surged through my being as I climbed knowing I would face this challenge with the power of my Aleisha, coiled, ready, resting. I could see her gleaming, satisfied eyes as she drank in the blend of Beno's blood, mine and the poison. Drawing it out of my ethereal being, leaving only enough which I was capable of dealing with.

CHAPTER 12

As I reached the edge of the bushes surrounding the mansion nestled comfortably at the summit of the hill, up against a steep incline rising sharply to a high cliff, I saw a soldier standing guard, watching. Beyond him, I saw others in various spots, barely visible through my eye piece. I would not have seen them without it. Stopping to rest and access my possible approach I again felt Aleisha come out and look up at me from her perch. Her thoughts again.

"Hide your visual aide, you will need it for your escape. Visualize me, now where you know I live in you. Let my power carry you. This is my realm, my power will deal with it through you."

As she returned to her hiding place, I found a spot beside a large rock visible in the night light and hid my visual aide. Then sitting down beside it, I closed my eyes and approached Aleisha's inner abode, the base of my spine. The inner serpent waiting to awaken. I felt the stirring, the deep red glow mingling with the light green of Aleisha's eyes. My body felt long, flexible, able to conform to any terrain, slip over it, move through any opening. My vision became even clearer than that seen through the visual aide. I found myself once again creeping on my belly towards a small opening at the base of the dwelling emitting a faint light. I moved within a few feet of the towering soldier gazing into the night. Would he see me? Then I was past him, unobserved. My body stretched as I reached the narrow slit of an opening, slipped noiselessly inside, dropping a few feet onto a concrete floor, then crouching, scanning the area.

The light was dim, but with my serpent vision, I could see a small stairway leading up to a door, reaching it, turning the door knob, I felt it open. Opening it just slightly, I looked inside. The light was brighter, there were sounds of splashing, laughter, a bathing area. As my sight adjusted to the light I could see several forms. Naked, in the dim light, playing, jumping in and out of the water. On the far end of the room, I saw several more forms in various stages of love making or should I say "Lustful Activity".

Love, to me, always inferred privacy. This was being displayed quite openly.

Uninhibited in their demonstrations of athletic gestures. The moans indicated extreme pleasure. Total immersion in their acts, oblivious to their surroundings. This was to my obvious advantage.

The general was not part of the group, then I saw him coming out of a small door to my left. His body was naked, sweaty as he stepped under a nozzle, turned a small lever and was drenched with a flow of water. His groan indicated the water was cold. As he finished and returned to the room, opened the door and stepped inside, I saw a film of steam emanate out into the outer space. This was obviously a variation of the sweat structures, I was quite familiar with. I wondered if it had similar spiritual experiences attached to it. I doubted it, my inner feeling still resonated with the secretive power systems I'd previously felt.

Stripping off my clothes, hanging them on a hook beside the door, I stepped inside and headed directly to a small pool of water steaming near the door, Miko had gone through. The hot water felt caressing, penetrating. I felt my strains of the night leaving. The minerals in the water filled my senses. I drifted with the heat and the music reaching me through the steamy air. The lusty activities some distance away grew furious as the music intensified in its beat, its tempo. I knew it was time to make my move towards Miko's presence. No one would notice me. Slipping out of the water, I went directly to the nozzle, turned the lever and felt the cold water sting my hot skin. Turning slowly under its pressured flow, I felt each part of my body being cooled, caressed. Then a warm hand touching my shoulder, sliding down my arm, resting on my bare bottom. The voice, feminine, sultry.

"Hi, Big Boy, want some company?"

She was large, firm, voluptuous and she was pressing herself demonstratively against me, undulating to the music now slower, deeper, erotic. I slipped my arm around the slenderness of her waist and drew her closer. My mouth touched the nape of her neck, then upwards to her ear, I moaned, amplifying my slight arousal.

"Yes, I would love to feel myself deep inside you, but now I must see the general. He has summoned me. Will you wait for me?"

I could feel Aleisha stirring in her hiding place, she would not be denied. I sensed a slight bit of jealousy in her presence. I feared for my companion who was drawing away now. Her voice a little higher in reaction to my direct proposal.

"Hurry, I'll wait over there."

She'd gestured towards the group still pleasuring themselves.

Watching my new acquaintance sway away from me towards the mass of erotic flesh, her voluptuousness barely visible in the dim light, I wondered if there was any limit to the animal desire I felt coursing through me. Transcendent to all my values and allegiances to those I loved, it flowed through my veins like hot lava undeniable in its insistency.

I moved my attention deeper inside myself through the higher heart realm up into the third eye realm, the crown chakra and beyond. Uniting with my ethereal, transcendent self, I felt its cooling effect. My mind agitated by the sudden flow of hormones, now stilled, settled itself into the focus of what lay ahead. My confrontation with Miko and whomever, whatever lay inside the door I was now opening, slowly, cautiously, just an inch at a time, only wide enough to slip my narrowed serpent-like body inside. The door closed behind me and I felt the intense heat. The room was full of drifting steam. I could barely see my own hands in front of me. I touched a bench beside me and sat. Breathing deeply, feeling the searing heat touch my lungs, again taking my attention inside to the cool place, the comfort beyond the physical limits, enhancing my tolerance level. Now I could stay comfortably for as long as necessary feeling the sweat begin beading on the surface of my entire skin area. I quieted my thoughts and listened. I could hear an occasional cough, a rustle, a slap then a voice, not Miko's.

"Congratulations on your successes of the night. My people are quite happy with your progress so far. I understand you have quite a little bunch of irritants caught in their little hole."

Miko's voice was steady, not jubilant.

"Yes, I have the leaders of all our resistance encircled and am applying a steady pressure. After this and some food I'll go out there and deal with them all. I'm doing what I must but I do not respect or agree with your tactics in dealing with Beno, that was very extreme and could have a backlash."

I felt my surprise rush through my body. I now saw Miko in a different light. Aleisha stirred, ready. The stranger's voice was now higher, excited.

"Just remember, General, do what you must in bringing the theater of activity under our control or you could end up like Beno. We will not hesitate to do what is necessary to achieve our ends."

As the stranger stirred, began moving towards me and the door, I heard the General grunt.

"Just stay away from my family, I'll do my part."

As the stranger moved, I coiled myself into as small a portion of the bench as possible. Visualizing myself invisible in the thickness of the steam. His hand touched the door, pushed, then reacted as if he felt me, hidden, coiled. His voice rang out.

"Are you sure your security is adequate? I have a funny feeling all is not right."

I knew he was sensing me, not seeing me, just knowing there was someone around who shouldn't be.

Miko grunted.

"The place is well secured. Your little orgy out there is probably unsettling you."

The stranger chuckled.

"Maybe, I think I'll sample a bit of it before we go up to eat. Will you join me?"

Miko disgustingly,

"I don't play with fire, like you. The disease sweeping our land knows no rank."

Miko's level of morality and concern again surprised me. I expected something else. I didn't really know what, but not this. I found myself softening to him, but this one only a few feet away gave me a cringing sense. Aleisha was moving down my arm to her perch, her launching pad. I restrained my impulse to flick her at his throat. Time enough for that, I thought, as he swept out the door. The door closed and I was alone with the general. Uncoiling slowly, I slid quietly toward his end of the room. I thought I heard a deep sob, getting closer, I could see his indistinct form slouched forward, his head in his hands. I was now right beside him, almost touching him, I felt sorrow not anger or fear, just a deep sorrow. Here sat a victim, not rampaging, ambitious warrior willing to wreak havoc gleefully, to the contrary one who had gotten himself into a situation discomforting, hopeless, inescapable.

Aleisha sat poised on my finger, as I reached out, touched his shoulder and whispered with a hiss,

"Good evening, General."

My hand stayed on his shoulder as he lurched up to a sitting position, his back against the wall, no where to retreat. His eyes moved down to my hand. He saw Aleisha, green eyes glaring back. I felt his shudder, he knew the danger. His breath quickened, large beads of sweat stood out on his forehead. Fear had its grip and was squeezing.

I didn't want to give the poor man a heart attack. Slowly withdrawing my hand with poised Aleisha, I assured,

"I'm surprised. After so much death around you, your own still brings you fear. I think I'll deny my friend here her pleasure for now. But let's have a little heart to heart, you know what I mean?"

His eyes and nod showed me his willingness under the circumstances. I wondered if he recognized me in the deep fog of the room. I queried,

"Do you remember me?"

His eyes peered squintedly at me.

"Yes, you were Beno's security man. I've been hearing a lot about you. How did you manage to get in here?" I felt the serpent energy surge inside. My eyes must have shone green as I saw him tighten up again.

"I have my ways but lets talk about your ways, or should I say your Master's ways."

He knew who I was referring to. He also knew I had heard their conversation. His eyes turned apologetically sad. His voice trembled,

"You know I have no choice. You probably won't believe me but I speak the truth. I respected Beno a great deal. We disagreed on many things but his commitment to the people was unquestionable. Above all else, he stood by his word. Few in this world do."

I felt sincerity in his being. I was beginning to open to him seeing his victimization, not respecting his weakness, but understanding. I suggested,

"Why don't you just get out of this mess? Gather your family if they are really threatened and join us."

His voice seemed grateful for the offer.

"Your offer is generous, but this is not possible. Much of my family isn't even aware of the threat. They would not leave their lives here for an uncertain future. I just couldn't ask them to, they don't even know my innermost feelings around this."

I could see the dilemma clearly. My voice was cautioning.

"You know, sooner or later you'll outgrow your usefulness to them."

We both knew the pattern, the most powerful always become uncomfortable at some point in time with those around them getting a little too influential. They preferred surrounding themselves with weakness, it seemed to enhance their limited power, abusive power, a bully's approach to life.

His voice expressed the hopelessness of the situation.

"Yes, I know my eventual destiny, but I have no choice. I've eaten at their table. I cannot deny my just desserts."

I enjoyed his play on words and somehow felt I could work with this man. Aleisha's glare had softened, she'd settled comfortably on her perch, still ready. I offered.

"My friend here seems to have lost her appetite for you. Would you be open to some compromise, a secret arrangement between us designed to bringing about a mutually agreeable resolution? Would you work with me on this?"

I felt myself moving into the ethereal dimension. My vision and attention slowly turned to the Auric interplay in the steam. The greenish swirling hues gathered thickly around us. I felt Aleisha tightening up, Her eyes glanced up at me. Her thought reached out.

"I will take back the serpent's aura for now and give you the opportunity to touch another's heart. This is what you want, isn't it?"

I thought back.

"Yes, that is what I want."

Aleisha straightened up, stood tall on her perch. Her eyes opened wide. I could see the greenish hues coming to her, away from the general, away from me. I saw the gaping mouth, gleaming fangs, the hue moving into her, disappearing.

My words were fast, as if our time together was short and a great deal must be related. I spoke of the need for planetary unity no matter what the form of rulership, the need for a centralized, benevolent authority open to guidance, a motion towards individual evolutionary processes growth full psychic awareness, the opportunity for each to participate in accord with their individual psychic skills. Finally on a collective opening to the possibility of more from the unknown aspects of reality. I found myself holding back the specific information on Galaxium and the workings of the Mahaj behind it all. I felt our hearts as one for the time.

The aura emanating from our heart centers was deep red, a warrior hue. The words flowed through me spontaneously. I opened my channels wide and flowed, not concerned with preciseness. The general imagery was more important now. The general's eyes were full, teary as I concluded.

"I see you eventually becoming a leader of healers moving into conflict not with the intent to conquer and control but to work with the conflicting factions towards a peaceful resolution. This can only be accomplished when the conflict within each one involved is healed. For you it will be an opportunity to balance the actions you now find necessary in the field of your command. This will bring you inner peace and strength, transcendent to the fear you now live with."

His voice emitted a warm but distrustful receptivity.

"I like what you say. My heart feels full, hopeful. But I just can't see the logistics of it all. It all seems impossible."

I assured.

"I won't bore you with the details, anyway it would take the fun out of it all. If you co-operate you'll soon see the changes for yourself. I'll convince General Meisha and General Kwan Yen to support you, work with you. This alliance will enhance your image among the people and your so-called superiors. Nothing need change too quickly right now. The changes must be gradual. I'll stay in touch with you through Meda. He is skeptical of you right now, but will co-operate when I explain the situation, the need. Tonight you must loosen the grip around us and allow me, Cinda and the rebels to slip away into the night. Call it a favor for loosening my grip on you here right now."

Aleisha amplified my point with a greenish glare. His voice got a little gruffer.

"I see your point. Under the circumstances I guess I really don't have any choice, but beyond that I would like you to know that I like what you have said. I tire of all the butchery and welcome the prospect of a stable, growth full peace. But tell me who the hell are you anyway, and your pet? How did you train her to do that?"

I felt Aleisha tighten up at the image of being my pet. I reassured her with a glance of appreciation for her independent will and co-operation.

"Once again, I won't bore you with the details. Someday we'll sit and I'll explain it all. Right now I feel we are running out of time and it's getting damn hot in here."

I slipped out of sight into the thickness of the steam, leaving him to ponder the situation but I knew he would co-operate. Now it was time to face the Master of the house. As my hand touched the door and began pushing it open, I heard his voice, deep, questioning.

"How do I deal with this fear that eats away at me? I no sooner come to grips with it, settle it and it reappears somewhere else, plaguing me."

I knew in that moment, I had an ally, his being had opened to me. The question, in its sincerity, was the beginning of the answer. My voice was almost loving.

"See it as part of yourself, the weakest link, but still just a part. Find the strong parts, support them and shine their strength and nourishment on the weakness, the fear. Be aware when it rises in you, see its temporal nature, how quickly it passes. I'll send you someone I've known for some time who works with the issues around fear. Open to her and co-operate with her processes. They will support you and enhance your own efforts. She will also be a link between us and I'll look forward to see what unfolds for you. I would like to call you "Friend" someday."

I could feel my words sinking deep into both his conscious and unconscious. A friend was in the making.

His voice trembled.

"Friend, I'm not sure what that really means anymore, however, I'll co-operate with your friend and you."

Slipping through the door, I felt the coolness of the large bath area. Aleisha lay concealed in her hiding place as I turned the nozzle and felt the cold sting of the glacier water. My body drank in the coolness, refreshing itself.

Stepping away, I felt the eyes of the group at the end of the room on me. My tantalizing companion lay on a small sofa, beckoning. As I moved to her I wondered if I could or even really wanted to go through with this part of the play. Her voluptuousness was inviting but something had changed, she seemed distant, in a haze. As I reached her side and sat down beside her, reaching my left arm around her already undulating hips, I saw it. A trickle, a trace left by the Master of the house while I was with the General. My appetite left me. I felt Aleisha moving down my arm to the trickle. I could see her darting little tongue sampling, then she thought.

"The disease is in this one, my poison can neutralize it. Do you will it?"

My thought was unthought, spontaneous.

"No, it must be this way."

Aleisha returned quickly to her hiding place. My voice quivered with the knowledge that I was speaking to one condemned to death by her own actions.

"It seems like you have already feasted."

Her smile was unabashed.

"I still have plenty left for you, Big Boy."

I was sure she did but I'd lost interest. As I stood to leave, her voice followed me invitingly.

"I guess you don't like sloppy seconds. I'll keep that in mind in the future. Mr. Maurice has invited a few of us up to his penthouse for drinks, would you like to join us?"

The door had opened for me in an unexpected fashion. Aleisha stirred eagerly.

"It will be my pleasure, I'll go and dress."

Slipping away, I could hear the giggles, chuckles, ohs and ahs. I felt somewhat on display, but what the hell, I enjoyed strutting my stuff. All those years in the milky aura physical readiness program had given me an attractive enough body. Might as well show it off? I glanced seductively over my shoulder as I swaggered through the door.

Dressing I spotted an area in the basement with dusty old bottles stacked in a neat array. Picking the oldest, dustiest, wiping it clean, my offering was in hand. The Master's own for his palate. I enjoyed the humor. The Mahaj always seemed to put what I needed in my hands with his divine humor and kept me from touching the unpalatable offerings. I appreciated the guidance, it left me free to dance rather than ponder my next step. I knew as I walked out through the door, bottle in hand, each step would be guided as long as I stayed open, responsive.

The room had changed, the lights were brighter, the naked bodies at the far end of the bath area had left. A small group of smartly dressed couples playfully stood waiting. My previous companion wore a bright red dress. Her voluptuousness was bursting out everywhere. A true creation of lust, her painted red mouth pouting seductively, her motions like an animal in heat, squirming, almost uncomfortable with the incessant need. Her voice drifted across the room lazily.

"Come, Stranger, I have someone here for you to meet."

She was pointing out a smaller, slender girl, younger than the others, dressed in a loose white outfit, frilly, an aura of innocence about her. Her eyes shyly scanned me.

The lady in red continued as I made my approach.

"Liza will keep you company. She's far less experienced than me, but you don't seem to appreciate my experience."

The group chuckled in agreement, moving to the door being held open by a young boy. Liza stepped toward me, her heels clicking sharply on the tiled floor, slipping her arm through mine, guiding me to follow the group's flow. Her voice was high, excited but strong.

"I hope you will find my company satisfactory."

Assuringly I offered,

"I'm sure I will."

The grimness of the picture suddenly struck me. The lustful curves of the seasoned, hardened veteran undulating up the stairs ahead of me and the innocent, willing girl beside me, shyly touching my arm with her fragility, her purity.

Yet hovering all around us, Death, knowing no bounds, indiscriminate of innocence or the seasoned. Willing to take both in its grip, its transformative grip. I knew as I looked down at my companion that soon she would mix juices with the collective gathered here and begin her final journey into the waiting arms of my old friend. I sensed the waste and my own helplessness in the picture at this time. Would the Mahaj move quickly enough for this one? Possibly, yet so many others faced the inevitable specter this moment in so many ways. This was but one.

As we came to the top of the stairway, I sensed a change in myself. I was beginning to move into the ethereal, my sight was starting to blur, objects were becoming indistinct. Simultaneously my ethereal vision was sharpening. I could see the auras of the beings in front of me. Various hues of red, orange, all surrounded by the pale green aura so dominant here. Everyone was taking off their shoes and moving in couples through the open door, the doorway into the Master's chambers. I could feel the beast within, waiting.

I whispered in Liza's ear.

"Go ahead, I feel a little dizzy from the heat in the steam room, I'll join you in a few minutes."

Liza's eyes showed concern as she stepped away from me, following the group. I stepped to an open window for a breath of fresh air. As she stepped through the door it shut and I was completely in the ethereal dimension sensing something approaching, an ominous presence, threatening. I could see Aleisha climb onto her perch, ready. She sensed it as well. Then I saw it moving through the cracks around the door, a greenish formless, permeating essence coming nearer. I felt scanned, appraised and found lacking. This ethereal being knew I was a threat and was moving in for the kill. My ethereal body was vibrating in readiness. I saw an image of my Reality Transformer, Rhona's feather beckoned, I brushed my little ethereal finger across it. The spell was cast. All I could do now was wait for contact.

The presence was beginning to take form, a vague ethereal form. It rose up before me, a sinister looking face with a gaping fang-filled mouth leaping at me from its coil. I felt its fangs sinking into my leg, the tingle of its venom. Aleisha's thought.

"My poison has immunized you from the poison of my kind. Let me deal with him now."

My little finger curled down meeting my thumb, the finger representing the ethereal dimension. I applied pressure then released. Aleisha's ethereal form flew high above the head of the attacker gleefully sitting back waiting for his poison to take hold. I felt no effect, just a powerful glow in my veins. Aleisha had foreseen this possibility and done her work well. Moham would be proud of his little servant.

Meanwhile I could see Aleisha spinning in the air above the attacker's head. A blur falling slowly behind him. Her eyes suddenly shone a bright red as she landed on the back of his neck sinking her fangs deep. The attacker's face showed a moment of surprise, then the poison struck, a blurriness in the eyes, a shudder, a green fluid pouring out of his mouth and nose. Aleisha drank deeply, filling herself with his essence. The essence of the fluid was enriching my friend, she grew larger, larger until she towered over me and the slumping attacker. Opening her immense mouth, she began sucking her victim inside herself. Her feast was short but so sweet. I could tell it in her eyes. Her thought.

"Now the way is clear for you. This was the diseased unconscious of your host taking form and striking out at you. Your host is not even conscious of any of it."

I knew the power of the unconscious and how it aligned itself with the will of the conscious, supporting, protecting, doing everything possible to fulfill the conscious wish. This specter had been created by a will focused on greed, selfishness, power abusive to its surroundings, success at any cost even murder. This was the one who had willfully made the decision to eliminate Beno.

Now Aleisha had consumed it, nourished herself with it and ruled where it once ruled. The door was now open for conversation, communication and possible resolution. I felt with Aleisha's rulership, Moham's will would be dominant in the unfolding of the night's events. I trusted in this, as I moved back into physical form, comfortably settled in and stepped towards the doorway. The sounds of the party inside reached out to me, oblivious of what had just taken place. I wondered how the outcome of this conflict would affect the emotions, thoughts and actions of those inside, now and in the future.

CHAPTER 13

Just as I reached the door, it swung open noiselessly, hinges well-oiled, like the naked bodies writhing down below now dressed, spread out in the room filling their senses with food and drink. An opulent array tasting the plentifulness of their host. Placing the old bottle of spirits in the hands of the young boy who had opened the door, I directed.

"Please give our gracious host my humble offering. Pass along my appreciation for his hospitality."

The boy bowed ceremoniously, closed the door and made his way to my host now dressed in a silk, black suit surrounded by a select group of admirers playing out their discreet parts of the play.

As I scanned the room, I saw no signs of security. There was a sureness of safety here, confidence in the forces that surrounded the building. A false sense of security in my experience. The only true security being the kind that flowed from within. External forms were all penetrable if one had the training and will to do so.

My eyes caught Liza's as she moved away from her small group hovering around a table full of an array of food and drink, and moved welcomingly towards me. Meeting by a large, tropical plant emitting a sweet perfume from its single bloom, her voice rang out to me, low, sweet.

"Are you all right now, has the dizziness passed? You look a little pale."

After witnessing what I'd just witnessed I had little doubt that my color was somewhat off, assuringly.

"I'm fine now, just a little thirsty. That steam room sure de-hydrates, doesn't it?"

Her smile was genuine, playfully taking my arm, retorting.

"Yes it does, makes me real hot too."

I nodded my head with a slight grin understanding her not-so-subtle innuendo. She continued.

"Come lets have a drink, are you hungry too?"

I felt Aleisha stretch in her hiding place still small in this dimension, but now in control in her grandeur in the ethereal. I thought I heard a big burp coming from under my arm. I chuckled, flirtatiously.

"Oh yes, I hunger for many things."

Her eyes danced shyly up to mine.

"Am I one of those things?"

I answered by running my hand slowly down her back to the base of her spine where the slenderness of her waist began to swell into her slim but full hips. Pressing myself firmly, momentarily against her as she turned, I assured.

"You are one of the most attractive things within my grasp here, unfortunately I'm a married man."

Her body stiffened slightly, questioningly.

"And you're not the type that fools around from time to time."

I toyed with my words.

"Fooling around is for fools."

Striking a pose in imitation of her voluptuous friend, teasingly.

"We'll see about that, Big Boy."

I was enjoying her quick wit.

I wondered how long it would be before it dimmed under the glare of her imminent fate. So innocently dancing under the watchful, waiting eyes of my old friend.

Just as Liza picked up a bottle off the table, placed a glass in my hand,

I felt a cool aura beside me. The voice of my host.

"Welcome to my little party. I see you've met my sweet little Liza."

My surprise turned to amazement as he gave Liza a big fatherly hug, continuing.

"She's the pride of my life along with her mother, of course."

This turn of events left me speechless, feeling a little toyed with yet I'd just assumed Liza was one of the girls available for anyone needing some entertaining.

My host offered.

"Here, have a drink of your own contribution. It happens to be my most favored vintage. You have excellent taste."

I sipped the rich, thick spirit feeling its glow begin at the back of my throat, creep down to my stomach and flow out to the extremities of my body. I thought I heard a big hiccup from under my arm. I finally found my voice.

"Yes, Liza has been a very gracious hostess but she didn't tell me how close she was to the master of the house."

My hosts smile showed his approval at my projected image of him.

His voice tantalized.

"I hope you find my rulership acceptable."

Assuringly, I offered.

"If its anywhere near that of your sweet little Liza, I'm sure I will."

Inside myself I knew I would place limits on his rulership but for now I was his guest and saw no need to be confrontive. He filled my glass again, now feeling safe, filled one for himself as well. A careful man. In this environment I was sure it was wise to be. His beady eyes questioned.

"What did you think of our General's speech, tonight? I'm sure I saw you sitting in the back."

I admired his powers of observation.

"I'm surprised you noticed me. The General has a very commanding presence and speaks very clearly, dynamically, but I wonder about his administrative ability in dealing with fiscal policy."

I'd played my hand right into his expertise. Assuringly, his voice hissed.

"Don't be concerned about that. I have all that under control. The General will be well advised, appropriately directed in fact."

I knew he would, not to the benefit of the poor, the ordinary worker and the other struggling factions, but for the already rich. Those with an unquenchable appetite for more.

I felt the attention of the room go to the door, the General had arrived with a few of his aides and security. There was no direct movement towards me. I sensed our heart to heart had achieved its purpose. He had meant what he said in parting, but I did not want to push it. One wrong word could tip the balance and I didn't want to do that, not with my friends still in their precarious situation.

My host suggested.

"Sample some of the food that's been laid out. Liza will see to your needs while I see to our newly arrived guests. I may have time for a longer chat later, if you're still here."

I knew I should leave soon. There was still a lot to do tonight. I felt Aleisha's impatience. We'd done what we came here to do. I sensed her stabilizing influence. Reactions to provoking stimuli would not be as erratic as before. This was definitely a step in the right direction.

"I do have important business in the morning and feel somewhat tired. Maybe another time."

He looked a little disappointed. I thought he enjoyed the tit for tat we played. His voice held a slight edge of impatience.

"Very well, until the next time."

He quickly moved away to the General's company. I could see him querying the General, glancing my way. The General nodded assuringly barely even looking in my direction. He was begrudgingly covering my tail. Liza took my arm and led me to the food. It was all appetizing, a feast fit for a king. I ate ravenously. Just as Aleisha had done earlier.

Liza flitted around flirtatiously emulating her voluptuous tutor who now hovered around the General's group, occasionally glancing my way with her seductive sweep. Rising from the table, full, I started for the door. Liza saw me leaving swayed seductively to me, her bare feet sinking into the deep pile of the lush carpet making a deep crunching sound.

"Leaving so soon, why not spend the night, you might enjoy it."

The invitation was sweet, almost too sweet to resist. My voice trembled slightly.

"Your not making it easy for me to stay faithful, you little temptress."

Our voluptuous companion had swayed up to us, her full lips broadened at my remark.

"Your teacher here has taught you well, don't let her lead you too far astray if you haven't already strayed too far."

Her voice teasingly injected.

"What, my sweet, virginal Liza, I thought you might start her on her journey to the fields of ecstasy."

Liza's shy eyes showed an interest in the journey, her voice beckoned.

"How's about it, Big Boy? Would you be gentle with me?"

My hand quivered as it touched her neck just below her short hair, pulling her close for an affectionate kiss on the forehead. My voice wasn't too steady either.

"That's the problem with commitments, they limit one's field of endeavor. The two of you have certainly stimulated my appetite but I must leave with this one unsatisfied."

Their looks of lustful disappointment were comically exaggerated for my benefit. Nothing like stroking the male ego in parting. Part of the art of entertainment. I felt very full as I headed for the door, my exit into another theater of activity unknown in its character, yet irresistibly beckoning me to enter. I waved a good-bye to the General and the master of this house, threw a small kiss to my flirtatious duo, hands on their protruding hips, lips pouted in their farewell kisses.

I was thankful for the training I'd had in self-discipline. It took all of it to walk away from the enticing scenario I was leaving as I stepped out the door following the young boy leading me out into the chill of the night, away from the warmth of the gathering. Sinister in essence yet so seductive, entrancing. The traces of weakness held, my self-discipline pushed me onwards.

As we rounded a corner in the stairway passed an open doorway into a large hallway, I heard music and the deep thump of drums, many drums coming out. I asked.

"What is going on in there?"

The boy replied.

"Some of my friends dropped over for a visit, want to take a closer look?"

As I nodded, he strode inside with me following close behind. The inside was dimly lit, the music and drums beat out a steady rhythm, pleasant, not professional. The feeling that anyone could join in, participate. A sweet smell drifted in the air similar to the smoke from the pipe around the camp fire back in the Valley of Peace. I could see the gathering was young, dressed in various arrays of color and style. Each finding their own expression according to personality and taste. There were several males and females swaying, dancing to the beat, each in their own space and feeling. Not interacting with one another, just moving in singular expression of the dance. The boy had moved into a circle, sitting on the floor passing around a small glowing object, smoke rose thickly around the group. Taking the smoking paper, he came to me, holding his breath offering it to me.

"Here, have some." He uttered through the restriction of his smoke-filled lungs. I took the object, sucked on it as I saw the others do, felt the burning sensation. My impulse was to cough but I held back, held the smoke inside for a moment and exhaled. Passing it back, I moved slowly towards the dancers. The boy glided past me as if on a cloud beckoning.

"Come, join us in our dance."

My head was feeling lighter than usual, my body tingled and Aleisha squirmed as if she was dancing in her own space.

I heard her thought.

"Hey man, I feel real high."

"Yeah," I thought, "me too, I haven't danced in a long time, why not."

Finding my own space, I closed my eyes and started moving.

The motion seemed to carry me with it until I was twirling, weaving amongst the others. Interacting unobtrusively, but still maintaining my own space.

The music and drums increased in tempo until we were all spinning in the dizzying frenzy of the dance. I saw flashes of familiar faces, old and new friends spinning, dancing with me, inside. The young group spun around me, occasionally brushing near, then whirling off away from me. There was no need to hold on to anyone or anything here, the intimacy was emotional, inside each touching ethereally, then just letting go. A meditation in motion. Feeling the collective psyche in celebration of each other's presence and our own. The frenzy ended suddenly.

Everyone around me, fell as if exhausted and just lay there breathing heavily. I sat down, rested and went deep inside myself. I felt myself floating within, clouds formed and cleared. Then I saw the General's face. It was sad, dejected, confused. I felt I had not given him enough, there was more, something missing. I knew I had to go back to him, open up and relate whatever it was I'd missed. I pondered what it could be. Fear was the issue, I'd spoken sincerely, genuinely.

I felt the small hand on my shoulder, his high voice.

"You are now one of us, your dance was as one with our way. Would you like to continue or stay here?"

I knew I must go back, take the risk.

"I forgot something up there, could you take me back for a moment?"

The trip back up was quick, holding the door open, stepping aside, the boy smiled.

"You enjoyed that, didn't you?"

My satisfied grin was answer enough.

As I scanned the room, I had the strange feeling I'd never been here before. Everything seemed different.

Everyone was busily interacting, lost in their own worlds yet communicating with each other's unique world. A deep sense of being unimportant. Just being gone for such a short time, yet forgotten so quickly, as if I'd never passed through. Feeling so much the center of it all just moments ago and now unimportant, forgotten. So much like life in general. We strut, feel our self-importance, then we're gone and everything falls into place in our absence as if we'd never danced our dance at all. I felt the steadiness of my observations, a dimming of my self-image, knew in that moment that all that really mattered was what was happening inside each of us. That is where we always lived. Our evolution was there, not out here in the temporal, yet here I was seeing Mr. Maurice and his entourage enjoying their dance of self-importance and the General picking at his food at the end of the table, alone, seemingly removed in his thoughts. I approached, leaned over the table as he raised his head, spoke.

"There's something I forgot to mention about our mutual challenge."

I knew by his eyes that he knew what I was referring to. Not the external scenario challenge but the inner one. I continued.

"When it rises in you, reaches out and creates an external reality, the opportunity is there to face it. Not try to squirm away from it and hide or aggressively attack and destroy its unpleasantness, but simply face it directly and as evenly as possible. Then you will see its true nature. It's weak temporal nature."

His look was one of understanding, I knew he had just faced it in his encounter with Mr. Maurice and had backed off into himself and was now feeling the emotion of lacking in courage. One step back plus the missing step forward added up to a lot of steps. Steps away from growth and inner stability. His voice was steady.

"Would you like a ride back to your companions? I have a truck full of medical supplies and food out back your friends could use, I'm sure."

My surprise at his offer was evident. He continued.

"Consider it a gesture of good faith. Your driver can be trusted. Introduce her to your friends if you like, she is very understanding and wise for her years."

I thanked him and left quickly. As I followed the boy leading me another way now, I wondered if I had even been noticed by the others, I'd felt invisible, just another shadow moving in the background.

As I slid into the passenger seat of the waiting truck, motor idling, Liza now dressed in a tight-fitting black suit almost invisible in the darkness, leaned over affectionately touching my cheek.

"Hi Big Boy, surprised to see me?"

My voice showed a little.

"The General said it was someone wise for her age, I didn't see anyone else in there who fit that description."

I thought a little ego building was in order.

My thoughts wrapped themselves around this new unfolding of events. Here I was heading back to my encircled, threatened friends with the daughter of the threat. An odd picture indeed. Was the Mahaj exercising his divine humor for my benefit or was I missing something. A cautious little voice from within suggested.

"Liza may be a spy sent to scan your friends, then hunt them down at a later date or worse yet, there may be a bomb aboard timed to explode and kill everyone in the compound."

Either alternative was an unpleasant specter, but then I recognized this voice was coming from the area within I'd recognized some time ago as my fear center. All thoughts coming from there were paranoid, untrusting in nature. I must once again let go and allow the Mahaj to guide me through all this as he always had in the past. I would take the normal U.I.A. precautions then trust in my inner impressions. Liza's voice broke into my thoughts.

"The General seems to be quite taken with you, if my father found out about this there would be sheer hell to pay. I sometimes fear for my father, he is extreme at times. I know extremity breeds extreme reaction and there are many around who begrudge him his success, wealth and power."

We were passing the area where I'd hidden my carrier, commandinglly,

"Pull over, I've hidden something here."

I jumped out as she stopped, retrieved the motorized vehicle, climbed in the back with it. Scanning the area, I saw it was near full of supplies, impossible to check it all but I sensed no danger. I returned to my seat.

Liza's voice questioned.

"What was all that about?"

My voice felt a little untrusting.

"Just tying up loose ends, I like leaving things as I find them, it feels like keeping your shoe laces tied up tightly, just in case it becomes necessary to run for it. Nothing worse than tripping on your own loose ends."

Her smile showed approval.

As we passed an open field area with a small treed hill in its center, I felt Aleisha stir and heard her thoughts.

"It is time for me to leave and for you to show your little Liza a bit more of yourself. This will be a good spot."

I spoke almost curtly.

"Pull the truck over there at the base of the hill behind that clump of trees."

I felt Liza tighten up a little, was she wondering what I was up to. Was she hiding something and now feared that I knew and might harm her here in this private place?

Assuringly.

"It's all right, I want to show you something, something that might affect your future in a growth full fashion."

Climbing out of the truck into the coolness of the night, the meadow around the wooded area we'd hidden in bathed in moonlight, I felt a deep sense of separation approaching. I'd gotten quite used to my companion in her little hiding place. Now I felt her slipping down my arm onto her perch as we climbed the short distance to the summit. Reaching it, I saw a small clearing with a broad, old tree, leafless, spread out before us like an old seasoned snake bathing in the moonlight. Sitting on a comfortable bough near its upwardly extended neck, I beckoned Liza to sit beside me, queringly.

"Do you believe in powers beyond your own?"

Her voice seemed surprised.

"Beyond my own? No, not really. There is much I'm not aware of I'm sure, but the power to learn is within me. I've attended the best schools and they've taught me to deal with life quite well, I think. What powers are you referring to?"

I knew words would have little impact on her well-trained mind. She would simply have to be shown. I reached out my left hand with my guest arching herself upwards in the light of the moon, her eyes glowing a bright green looking up to the stars. Liza's trembling voice as she stiffened.

"What is that, are you trying to scare me?"

My reply rang prophetically as I stretched my arm up to the heavens.

"Behold, the powers beyond your own."

It started as a small dot on the horizon coming up out of the zenith of a distant mountain, dark ominous in essence, getting larger as it came closer. As it flew between the moon and us, we could see its great outstretched wings beating slowly, steadily. Then soaring high above us, it circled, beginning its descent. An ear-piercing shriek, a scaly rattle as it adjusted its approach. A large reptilian bird-like creature with two eyes, one a deep red, the other a deep green, both moving independent of the other. One scanning above, the other below. This one would not be surprised from either above or below. I felt the deep sadness of parting again. Aleisha turned her eyes, now a soft mixture of green and red towards me, her thought.

"Well, old friend, the time for parting has come, but don't be sad, we've had a great time, haven't we? We showed them all a thing or two. Remember I'll always be with you, coiled, ready. You know where. Play with me whenever you like. Out here your little Liza will carry my essence, she will now serve you as I serve Moham."

Glancing at Liza sitting motionless, dazed, I saw the same hue, the mixture of red and green in her staring eyes. She was absorbing more than just the unusual vision in this dimension. Aleisha was now becoming a part of her, ethereally

The creature was now hovering high above us. Then from his outstretched talons I saw two small bird-like creatures with wings beating so quickly that they were almost invisible. Emitting a low hum, they descended quickly, one picked up Aleisha's head, the other her tail and lifted her gently from my little finger, leaving a slight tingle. I could see Aleisha squirm a little, her thought as she smiled down at us.

"It tickles like crazy, I never get used to this part. Farewell."

Up they all went into the waiting talons of the one, hovering. I caught a glimpse of Aleisha once more peeking out through the great dark claws. A playful wink and they were off in a sound of beating air and the clatter of scales, back towards the zenith of the far off mountain. We sat in the silence of the night watching them disappear. I again felt the parting, the absence, the loss of a companion I'd gotten used to, learned to appreciate on many levels.

Closing my eyes, I moved deep inside myself to the place she assured me she would always be. Down deep at the beginning of my energy body, the first chakra, the coiled serpent within. As the glow started, warming me from below, I felt a cool, shivering hand on my shoulder. Her voice quivering.

"What are you doing, you seem to be disappearing, don't just leave me here alone."

I realized whatever experience I was about to have with my inner Aleisha, Liza would have to be a part of it. Stretching out my left arm, invitingly.

"Come sit here between my legs where its warmer on this branch and join me in this experience. Fear not, everything you will see and feel will be quite natural, you are never challenged beyond your abilities in this realm."

As she hesitatingly sat and leaned back into the warmth of my thighs, I felt her chill. Her energy had withdrawn and fear was her dominant emotion. Running my left hand down her spine to its base, I pressed firmly. At the same time, placing my right hand on her forehead, the sweet little forehead I'd recently kissed farewell, I pulled her close, wrapping her in my warmth. I could feel her beginning to relax. Wrapped together, I again moved my attention to Aleisha's realm inside myself. I felt the glow begin to move upwards through me, through my hands, into the base of Liza's spine upwards. I knew now we were as one, her body melting, warming, letting go, just relaxing in a growing trust in me.

I felt myself being drawn deeper, deeper, a light resistance. Liza was moving in with me but her well-trained logistic mind kept interfering, questioning, pondering, looking for the logic in it all. Yet there was none to be found. Unknown terrain to be explored openly. A quiver, then a letting go, a sense of co-operation and we were inside bathing in the pale green light of Aleisha's aura.

There she was, waiting for us. Aleisha in all her splendor, coiled, beginning to unwind, her regal head now wearing a small golden crown, on her back two small furry saddles. Her voice I'd never heard, like the breath of a hot summer breeze moving through the trees.

"Welcome, come aboard. I'll take you for a ride through many kingdoms. There's someone up there who wants to see you. It will be my pleasure to be your carrier."

Liza was now relaxed, eager to see more, trusting. As we settled into our comfortable seats, Aleisha uncoiled herself reaching up to a descending swirl of lime green vapors. A funnel inviting us to ascend, we flew, Aleisha effortlessly undulating in the power of the pull upwards. Her voice rang out like a tour guide.

"We are now entering the Kingdom of Ego."

I felt that I was somehow inside myself experiencing from within, yet still the body in which it was all taking place. The center we'd come to was the belly. The area of the womb, the center of motion, the point of balance.

She continued.

"Here is where physical form comes into being. First in seed form, growing into a form ready for birth into a new unknown world where a fitting persona develops around the experiences that external dimension bestows on it. Here is the realm of pure consciousness uncontaminated with self concerns. That all comes later, out there. We know it generally as survival."

The colors around us were changing gradually into a deep creamy hue, a variation of the Milky Aura on Javada. I felt the power of motion all around me. The surge of spontaneously moving with the currents of the universe, in form, in harmony with the will of the Mahaj. Aleisha below us was filling herself with the nourishment, emitting a warmth creeping up through us, from between our legs upwards. I thought to myself.

"Hot little serpent, aren't you?"

This time her thought.

"Too hot for you to handle, Big Boy."

As we drifted in the warmth of the mother's milk, nourished, caressed, encouraged to grow, I felt another essence descending, greeting us welcoming us to continue upwards.

Aleisha, looking over her shoulder, up at us, querying.

"Are you ready to continue? We are all invited to the realm of the heart. The lower heart which provides nourishment to all that we have just passed."

I could feel Liza's eagerness ahead of me nodding her head, now feeling the fullness of her potentiality. I wondered who waited for us, up above.

The descending essence gently turned into a beige-colored cloud hovering before Aleisha's entry. As we slipped into its cover, I felt the surging emotion of this place. Floating upwards, the sense of loving, caring, protection, courage, a willingness to openly love and nourish all in and below its domain. An underlying vulnerability, willing to risk despite the threat of rejection and the resulting emotions of pain. A feeling of respect flowed through me. Not wanting to be a bull in a China shop at all costs. The resulting stillness, just watching, feeling at peace in a most fragile strength. The overwhelming presence of femininity, under me, in front of me, all around, and finally emanating in and through me.

Bathing in the aura of full heartedness, feeling our fears soothed, our deep old child hurts caressed and healed. A place of resurrection, renewal, comforting. As we drifted upwards in the beige opulence, I saw ahead, above us, a turbulence, a boundary, unlike a wall, more like a riptide. Two currents within the same ocean. A boat, a sleek, maneuverable sailboat riding the edge of the current playing with the subtle innuendos of water and air. As we glided through, Aleisha's power moving us effortlessly with just an occasional fluctuation to each side in response to the turbulence created by the meeting of the two oceans, I saw two familiar figures waving up to us. It was my two Javadian leader friends. The Milky Aura Leader at the helm playing in the currents and the Beige Aura Leader, one hand on her heart, the other waving joyfully in welcome and farewell.

Aleisha again looking back, educating.

"We've just passed the boundary between the lower heart realm and the higher heart realm. We have now arrived in the spiritual heart realm. The part of each of us nourishing and being nourished by the transcendent realms, the spiritual realms, the ethereal."

I could feel the emotional change in the climate. The heaviness, overpowering almost suffocating love feelings had changed into a clearer, fresher sense. Still full of the comfort and warmth but now somewhat aloof, freer, unconditional in essence, nourishing without need. A steadiness, no risk of betrayal and pain here. Self-sufficiency with no expectations. Just a calling to move higher.

Aleisha, looking back gleefully.

"This is real nice, I'm glad the two of you have come. It's never quite the same alone. The next two realms are so sweet, hold on."

With this she flicked her sparkling green tail and up we went into a darker beige, almost orange hue. It felt like floating into a sweetness, bathing in an ambrosia, a sense of intoxication with intense clarity.

She continued her guidance.

"This is known as the Nectar of the Gods Realm. Full of such sweetness. Open yourselves to it, drink deeply."

As I opened, I felt my heart realms uniting with this newness. A flow of richness, back and forth, an intermingling, a deep throat kiss from the Gods. Sweet indeed. The sense of deeply-rooted power. Then feeling oh so full of this unknown nectar, I heard the gentle sound of the universe from above, calling us. The slight ring of celestial bells rising from the constant hum of the universal motion, moving through us in its all-pervasiveness, its everywhereness unobtrusive, yet undeniable.

The sound was increasing in intensity filling everything, everywhere. I felt so full of it, bursting at the seams. Aleisha was bounding upwards towards its source. Yet it seemed like it came from everywhere. Ahead I could see a swirling vortex, an opening of colors moving shut then open for a microsecond, we were heading directly towards it. Aleisha seemed to be timing her approach carefully. Her voice rang out above the deafening sound.

"We are approaching the realm of duality at its source, the place where form and formlessness meet, the place where separativeness and oneness intermingle, then return to their spheres."

As we hurtled towards the opening it closed before us,

I felt its resistance, its probe of our beings, then just as we were about to crash into it, it opened just large enough to allow us to slip in. I admired Aleisha's faith, her confidence in the timing as she quickly tucked in her tail just before the vortex closed on it. I thought I heard its brush in passing, a close passage, a tight fit. A sense of being here just on time, not a moment too late or too early.

The silence inside our new realm was almost as deafening as our approach, just this low hum intermingled with a high buzz. The sound was more like a feeling moving inside and out, perceived without boundaries as if all separation was dissolved, perceived and perceiver as one. Logistically impossible yet here it was in manifest. The gently intermingling colors emitted a flavor as sweet as the Nectar Realm. The sense that all we'd just passed was here in the collective, potential to manifest at the slightest will.

Aleisha's smiling remark.

"You are both on the edge of form and formlessness. Here your every wish is possible. Enjoy your illusion of form experience, you will be called into the other soon enough. What would you like to experience?"

My thoughts went blank, after what we'd just passed through, how could I wish for more. A sense of openness to the infinite imagination, wanting it to give me what it would, rather than my limiting it to my imaginative process.

Then I heard Liza's voice.

"I would like us to bath in the oceans of bliss down there."

As she pointed downwards, I first saw nothing but undulating colors, then I saw a turquoise ocean with gentle white caps regularly surfacing. She continued.

"Some hot, caressing white sand to lie on."

I could see a tropical island with immense stretches of white sand forming.

"The hot radiance of the loving sun which nourishes this place."

The area above and around us turned into a vast light blue sky with a blazing sun warming us, inside and out. It felt like an externalization of our own burning spiritual collective heart. Aleisha had descended to a patch of firm, white sand, settled herself and stretched out, letting us easily slip out of our saddles onto the warmth of the sand. I was suddenly conscious of our forms again, now naked, radiantly glowing with the exhilaration of the experience, the fullness of the nourishments we had passed through, a feeling of child-like innocence.

Aleisha's eyes, a little tired as she spoke.

"Play in your paradise, children. Abandon yourselves to your inner joy and dance in this place forever if you like. I'll wait for you in that garden over there, I'm a little tired after all that."

I felt a deep appreciation and concern for our most gracious, energetic hostess. Her vitality and understanding of the subtle currents of this place had brought us safely to our resting place. I knew this would be a temporary stay, someone waited somewhere, I could sense it, but for now what a place, what a feeling. We ran, played, explored, found unimaginable treasures. Played games of creation and destruction, knowing it was all an illusion. No harm could be done or come to us. Bathing in our own emotional ocean of bliss, warming ourselves under our own protective, nourishing Heart Sun. Tasting the sweet nectars of our own god-like nature surrendering into the deepest recesses of our own beings.

Like innocent children exploring our own little Garden of Eden. No past to remember, no future to ponder and control, just now, the moment which always was and always would be. Looking into Liza's playful, now turquoise eyes, I remarked.

"I like your creation, you have a very sensuous imagination."

She danced away gleefully, her voice rang like Aleisha's.

"I'm just a child of the universe, unlimited in nature, boundless in my bounty."

Aleisha's voice rang out from the nearby garden.

"Come in and eat when you like, I won't even tempt you with the apple of right and wrong. I got into enough shit over that some time back. Play on under your sun of unity, duality will wait."

We went in and tasted all the offerings. As sweet as the ambrosia we'd tasted on our journey. Each bite met with an inner excretion of sweetness. Two worlds meeting, intermingling in flavor.

CHAPTER 14

As we sat filled to the brim, listening to the sweet song of the garden birds, feeling the caressing warmth of the ocean breeze, Aleisha suggested.

"Would you like to see the infamous tree with the forbidden fruit? Now that you are full to overflowing, you won't be as tempted as most I have brought here."

Slipping quietly, noiselessly through the undergrowth of the garden towards a clump of trees, an orchard in the center, she led, we followed hand in hand still like children unconscious of our nakedness, no sense of self-consciousness, free of the concerns of self-images. As we stepped through the circle of sentinel trees into a clearing, we saw it. A large old tree standing alone in the center. I felt an immediate intensity, an almost ominous chill ran through me. I'd heard the myth surrounding this unusual creation. The creator had placed this one tree here with the specific instructions that the fruit of it was forbidden. One could look, touch, but not eat of it. Some could not resist and were thrown out of the garden of plenty to forage throughout creation on their own, striving, trying to fill themselves, yet unable to fill the uneasiness, the place deep inside only the creator could fill. Yet the creator in his infinite compassion and wisdom always showed the searcher a way back and now here we were standing before the temptation again.

I thought to myself.

"It's a nice enough tree and the apples look delicious but what's the big deal. The array of fruits and vegetables we had just filled ourselves with, were unimaginably tasty. Why would I even consider standing in contempt of the creator of all this beauty just for a taste of the forbidden fruit."

Aleisha read my thoughts and sent hers.

"You are as children right now, cared for, protected, happy in your innocence. But you are dependent upon the graces of your benefactor. For some, this is not good enough, they want control over their destinies, they want to create and destroy according to their own will and imagination. The fruit of this old tree gives one the power to do this, but the cost is high. Surrendered innocence is replaced by willfulness. A seriousness replaces your present joy, but most of all the fullness in your heart where the creator now lives and radiates his love is felt as an aching emptiness missing its absent guest. The time is then spent trying to fill the gap with external stimuli, relationships. A constant search for more yet the more only deepens the emptiness, until like you, one begins the process of letting go. Living in faith once again, opening the inner door for your absent guest to come calling once again."

Aleisha's thoughts had filled my heart to overflowing. My being was so full of a feeling so rapturous. No comparison can be found to relate it to anyone. An orgiastic culmination of emotion in flesh and spirit. Through my tear-filled eyes I could see Liza, as if entranced, moving towards the tree, seemingly unaware of the danger. Her hand reached up, held a beautiful red apple for a moment. I felt myself opening my mouth to yell "NO" but no sound came out.

Aleisha's thought.

"You cannot stop her, it is her destiny to go back and serve the creator through her strife. Her world needs her now. After all this, she will have a positive influence despite her inner turmoil. You will be there to help her through and eventually bring her back far wiser, seasoned."

Aleisha's assurances were little comfort as I watched my sweet little Liza turn the apple once and pull. I heard the snap as it left its perch, then the aerie sound of her flashing white teeth piercing the outer flesh sinking deeper and deeper into the juices of the forbidden fruit. She turned to me with the same look Aleisha had when she had drunk deeply of the green fluid of Mr. Maurices's, Liza's father's unconscious creation. Holding out the bitten fruit.

"Come, my love, eat with me."

As she spoke, waving her hand high above her, a rainbow of sparkles formed around her head, like a crown of stars. I felt her power, her radiance, the goddess of my dreams, every love I'd had, standing there before me beckoning me to join her in the dance of creation.

"Come, rule at my side. Together we will be invincible. A complete circle of the masculine, feminine nature of the universe."

My heart leapt at the vision, but the deep inner voice.

"It is forbidden."

I knew I could not turn away from the unlimited nature of my inner guest but now I understood the power of the tree. The temptation was almost irresistible, but I was full and somehow had the presence of mind to inwardly know the cost would be too high.

I would not walk in this creation, this garden, in contempt but in openness watching the miracles of unlimitation in essence unfold around me. This was now my joy, not to create and rule but to simply witness the creator's hand as a child, cared for and protected.

Then my sweet little Liza turned away from me, hiding her eyes. She had seen my nakedness and my reluctance to join her. Her disappointment and shame swept through me like a cold winter storm.

Aleisha's thought.

"Liza and I can go no further on this journey, but I feel you will be leaving us soon. We will be here to welcome you on your return."

As she slipped quickly through the tree sentinels, Liza followed, still not looking at me, now stooping with the weight of her self-inflicted responsibilities and yet somehow I felt it was all harmonious, not really her choice, her attraction to power like her father was not to be denied, but played out in her evolution.

I knew as I stood here in the center of it all, that it was by grace alone that I was able to resist. Had Aleisha not forewarned me, had I been hungry, starved, had

I been irresistibly drawn to Liza's beauty and vision, had I forgotten the most precious experience available was the fullness within above all else, then I to may be stooped with the power to create and destroy. The inner tools I'd been given in my travels up to now were sufficient to deal with any challenges I might face. The aloneness I now felt was not unpleasant, not a loneliness, I was full of company, divine company. No need to reach out for more, yet ready to respond openly with no fear of loss or need for gain.

I wondered how and where I would be called to go now, in this realm of infinite possibility and potentiality.

As I gazed lazily at the magnificence of the old tree, I felt a oneness with its history. The myths of temptation it had generated over the centuries and the question

"WHY?"

Why were beings brought to the edge of contempt, tested for allegiance to the creator. It seemed like such a childish game for such a grand presence. There must be some deep hidden truth behind this phenomenon, something that when faced and seen, opened well springs of evolution, possibly a deepening of spiritual experience. Yet in the eye of oneness, all separation was illusionary, so all this really didn't exist. Just a game one played with oneself. What sense in the torture of failure, what real accomplishment in success. The pondering was overwhelming, my mind raced through the issues, the scenario in circles ending nowhere except where I started. A sudden drowsiness fell over me, just then I saw a cloudy object drifting towards me from the edge of the sentinel trees. As it reached my side, I watched it form into a small bed, a bed for one with a golden embroidered pillow. Looking closer I saw a monogram.

"Sweet dreams from your sweet little Liza."

Laid next to the pillow, a satin set of clothes. Liza no longer found my nakedness acceptable, I put them on and lay down on the softness of my bed, lay my head on her well-wishes and quickly fell into a deep slumber. The last sight was the old tree standing alone in the clearing watching over me.

The dream had an immediate sense of excitement, the exhilaration of flight, in my hand lay Liza's apple, partially eaten.

Aleisha's reassuring voice.

"You must be very hungry, eat the rest of it and join Liza and I on a flight to the realm of the gods. They are calling you to join them."

Without thinking I raised the fruit to my mouth and bit in deeply. The sweet juice permeated my senses. I felt a powerful glow beginning down deep at the beginning where this whole journey began. Then a flash upwards through all the realms we'd passed through. A sense of openness, infinite space within and without. We were once again in our saddles comfortably sailing along. Liza ahead of me, her sensuous athletic body moving gently with each of Aleisha's contortions. I felt the arousal, the need to be closer to her, to consume her, to own her in every way. To rule her life as I would my own. The feeling of importance in my decisions, the confidence in my own powers to face any challenge and dominate. Rule with inner power-despotically, no room for debate or a questioning of my authority. I was now as god, capable of creating and destroying worlds at my slightest whim. Serious business yet

I felt the exhilaration of its prospect. Here with my serpent and my obedient love, off to conquer and rule.

Aleisha's eyes gleefully glancing back at us, her voice ringing out.

"You no longer need me. You are gods capable of flight on your own."

With this she arched herself and bucked us off her back, slipping away behind a nearby cloud. The suddenness of hanging momentarily in the air, seeing the rocks below waiting to meet our fall, yet there was no fall. Just drifting, high, comfortable, but the inner need for more experience. The hunger for exploration. Liza flew ahead, waving.

"Come, we're off to the God Realm, I know where it is."

Not having wings, I wondered how I would propel myself.

Aleisha's thought from behind the clouds.

"Use your will, it is now omnipotent." I willed my flight. The movement was instantaneous, like a blink. There we were gliding over castles, realms within realms. I felt a welcoming, an open door down below, but it was the flight I wanted. Turning, hovering, moving higher and higher until there was nowhere else to go. Beyond clouds, just infinite space above. Liza's voice.

"Your old friend Moham waits for us in his castle down below. He has prepared a feast, a celebration."

Yes, I thought, it is Moham's presence I want to experience. Fill myself with his power, explore his creations. A blink and there we were descending, floating down to a small group standing in a court yard, welcoming us, waving. There in the center of the group, stood my old friend dressed in celebratory robes, arms outstretched in welcome. I landed in them and once again felt his great hug. His power flowed through me filling me with the intensity of his presence.

We drank, ate, walked in his garden. He told us stories about his creations, his realms, his rulership and his concerns.

I felt a part of myself resonating with him, it was my fear center. I queried.

"Moham, is fear a part of your rulership?"

His face dimmed.

"Yes, I use it to maintain control. It is a very useful tool, but it only works on those who already have it deeply instilled in them."

I could feel the aura of fear descend on us like a black cloud.

He continued.

"This is my greatest challenge, once used fear fills the realm in which it is used. I've learned to live with it, but it is a restricting influence. Not pleasant in its essence but you will soon know all about that. It's a part of being a god, only children play in their innocence. We have work to do, responsibilities for our creations."

I felt the weight of his words, his vision. I felt the presence of my own fear center. I felt the heaviness of my own upcoming responsibilities. I wondered if the bite was worth it.

Moham had a far-off look on his intensely lined warrior face. The scar on his neck stood out a livid white. I queried.

"Where have you gone?"

Coming back, glancing sideways at me.

"I was remembering a time back when a planetary system I'd created reached a level of turbulence in its development where in self-destruction was a possibility. I went there with my new bride, a lovely creature, so sensitive, so caring. I knew the risk, I would have to use my powers, including fear through the projection of channeled anger to bring affairs under control. The result would be a realm steeped in the cold grip of fear. I did this formulating a system based on the fear of insecurity. Values were formed around the competitive mode and control was maintained through laws severely enforced by punishment. I very quickly brought about a state of stability but fear was the ethereal vapor we all had to live in. I have over time adjusted to its presence and can maneuver quite ably in it. My psychic defense systems are developed to a stage beyond coping, in fact I thrive on its presence. It's simply a matter of finding the abused helpless, scared child inside yourself and hardening him up, making him tough enough to deal with any threat. Then through the projection of anger, assertive aggression, you strike the vulnerable child in those around you, make them cringe, bring out their defensiveness, unbalanced defensiveness and then forcefully rule them in their confusion. It works every time, yet there is a cost, you find yourself surrounded by helplessness, dependency. Everyone becomes too afraid to think and act for themselves. My will, of course, became omnipotent and I ruled as benevolently as possible under the conditions.

My bride, however, did not have the ability to deal with our auric surroundings. The sweet, tender thing absorbed too much of it and grew sickly. Her time was spent in so much pain, the pain I felt as if it were mine. She, to, in time began to fear me. The fear seemed to bring out anger in me. Like an animal in the wilds, I wanted to strike out and devour her and I did in many ways. When I saw how destructive our love had become I had no choice but send her away, back to her home planet. We see each other from time to time but it just isn't any good now. I feel her cringing whenever I look at her."

I felt the sorrow in his heart, his great warrior heart and I knew the cost was just too high. Giving up the fullness of the carefree child, cared for, protected for this, the power to create within the confines of our limited imagination and in the process losing all that we love and are loved by.

His words were once again strong.

"My friend, learn from my experience, beware the power of fear, use it sparingly. You have a unique opportunity on the planet you now find yourself on. You have made inroads into each power realm. The rebels find you and your skills interesting, Mirabel is very fond of you. Cinda, of course, as your wife brings the support of all Beno's followers, but she herself is too young, too impulsive to rule just yet. Look what she did with the eyes of her victim, the whole planet may end up blind in time. General Miko is quite taken with you, using your understanding of fear has given him an insight, a hope around his issues. He will co-operate with you to the extent of his limitations. Now, armed with Liza, you have a direct channel into the wealthy, powerful segment of the society. Its all laid out very nicely on your plate.

I've found it very interesting watching it all unfold for you. You seem to dance somewhere between full utilization of your will and total acceptance of your Mahaj's will. The blend seems to be working quite well. It is an interesting study for me. Marty and I have discussed the possibility of putting you in charge of a little experiment we've had in mind for some time after you finish your present project.

Galaxium's approach can be made quite smooth with your involvement and Javadian guidance. It is not time to play as a carefree child, you have a responsibility to those down there you have touched. The Garden of Eden and beyond will wait. Realms of Reality will be affected by what you do now. Take it seriously. Use your powers consciously and there will be no harm. Even anger can be used to pierce through resistance when need be. But, it must be directed like a beam, not just released aimlessly. It's all a very delicate balance, this god business."

I once again felt the weight of his words, his direction. Was it really time for me to grow up from being a child of the universe, grasp the reins of power and disperse my will with every ounce of wisdom I had? A benevolent monarchy would indeed facilitate Galaxium's approach creating direct channels through a centralized administration with all aspects open to the power of the Mahaj, a balance of my will and more. A very tempting exercise, indeed. Playing out all my inner fantasies around power and rulership all under the umbrella of service. Was there a right or wrong around all this? How could I be sure that a motion in this direction was universally harmonious and how would it affect my long-term spiritual evolution? As I pondered the issues Moham stepped back, watching, knowing my inner dilemma. Moving with the Mahaj was always so effortless, the results always so harmonious, the inner feelings so relaxed, loving. Use of my own will up to now was always in response to conditions arising around me pushing for decision in the moment. A reaction to threat or intense appetite. The sense that even this willful action wasn't really mine. The Mahaj set up the scenario, gave me the appetite and made the decision to move in a certain direction almost inevitable, little choice if any. I remembered my last deep wish on Javada and the evolution it initiated. We had all spent a great deal of time in purification processes, deep meditations and inner warrior exercises. At a point of clarity, a time of intuitive awakening, we were sent off to private places to meditate on our relationship with the Mahaj and what we truly, deeply wanted from it all. My place of seclusion was a deep forest at the base of a gently rolling foothill. On the last night, I built a large fire, drew out a large circle in the ground and relaxed into myself, searching for my deepest desire. A sense of trust enveloped me, almost immediately, a sense of a wholeness, being completely at home within myself. No need for any more. Then feeling a glow in my third eye area, the center of my forehead, I heard my own voice utter.

"May my will and yours grow to be one."

I now saw standing here with so much on my plate and yet feeling open to releasing it all, the power, the sense of the importance of serving, my way of seeing reality, my wish had been granted.

Above all else, I felt my will had grown into a synchronicity, possibly a reflection, but more like a synchronistic arising with that of the Mahaj. If I stayed in tune with my inner realms, my intuitive sense, my will would be a portrayal of the greater, a harmonious expression of the creator and the created.

A relaxation suddenly came over me, as Liza joined Moham and I after her romp through his garden. She was holding a fully bloomed flower in her hand which I assumed would be an offering for our host, instead she stepped up to me, looking up almost child-like, offering it to me. Her voice soft, humble.

"Take this as a gesture of my appreciation for bringing me here. I will always be grateful to you for this."

As she danced off with Moham's guests, I knew her appreciation was genuine, I felt sure of her allegiance upon our return to service. At the same time, I felt a strange uneasiness holding the flower, feeling the projections of admiration, respect and love.

Moham's voice boomed.

"It takes a little getting used to, all this worship. It sometimes feels easier dealing with the shit and abuse. The warrior in us thrives on it. This stuff feels a little too mushy sometimes, but its genuineness has its appeal, not to mention the love."

I woke with his words still ringing in my ears. Liza was kneeling beside me holding my left hand. She was fully dressed in a loose flowing gown studded with stars and the colors of a rainbow. Her eyes were no longer child-like, playful, but beamed out an intensity, a need. Her voice committed.

"We must go back, there is so much to be done. There are so many who need your guidance. I swear I will serve you with all my power and make your will mine."

I felt her sincerity and need but knew there was more for me here. Something unfinished, waiting.

"Aleisha will take you back if you like, bath in the wellspring of your heart-realm, nourish yourself, you will need all your inner strength for your service. Seek out the one who lives there in the seat of your soul. Familiarize yourself with your femininity, it is part of your destiny, then rest with Aleisha in her resting place. It is a powerful place and you will need the power combined with your inner strength."

Her eyes disappointedly turned away as she obediently left my side and disappeared through the tree sentinels. I wondered if I would return to her or was this our final farewell.

The cloud I'd slept on slowly dispersed setting me down gently on the softness of the garden. The old tree standing in front of me emanated a glow of completion, it had done its work, showed its power, given me an understanding of its fruit. Now it was time to leave, but where and how? I knew I was running out of inner chakras, all that was left was my intuitive center, the third eye and the doorway through the crown into the infinite. I felt drawn yet held. Was this a step with no return? Was I ready for that? This realm lay beyond my will, just my willingness seemed enough. I'd brought Liza this far and she seemed content with her journey, ready to return, but my call upwards was growing stronger, stronger than the resistance.

Lying there, not wanting to move, not knowing where to move to, gazing up at the heart sun, the sun created by Liza and me in our child-like play. It's warmth seeped deep into me, I felt a longing for the return of that time, that carefree play in the ocean of bliss, the hot sands of time, the waves of ecstasy sweeping over us in their rhythm of constancy. Now Liza was gone into her realm of power and responsibility and I lay here alone, waiting. As I felt her absence deeply, the sun began dimming. The garden was quivering, turning slowly vibrational, disappearing. I felt myself floating alone and free in space, dark space, yet luminous in its essence. The darkness felt comforting like a nourishing womb and I like a grown fetus ready for birth, eager for the next step into the unknown.

The sense of motion in the darkness, feeling my essence moving through space, a glimpse of a far-off spark, then a steady light growing larger, closer. I was moving, now completely transformed into my ethereal center body, into the light. It was more of a feeling than a visual sensation. A constant rhythmic emanation coming into my third eye, permeating the entirety of my being. I thought.

"This must be the Realm of the Intuitive Light, the source of Creativity, Understanding and Wisdom."

Feeling full to overflowing, I gazed into the brilliance, consciously absorbing, knowing I faced a power beyond all the known. The seed place where all known reality began. A spark of creative genius, a thought, a train of thoughts and then the physical reality unfolding.

A familiar voice gently brought me out of my entrancement. I looked deeper into the brilliance, expanding my vision. A figure slowly took form, almost invisible, vibrational yet distinguishable enough for me to recognize. It was my old friend, Marty, with his hands outstretched, welcoming me.

"Well, you finally got here, I thought you'd never get free of all that temptation down there. Had a good time, didn't you?"

I could only nod, a little dazed by it all.

He continued.

"I see Moham took you on quite a ride. Even tasted a bit of his power realm without taking an actual bite. That was interesting. An astute use of the dream-state. Having the experience without incurring any karma. Now that you are here, I guess it's my turn to entertain you. However I must warn you, if I show you the entirety of the remaining realms you may not want to return to your service. This intuitive, third eye dimension is the gateway to infinity, formlessness, eternal life beyond transition. You have passed through the centers of your energy body, felt the resonance of the holy word, that creates, sustains and destroys. You've tasted the sweetness of the God's nectar.

You've heard the inner thunder of the universal voice. Now you bath in the light, the feeling of it, this is my kingdom, welcome. You can pass through this and the crown."

As he spoke he waved his hand high. Above us a golden circle of light formed. I caught a glimpse of turquoise blue and sparkles, each like a star, twinkling.

"However if you choose to enter, you may never return. It is difficult to leave immortality, eternal radiance for the transient nature of form. I feel you are being called, but once called, the door will always open for you on approach. You have the key, the knowledge, it is your choice."

I sensed the grandeur of what lay ahead, the unimaginable experience of infinity, lying beyond the realms of beginnings and endings. I felt the resonance of its solidity, its rapturous emotional essence, its absolutely irresistible call into itself. My friend standing at the gate waiting for my answer.

I thought.

"What about my service somewhere back there, already dimming in my consciousness. My help would ease all the upcoming transitions. All the inroads had been given to me by the Mahaj in his approach. Now I was free to choose. Would this step through the crown into infinity be selfish? Did all that melodrama back there really matter or was this my destiny, to move forward, merge with my trueness, be one with all that really was? To re-identify with the universal self. Was that dissolution, the end of self or a growth into the ultimate potential of life?"

Marty broke into my train of thoughts, smilingly.

"The process from this point on is virtually effortless, blissful, the path of all the masters, choose and speak, my friend."

ABOUT THE AUTHOR

The author is a practicing holistic health consultant utilizing a unique blend of eastern metaphysical, western psycho-physical, self-developmental systems designed to naturally optimize the individual human potential.

As the director of InnerScapes2000.com a non-profit concern, he is surrounded with active participants holding a similar vision of freely sharing their understanding and support in their community.

The Pacific Northwest is home for this group of well-meaning individuals spontaneously drawn together in support of their timely, worthwhile offerment.

Anyone touched by the fabric of this swash-buckling adventure is welcome to connect if they so wish.